AFTER THE FLOOD

First published 2022 by
FREMANTLE PRESS

Fremantle Press Inc. trading as Fremantle Press
PO Box 158, North Fremantle, Western Australia 6159
fremantlepress.com.au

Cover images Jordan Cantelo, jordancantelo.com; focusphotoart
at iStock, istockphoto.com
Cover design Nada Backovic, nadabackovic.com

 A catalogue record for this
book is available from the
National Library of Australia

ISBN 9781760991012 (paperback)
ISBN 9781760991029 (ebook)

Fremantle Press is supported by the Western Australian State
Government through the Department of Cultural Industries,
Tourism and Sport.

Fremantle Press respectfully acknowledges the Whadjuk people
of the Noongar nation as the traditional owners and custodians of
the land where we work in Walyalup.

DAVE WARNER
AFTER THE FLOOD

FREMANTLE PRESS

For Anne Tyler and Don & Meg Williams

PROLOGUE

Mariana County, Brazil

It would be pork tonight he was pretty sure. When they spoke earlier, before she finished her shift, Gabrielly wouldn't tell him, having some fun, teasing it out, but it was Thursday so he figured pork. He liked the way she cooked it. In fact, her mother cooked it even better but he wouldn't tell his girlfriend that. Back in Australia his family had never eaten much pork – lamb and chicken was more the go.

'Are they our people?' From the porch of the hut where his office was located, he could see a cluster of hi-vis vests down at the wall of the tailings dam.

'No. Engineering bring them in.'

His assistant Victor leant his forearms on the railing and blew a stream of smoke into the thick, warm air. The sky was pale blue today but that didn't mean it wouldn't rain. It rained at the drop of a hat here, heavy, like somebody had tipped a bucket of nuts and bolts out of the sky. He'd not worked Far North Queensland but he'd had stints in the Kimberley and the Pilbara back home and he'd seen a cyclone or two but that was more sheeting rain. 'Slovakia,' he thought to himself. They ate a lot of pork in Slovakia. He'd gone there late '90s after he'd been retrenched in Kalgoorlie. Jobs were thin on the ground, especially for HR in the mining industry and he'd been lucky to snare a job at all. It had been brutally cold. He couldn't do that again. Well of course he wouldn't anyway, not with Gabrielly. He'd never leave her. As soon as they were married, he would see about getting her back to Australia, some place with this kind of climate, up north.

He now liked humidity, had come to see it as a balm. There was no rush though. He wouldn't want to uproot Gabrielly from the village, her family, her friends. But in six months there would be another family member to consider. Better his kid was born in Australia. Somebody had said that you can't fly when more than five months pregnant or something, so, there wasn't oodles of time. They would need to organise things. Well, he would need to organise things. Gabrielly was worried about her family, her mother in particular. Her father worked at one of the local farms and before Gabrielly's job, his pay had barely supported the family. Gabrielly had two younger brothers still at school. Her wages had improved the family's life dramatically. Her father had not taken him up on his offer of a job at the site. Mainly by sign language he'd explained to 'Paulo' as they called him here, that he had worked his whole life on farms. He'd poked himself in the chest, jutted his chin as if to say, that's who I am and I'm not changing now. It was a man-to-man discussion, no women around, but later Gabrielly had confirmed he'd got it right.

'He's worked his whole life, digging, harvesting vegetables and helping with livestock. The machinery at the plant is a different world to him. He doesn't fit there.'

So, unable to help the family in that way, 'Paulo' had assisted by buying the boys shoes and clothes. He also made sure he always brought some sought-after delicacy to the house.

It was funny how your life could turn so quickly. He'd begun to think he would never find that special partner. You hit forty-one, still single, barely had a girlfriend your entire life and you're in an industry with ninety percent men. You don't rate your chances of finding somebody. He could have still been playing cards with the other loners, thinking wistfully about girls he almost dated back in his uni days. Instead, he'd taken the punt and decided to risk egg on his face. Truly he didn't give himself much of a chance, big-boned, and let's face it, pudgy, while she was slim with the most beautiful brown eyes. They had flashed at him when he'd confirmed her for the cleaning job, so happy, like he'd tossed in a car as a bonus. That's the first indelible impression she had made upon him. You had to be careful these days too, especially in HR. There were a lot more women in the industry than when he'd started but still only a handful, so personally he'd never been in this situation before, where you actually fancied an employee. But he knew guys from his uni class who had gone into retailing and insurance and had risked getting themselves into hot water because they'd asked a fellow employee out on a date. It was unfair and stupid really. Where were you supposed to meet anyone if you weren't a social kind of person? In the end he'd decided he didn't have that much to lose. It was Brazil, middle of nowhere and he was the highest ranked HR employee.

And he was lonely.

And she seemed to like him, smiled at him when their paths crossed and so he'd asked her out to lunch one weekend and she'd said yes. Then everything had fallen into place. And tonight, they'd be having pork for dinner – bet on it.

Something, a shout or some other sound, drew his gaze past the smoking Victor and back across the sloping valley to the tailings dam whose wall was built in an S shape. Did he imagine it or did it just move? No, something was up, the men were scattering, shouting now, running back up the slope towards the offices. And then the dam wall just dissolved and red sludge began to pour out like lava and slide down the mountain. His brain calculated in that scintilla of a second it was his future happiness pouring out of that broken dam, his blood, his plasma, the life of Gabrielly. His insides were hollowed out as if readying his body to be embalmed in grief. Everything was slow motion, unreal. He turned and dashed back into the office. Even as he shouted that the dam had burst, he was realising that there was no phone to connect with the village. His eyes lit on the two-way.

'Martha, Martha are you there? Over.' Martha was in the motor-pool five hundred metres down.

Her crackly voice came on the line. 'This is Martha. Over.'

He blurted out what had happened. Luckily, she was already on her little motorbike. It wasn't necessary to tell her to ride for the village and raise the alarm, she took that initiative the instant she knew but all she had was a small bike on the dirt backroads that led to the village. The fall from the dam into the valley was steep and it would move as rapidly as a crocodile after an unwary bird. He stood there shaking. As the level of the watery brown fluid in the dam rapidly dropped, his fears raced to this throat.

It was hours before he could get to what was left of the village, and then only because he was able to hitchhike on one of the company choppers. The dirt roads one usually accessed the village from had all been washed away. Martha had been forced to pull up about two kilometres short on the main road that was high enough to become a virtual bank of the new brown, muddy river. The fall from the tailings dam, down the mountain to the valley was steep and the goo had moved with surprising rapidity. He prayed that Gabrielly would be spared but when he heard the early reports from those flying over the scene he had thrown up in the basin, his legs trembling, his jaw quivering. All but a gram of hope had been crushed. Then came news that many villagers had got to higher ground or to upper floors and roofs of houses that had survived, and he had dared hope.

But as the helicopter made that first pass over what was left of the village, he felt both despair and bile rising. The houses looked like shavings on top of a chocolate mousse. Some dwellings had gone entirely, many more were nothing but a façade, their walls dissolved back into the clay whence they had been extracted and baked. Where the little grocery and supermarket had stood was a mud flat. Gabrielly would always be in there, gaily chatting with other locals. Cars were strewn around, mostly pushed to the perimeter of the village, nothing of them visible below the windscreen.

Rescuers in fluoro vests and gumboots were wading through the shallower areas. He caught a glimpse of one person, so covered in mud he could not tell if it was a man or woman, their arm around the neck of the rescuer guiding them out. Where the helicopter was landing on higher ground, a makeshift triage had been set up.

Other helicopters were arriving or evacuating the injured. It was like a Vietnam movie. Villagers stood aimlessly, soaked, muddy, some clean as one of his freshly laundered shirts Gabrielly would insist on doing for him, but all with haunted faces so they looked more like a painting than real life. Right as the chopper put down, he spied Gabrielly's mother clinging to one of her neighbours for comfort. For an instant relief flared.

Yet there was no sign of her. He swivelled and pivoted.

'Gabrielly!' he yelled through the open hatch but of course it was drowned by the noise of the blades. He was still yelling it as he charged out of the stationary helicopter but he didn't realise that. How could he experience anything in the present when his life was now doomed to be forever hostage to the past?

1 THE KIMBERLEY

Wednesday 10 November 2021

'Look at this lot. Guarantee you they're all on a government handout.'

Shepherd shut the door of the paddy wagon with extra force and pulled his belt up higher like he meant business, which he guessed he probably did. His promotion to detective sergeant did not reflect any shortening of the traditional gap between Shepherd's actions and his thoughts. Uniform constable Nat Restoff followed in his wake. Already Shepherd was missing the car air-conditioning. The earth was dry, hard as a London mailbox and almost as red. So far this spring, the rain had fallen in thimbles. Each year your body had to get used to the wheezing humidity all over again. There were less than twenty protesters, chanting with placards, vegans out to make you feel guilty for enjoying a steak. Well, they were going to be disappointed. Not much in life made Josh Shepherd feel guilty. Potentially the biggest problem here was the abattoir workers. Corralled behind their supervisor, a few of them were brandishing boning knives at the protesters. The supervisor was trying to calm them but threats and swearing were breaking ranks.

'Go and suck on your ice, you deadshits,' one of them yelled at the protesters.

The cameraman immediately swung towards the hothead.

This job could have been left to the uniforms in Shepherd's not-so-humble opinion. It did not need anybody from the detective squad but Clement had told him that Scott Risely, the boss, wanted a detective presence. A month or so back somebody had torched the cars of the night-shift workers but no progress had been made on the case. Jo di Rivi and Graeme Earle had run that one, maybe that was why? Now that di Rivi was a detective you couldn't turn around without bumping into her. She was getting all the good jobs. 'It's terrific to have a woman's perspective' and all that crap. She and Earle had flown up to Halls Creek on some mining site break-in. Cushy. Most of the day you spent in the plane there and back with a few questions at the crime scene and a free lunch in between. They'd probably strike out there just like they did at the abattoir.

But this job did have its compensations like the fact this was going to be on local TV. Never hurt to have your mug flashed around the place. Even better, the reporter Amy was very, very attractive.

Whenever their paths crossed Shepherd took the opportunity to strike up a conversation. He'd heard she was single. Well so was he, and in Shepherd's world view, a reporter on the crime beat and a newly promoted detective sergeant was just a natural fit. Amy – he wasn't sure of her second name, it was long and complicated like a Sri Lankan leg spinner's – had given no indication that she found him of the slightest interest but he wasn't rushing this one, he was going slowly, slowly, not giving her a chance of a pre-emptive strike.

He'd learned that lesson.

Let them acquire a taste for Shepherd before you put them on the spot and asked them out, because once they've rejected you, that's it, there could be no going back. See, if you tried a second time and got rejected again you were just a fool or a nuisance. Every time Amy covered one of his cases at the court, he would throw out a line hoping to get her to nibble, and every time she would smile politely and then move off as if she had urgent work to do. Her short yellow skirt contrasted against her dark skin. Today she was looking especially alluring.

'Animals ... Deserve ... Better,' chanted a core of protesters. Shepherd felt their eyes turning his way. He liked the attention. Placing himself somewhere equidistant between the warring factions, he planted his feet and held out his hands as if pushing down their invisible anger.

He was mirroring as closely as possible what he'd seen the Roman centurion do on the Netflix show he'd been watching this week when the Roman peasants had been causing a stink.

'Hey,' he said. 'Calm down, the lot of you.'

'We're calm. They're the ones threatening us with knives,' said one of those seventy-year-old greybeard types from underneath his akubra. Every rally had one of these: rimless glasses, short-sleeved check shirt, Pommy accent. Used to be a professor of something at some uni, odds-on. They'd always have the wife there too in a big sunhat. Yep, there she was. The rest of them looked like they'd crawled out of the same sleeping-bag at a music festival. Young, scraggy, unwashed.

'How'd you like it if we threatened your jobs? Oh, that's right, none of you work!' An angry young worker, saliva flying. Shepherd would like to have seconded that but then Amy was watching and he was on camera.

'That's enough.' This time he scuffed his feet, imagining Roman sandals on them. In fact, he was wearing his near-new shiny black leather shoes he'd bought to go with his promotion. He remembered this, regrettably, a fraction too late after he had already done the scuffing. Damn, a whole month and they hadn't a mark on them till then. This increased his anger towards both parties over whom he was presiding.

'You lot,' he pointed his finger at the protesters, 'have got your pictures,' a gesture at the cameraman. 'You're interfering with work being this close to the shed.'

'We're not stopping them working.'

Hmm, a bearded layabout. Shepherd gave him his best 'I've-got-your-number' look.

'You are an OH and S hazard.' Shepherd had practised the words Mal Gross had drummed into him as he was climbing into the wagon. 'If you want to protest, you can do it two hundred and fifty metres away. Over there, away from traffic.' He pointed to a patch of sand with no protection from the blazing sun. He swivelled towards the workers behind him. 'You lot get back to work.'

He couldn't help throwing a glance at Amy and was impressed to see she was actually watching him with some interest.

'We're doing nothing wrong.' A woman this time. Long straggly hair, singlet, tattoos, shell-necklet. Probably sold scented candles at one of the markets and declared nothing on her dole form.

'If you don't move, we will have to arrest you and nobody wants that, right?'

He looked at the camera. The very reasonable request of Detective Sergeant Josh Shepherd would be clear for all to see.

'We're not moving. If you want us over there, you'll have to carry us.'

It was the frau of greybeard. She sounded like the Queen. Shepherd was about to lose his cool when he felt Restoff touch his elbow. He looked around. Restoff gestured that he wanted a quiet word. Shepherd moved a pace back and lowered his ear.

'You see the kid at the back?' Restoff kept his hands on his hips but he tried to point with his chin. Shepherd turned back to the protesters. His gaze focussed on one of them wearing a t-shirt with a picture of a sheep above some greenie slogan.

Shit.

***

Sitting in his office confronted by the deflating sight of a stack of unfinished reports, the void in Clement's life was laid bare. The football season had ended and with it had gone the best way to soak up those gap minutes when you didn't want to think about your life and its futility, or at least everything that it ought to have but didn't. Instead of confronting those big questions you could divert your waking thoughts to football selections. He had finished runner-up in the footy tipping comp this year. Two weeks out he'd been sitting in second position and had been faced with the eternal question: should he go for broke and try and win the big prize and the accolades but maybe miss out on second? First prize was three hundred bucks but the bragging rights were immeasurable. Second prize was eighty bucks, basically your entry fee back from this year and your fee for next year. Clement wrestled with the dilemma for the whole week before playing safe. Result: overall second, eighty bucks and months of regret. And worse, now that he didn't have that psychological polyfilla of the tipping comp the cracks had opened up like they were this minute.

Obsessing about the tipping comp is what occupies lonely single men, he reflected. That's precisely what you are, Clement. It had been his old schoolfriend Bill Seratono who had convinced him to sign on. The first month or two of the season, he had not taken seriously. Back then he still had a life, was dating two women, not on the sly either. Dating was a polite word. He was sleeping with them, sometimes even the whole night. For Clement this was a novel experience. There had been previous times where he'd dated a flurry of women to try and forget Marilyn, his ex-wife, but not simultaneously. It wasn't like he was trying to play the field, it just happened. He had been, to use an old-fashioned word, courting Lucinda, a divorced doctor. They'd had some dinners and canvassed sex. It was pretty well accepted they would go to his seldom-used house in Derby and enjoy a consummation weekend in the imminent future. But just days before the long-awaited event was scheduled, he got a little drunk at the Anglers and so did Melissa, a petite blonde tour guide. Bill Seratono offered to drop them both home. Clement got out at Melissa's determined to walk the thirty minutes back to his own place. He never made it. He woke in Melissa's bed beside a furry toy bear. She asked him if he was in a relationship and he said he was, though that was, he supposed, an exaggeration. She didn't care. After wrangling with various options, including silence, he came clean to Lucinda, expecting her to toss away their planned lovers' weekend like old fish heads. Instead, she gave him a long spiel about how she wasn't falling into the same trap she had in her marriage where her husband had wanted to control her. She didn't want to control Clement, but she needed sex. She pretty much demanded their hours of groundwork reach fruition in the cot.

And it was a very enjoyable weekend. Somewhere in the midst of it Clement studied himself in the mirror and wondered if this could be real: two women, great sex, and he still had to put out nobody's garbage but his own. Lucinda had told him it was up to him if he still felt the need to see 'other women' – like he had a string of them. Of course, she meant Melissa but Clement was too blind to see that or deliberately chose not to interpret it that way. Actually, he had no plans to see Melissa again but then she called him and invited him over and Clement found himself wanting to explore the road less taken. Or maybe both roads at the same time. The situation hadn't lasted a month, or in football parlance, four rounds, when Melissa had given him the ultimatum: Make me exclusive or I walk.

She walked.

Almost immediately Lucinda became less and less agreeable in following any suggestion of his as to how they should spend their shared time. If he wanted to go out, she wanted to stay in. If he was tired and fancied a night in, she would want to head out. The decline was swift and the parting far from sweet.

Deep down Clement accepted that it was never going to last. Not for him. In those dangerous hours when it was too early to kick back with a beer and a loved album, football became his lifeline. It was amazing how much you could avoid thinking about, if you just restricted yourself to nine all-important games of football each week. Those long stretches waiting for a DNA test to come back or to give evidence at a trial would see him studying the teams' ins and outs, and their win rates at particular venues. It made life tolerable. There would always be a scar to show where he had finally ripped Marilyn from his heart but he no longer brooded about her, just experienced the occasional dream where they were together still. He would wake and assure himself that there was nobody in his bed but him, nobody in his life but his daughter, his parents, his old mate Bill and those with whom he worked. He accepted he was solo now. It frightened him that he may never again be part of a couple. He wondered if that solitary month of his life with two lovers was a final gift of the gods before he was expelled to a barren island. More and more often he would catch himself studying some shuffling old fella on his way around the supermart with a small shopping basket bereft of anything but milk, bread and sausages.

That image disturbed him and made him determined to resist that outcome. He had taken the challenge to cook for himself something more adventurous than pasta or a barbecue. Now prawn and fish, in curries or wok, had become his specialty, albeit closely guarded. He wasn't yet ready to go public.

I really should concentrate on these reports, he urged himself, trying to avoid looking too closely at the stack of boring paperwork waiting to be written up. He gave up and reached for the first file with resignation.

'Just had Josh on the phone.' Mal Gross, the senior sergeant who ran the station's administration, was bustling over. Those words were enough to get Clement tense.

'Tell me he didn't arrest the protesters.'

'No, but there's a problem. You heard from Graeme?'

Graeme Earle, Clement's usual partner, was at Halls Creek with Jo di Rivi following up on a theft of explosives from a mine site. Halls Creek was seven hundred k east of Broome, too far to drive but less than two hours flying, so Earle and di Rivi had left early in a light plane.

'No I haven't. Why do you want Graeme?'

Outside it was steamy but Clement had the air-con blasting full as he drove. The kid had pulled a jacket over his t-shirt and sat huddled as far away from Clement as he could squeeze himself. Clement had left a message for Graeme Earle to call but he hadn't yet. According to Mal Gross, he and di Rivi would still be in the air. The boy stared sullenly ahead through the windscreen, avoiding eye contact.

'You can't just skip school you know.'

'I know. It would look bad for Dad.'

Smart-arse. Rhys Earle was only a year or so older than Clement's daughter. He was glad Phoebe had never been a problem kid. Then again, up till now neither, so far as Clement knew, had Rhys.

'Animals have rights,' said Rhys.

'The abattoir wasn't breaking the law. They weren't maltreating the animals.'

'Tell that to the animals. I reckon being slaughtered isn't exactly a life choice.'

Clement tried to ease around the subject. 'I didn't know you were vegetarian.'

'Vegan. Why would you? Dad wouldn't say anything. He doesn't even want to acknowledge it.'

'There are other ways to protest, you know.'

'Write an essay?'

Clement fought the temptation to snap back. 'Sure. Instagram or whatever.'

Rhys Earle shook his head the way a soccer fan does when his team misses a penalty.

'You guys are always on the side of the rich and powerful.'

You guys? Clement felt sorry for Earle. At least Phoebe respected the work her father did.

'We're on the side of the law.'

'Which always favours the rich and powerful.'

'I don't know that the abattoir is that rich or powerful.'

Rhys stared ahead, letting the silence smother them like a dust storm.

Clement's phone buzzed. He saw it was Graeme.

'Yes,' he answered.

The boy knew who it was and didn't move a muscle.

'Is he with you?'

Clement could hear the tension in his friend's voice.

'Yes, we're five minutes away.'

'Bring him to the station. We're back. I'll take it from there. Thanks.'

From the back door of the station Clement watched the heated exchange between Earle and his son in the staff parking area. Then the boy climbed unhappily into the vehicle and Graeme Earle shut the door and walked around to the driver side. Kids. Clement didn't believe he'd given his own parents grief. Well, not at that age. He recalled how upset they had been when he'd told them Marilyn and he were separating. He noticed the way his mother had wrung her hands, and how his father, rather than meet his gaze, directed it down to an ants' nest in the back paving. They loved Marilyn. It occurred to Clement at that moment this was the first time he thought about how it must have devastated them. Up till now, he'd only ever thought of it from his point of view, how embarrassing it was to him to have to tell them. But now he imagined what had happened when his car had disappeared from their driveway, how their arms would have gone around one another, his mother likely tearing up, his father anxious for his grand-daughter's welfare and for his son.

He turned back inside. Jo di Rivi was at her desk. He was proud she had made detective. She deserved it and every one of the staff was equally pleased for her. Well, with the probable exception of Shepherd. Clement knew the basics of the case she'd been in Halls Creek for. Lizard Minerals was a small mining operation. Their bulk storage shed had been broken into and a bag of ammonium nitrate taken.

'How did it go up at Halls?' he asked. Neither felt inclined to address Graeme Earle's family issues.

'Bit more complicated than we realised at first. Besides the bulk storage, a booster was taken from one of the two portable magazines.'

Clement wasn't a mining man but he knew a booster was a TNT charge that would trigger the ammonium nitrate. He presumed the other magazine had contained the detonators. The magazines and the bulk storage shed were separated to prevent accidental explosions.

'Inside man?' he postulated.

'Our first thought. There are only two possibles: the explosives handler and the mine supervisor. They don't have criminal records and we didn't get any vibes from either of them. The keys were locked in a safe. There is a working camera at the perimeter fence pointing at the shed and it shows nothing untoward. You know how they got in?'

'Siegfried and Roy,' said Clement and then realised di Rivi had no idea he was talking about magicians. He waved her continue.

'Dug underneath and came up through the floor.'

Criminals did not lack for ingenuity.

'No concrete apron?'

'No. They're those portable magazines that sit a few centimetres off the ground on chocks. Couple of shovels and you're underneath it in fifteen minutes. They cut a square out of the aluminium floor to get in, then covered it with boxes when they left. Nobody noticed till Graeme and me moved the boxes away. They'd already done a stocktake. One bag of ammonium nitrate missing. They weigh about four kilos so they're easy to haul. We thought we better check the other sheds too. Detonators weren't touched but they did the same thing to get the boosters. Filled in the hole when they left and nobody was any the wiser. Could have been up to a month ago.'

'Did the thieves risk blowing themselves up?'

'Not without detonators. It would have been noisy getting in, but at night there's nobody around except goannas.'

Clement was thinking somebody had to know a little about the operation.

'Get a list of past and present employees and check for criminal records.'

'Graeme's already got a list of current employees. I was about to get onto that.'

'It might be a long shot. Anybody who worked there could have innocently mentioned stuff at a pub, but check anyway.'

Di Rivi said, 'We took prints too but I reckon if the culprits are in the system, they're not going to leave us anything.'

'That's true. But have a look and see if there is anybody whose prints ought to be there but aren't. Sometimes these dummies wipe off their prints and it's like a neon sign.'

'Will do.'

So much for a day of investigative excitement. Clement was bored. Maybe he should never have left Perth. At least he would be close to Phoebe. Perhaps he should go back to the city? He shoved that thought aside, replaced it with an easier dilemma: what to cook for tonight's solo dinner?

Clement saw her too late. He'd been focussed on the meats in the supermarket freezer still tossing up, chicken or beef. One of each, he decided, but as the styrofoam trays hit the bottom of his plastic basket, he looked up and there she was, staring at him from the other end of the freezer.

'Hello, Lucinda.'

Her eyes levelled at him reminding Clement of a black-and-white movie he'd watched a couple of nights ago when the German battleship *Bismarck*'s guns trained on the British cruiser *Hood*.

'Hello, Dan.'

If you took a sea sponge from the ocean and laid it on a hot rock where ants could swarm over it and denude it, it might eventually become as dry and hollow as the tone with which she imbued those two words.

'How have you been?' he asked, the uncomfortable plastic basket swinging off his wrist.

'As if you give a damn.'

She turned her back to him and pushed her trolley in a different direction.

It left Clement shaken, guilty. He hadn't meant to hurt her. He wanted to tell himself that he hadn't realised she had invested in him but was that really true? Didn't he sense a vulnerability within her, way back at the beginning? She'd come on as gung-ho and he thought he'd bought her grab-you-by-the-balls act as genuine but now he wasn't so sure. Dating was a mined sea lane that he'd believed he'd long safely traversed until Marilyn cast him adrift.

He waited several minutes, loitering by the dairy section. Only when he saw Lucinda disappear into dusk did he progress to the checkout. At least tonight there would be nobody to offend but himself.

2 THURSDAY MORNING

A layer of fine glass covered the floor like jelly crystals, the only exception being what remained of the window that had been smashed after they had sawn away the outside bars. The small secure medical fridge had been forced open to get at the vials. The crime-scene crew had already been through and fingerprint powder was all around. Josh Shepherd was thinking that between the glass and the powder, his shoes were going to suffer further. He was also thinking that Saturday was a big game coming up and the skipper had better make more use of his bowling than he had so far. Last season Shepherd had taken the second most wickets and more often than not he had been one of the opening bowlers. This year he was being called on as first-change. 'Relegated' to first-change was how Shepherd thought of it.

'The nurse found the mess when she came to open up,' said Daryl Hagan. Two uniforms, Hagan and Beck Lalor, had called it in. Clement had told Shepherd to take charge.

'After the drugs,' reckoned Shepherd.

'Not to use,' said Beck Lalor, heading over from where she had been talking to the community nurse.

There had been a time Shepherd had set his sights on Lalor. She had a wide-face with large eyes and curly light-brown hair that he liked. She'd never responded positively to his overtures though and so Shepherd, true to his code, had backed off. Shepherd had no desire to make a nuisance of himself if there was no likely payoff.

Still, it was a pity, those curls were attractive.

Lalor continued. 'The nurse, Claire, tells me that this whole batch that has been destroyed is for vaccinations: whooping cough, measles et cetera.'

'They didn't take any drugs?'

Shepherd couldn't keep the incredulity out of his voice.

'They keep no addictive drugs here,' said Lalor.

'So they went to all that trouble – cutting the power to the alarm, sawing through the bars, for nothing. They got in a funk and smashed all the vials up. Dipsticks,' said Shepherd, placing them in the same bag as his cricket captain who was too stupid to use Shepherd to his best advantage.

Hagan raised his eyebrows to Lalor to show he understood the significance of the destruction.

Lalor said, 'I'd say there's a fair chance that they're anti-vaxxers.'

'Crazies who reckon that vaccinating kids gives them major diseases,' translated Hagan.

'I know that,' snapped Shepherd.

But Hagan didn't think he had known it.

'They got a camera anywhere?' Shepherd scanned the ceiling, hoping.

'No,' said Lalor. 'But Claire says they had a young woman a little over a week ago standing outside lecturing the people coming in that they were threatening their kids' futures.'

'Local?' Shepherd was poking here and there as if he might uncover a killer clue.

'Claire didn't actually see her. One of the clients reported it to Claire and by the time she went out the woman had gone. She's getting us a list together of the clients who were in that day.'

'Good work,' said Shepherd. He didn't want to be one of those fault-finding superiors, he could afford to be magnanimous. 'I want you guys to check the witnesses out, see if any can give us a description. We can get an artist if we need.'

'Fair chance they'll get a print.' Hagan nodded at the dusted drug-safe.

'But if they don't, I want to have some other avenues. This could be related to the abattoir.'

Shepherd enjoyed demonstrating to the uniforms that there was a gap between the respective abilities of them and him. The last thing Shepherd wanted was to have to interview a bunch of snotty-nosed kids and their mothers. The uniforms could do that. Meanwhile, he would slip over to the local TV station and get a copy of the footage Amy and her crew had taken the day before at the abattoir protest because, let's face it, it was going to be one of them who had done this. Quite likely the tattooed one who probably sold scented candles, or the no-hoper bloke who looked like his occupation was dealing eccies at open-air rock concerts. And how good was it going to look when he cracked this case and the hitherto unsolved torching of the workers' cars. That would make everybody sit up and take notice. From his pocket he extracted his wallet and then the business card he had made Amy hand over the previous day before he had taken his leave of the abattoir. He tried to read her name. Amy Wickramasinghe. Nope, he'd never remember that surname or would offend her getting it wrong. It would just be Amy. He dialled.

'Yes?'

She had a nice, deep voice for such a slim young woman.

'Amy, it's Josh?'

'Josh who?'

'Detective Josh Shepherd.'

'Oh.'

'I think we might be of mutual benefit to one another.'

There was a long pause.

'How?'

'Why don't you come to the early childhood clinic and you'll see. You may want to bring your cameraman.'

It had not taken Beck Lalor long to locate the witnesses recommended by Claire from the clinic. They confirmed what Claire had said. A young woman, probably early twenties with long dark hair, had been standing outside the clinic as parents were going in, haranguing them that they were poisoning their kids and being puppets of multinational pharmaceutical companies. The young woman had been wearing a t-shirt and jeans and was 'kind of grimy'. Savannah

Duggan, a young mother with two little kids crawling over her, was sitting in the station-house kitchen while their sometime artist, Lilly, drew the woman from Savannah's description.

'She was full-on,' said Savannah, who like many Broome locals, had an incredible delicacy about her features, with high cheekbones and sharp chin. She paused to study the drawing. 'I couldn't see her ears. Her hair was kind of covering them.'

'Are her eyes right now?' asked Beck Lalor, munching on a biscuit. Might as well get something out of putting in the effort that Shepherd had conveniently avoided.

'Yeah. That's better. Angry. She was real angry.'

Lilly worked fast. Clement had found her making pocket money drawing tourists and suggested she offer her services to his department. There were lots of times when a sketch artist would come in handy. Lilly had agreed. It was a smart move by Clement because the town itself was bereft of the kind of constant CCTV monitoring you might find in the cities.

'Is that close?' asked Lilly turning the sketch for Savannah to study.

Savannah nodded. 'That's the bitch.'

***

Things had worked out perfectly, thought Shepherd. Amy had arrived and got her cameraman to shoot footage, then done a report on the spot. He'd hung about with the excuse he was waiting in case the techs came back with something, though truly it would be a while before they had any information.

When Amy was done, he'd said, 'Did you bring what I asked?'

She had. She handed across the thumb drive.

'That has all the footage we took at the abattoir yesterday.'

'Terrific. Did you take names?'

'A few,' she said. 'Not everybody would give their name.'

'Nah, probably on the run from somewhere or illegal entries.' Her expression at his quip was not reassuring. 'Just joking. I might need to check with you. I mean chances are it's one of the protesters.'

'You want to say that on camera?'

He was about to commit wholeheartedly but seeing as he hadn't run it past Clement yet, a faraway bell sounded.

'Not just yet. After all, it may not be them. It could be some stupid junkie. I'll bring you back the USB when I've downloaded.'

'Don't bother,' she said in a tone that called upon Shepherd's deeper layers of skin to withstand.

'No bother,' he'd countered.

Now he was back in the station and the first person he saw was Beck Lalor brandishing a large pencil sketch.

'This is our clinic suspect. No name, only seen her the once so may not be local.'

Lalor tried to hand it to him. Shepherd kept his hands low like he was facing a clever medium pacer on a zippy wicket. One thing he hated was photocopying.

'Could you get copies done and bring me one? Thanks.'

A few minutes later he was at his desk carefully checking all the protesters who had been filmed against the sketch. He couldn't spy her. That didn't mean she wasn't associated with this lot. He called Amy again. She was busy cutting her story on the clinic break-in but he was pleased she hung five to give him the names she'd taken. There were only a few.

'I think your best chance might be the older couple, the Meadows. They seemed to know most of the others there.'

He remembered those two, the professor and his wife who spoke like the Queen.

***

The cheap electric fans had done their best but they had not cooled Clement sufficiently to allow him a decent sleep. This time of the year he always found tough, coming out of the more pleasant winter and early spring. Or maybe it had been the encounter with Lucinda that had made him restless. At least as far as he could recall he hadn't dreamt about her. Sitting at his desk, he felt hungover, although without the comfort of knowing an alcohol-fuelled good time had preceded it. He wasn't drinking much these days, just a few beers. Graeme Earle was working away on the mine heist and this morning they'd not yet chatted socially. Clement wanted to offer support to his partner as regards the Rhys situation but he wouldn't push. If Earle wanted to seek advice or comfort, he would. Clement was bored out of his skull. He noticed Shepherd heading out.

'Where are you off to?'

Shepherd explained. Clement was pleased that Shepherd had thought of going through the TV footage looking for the culprit but he suspected there might have been a base motive as well. He'd overheard Shepherd waxing lyrical about the reporter's looks to one of his mates during a phone call.

'I'll come with you,' he said. It annoyed him that they'd not cleared the earlier incident of the workers' cars being torched and it seemed possible that the break-in was related.

The townhouse was recently built, one of a small development near Cable Beach. A Hyundai sat in the driveway. The garden was a colourful mix, mainly native hibiscus and wattle, a couple of English-garden type plants. Clement rang the spotless doorbell beside the metal flywire door. The interior was in shadow. A tall man with thin bony legs in faded shorts, a natural stoop and a crown of thinning white hair came to the door and opened it with curiosity painted on his long face.

'Mr Meadows?' asked Clement.

'Yes.'

Clement introduced himself and Shepherd. Meadows was patently concerned to find police at his threshold. Clement heard a shuffling from within, possibly the wife trying to overhear what it was about.

'You were at the rally yesterday,' said Clement.

'We did not break the law.' Meadows looked accusingly at Shepherd as if he'd lied.

'No, we are grateful for the protesters' cooperation,' said Clement diplomatically. 'But somebody did break into the early childhood centre overnight and smashed it up fairly badly. We think it might be anti-vaxxers and we hoped you might be able to help us.'

Clement finished with a polite upwards inflection and gazed at Meadows with the look of a villager asking a favour of the squire.

'Please, come in,' said Meadows.

The interior of the Meadows' house was a weird hybrid, as if they'd been shipwrecked and furnished their home from the contents of other passengers' trunks that had floated onto their beach. From the middle-class British trunk there was a small floral sofa and matching armchair, a blue-and-white striped Doulton teapot, an Edwardian sideboard topped with bric-a-brac including a Di and Charles mug, and several high-glaze rustic pieces including a miniature thatched cottage and a pig. The imaginary trunk of the local crew that had washed up on their beach included a Tiwi design throw rug, a cane coffee table, several watercolours of mangroves, ceiling fans and the clothes on their backs. In his youth Clement had been surrounded by this kind of mix, unofficial aunties and uncles who had drifted to Western Australia after years in Malaya or Singapore. They would all come back to Australia after their time abroad but their possessions and clothes were forever altered.

Stephen Meadows, who had quickly introduced himself and his wife Hazel, wore a batik short-sleeved shirt. His long feet were encased in sandals. Hazel wore a kind of cotton kaftan in vivid colours.

Stephen Meadows poured tea from the Doulton. Clement was aware that he and Shepherd looked odd jammed into the two-seater sofa side-by-side but that's where the Meadows had directed them. Hazel hovered in front of them with a plate of slice that looked healthy. Clement was happy to indulge, even though caraway seeds and semolina weren't high on his wishlist. Shepherd made do with the tea and extra sugar. Clement had run through the witnesses' account of the young woman harassing the mothers.

'Well, Inspector, we are not anti-vaxxers, quite the opposite,' said Stephen Meadows. 'You'll appreciate that people who might oppose the abattoir can come from very different streams into one large river.'

Hazel said, 'While we believe everybody – loggers, meat-workers, you name it – is entitled to freely express their opinion, I'm afraid the anti-vaxxers talk a lot of stuff and nonsense. They get all this rubbish off the internet and treat it as gospel.'

'This is the woman we'd like to speak with,' said Clement producing a copy of the sketch. Stephen Meadows bent forward and frowned at it as Hazel peered over his shoulder.

'I'll get my glasses,' announced Meadows. He appeared to find them beneath a large barometer that once again echoed with Clement. His mother's family had been in shipping and, in that circle, a barometer on the lounge room wall was common.

'Yes, I'm sure I have seen her,' said Hazel. 'Take one,' she urged Shepherd, poking the plate of slice under his nose. This time he obliged.

Stephen Meadows now with eyewear got close to the sketch before announcing, 'Hazel's far better at faces than I am. She looks familiar but then, lots of young women look similar.'

'No, I've seen her.' Hazel held up a finger as if to silence her husband while she thought. She nibbled on her slice. 'The mangroves?' She turned to her husband for confirmation. His mouth formed an O.

'Yes, could be.' He pointed at the watercolours. 'Hazel did those.'

'They're excellent,' said Clement. He was not trying to curry favour, he was genuine.

Hazel beamed. 'Thank you. It's just a hobby. There was a marina planned that would have affected the mangroves. We protested. I think that's where ...' She immediately turned back to the matter at hand. 'Or am I making it up? No, I'm sure she was there. Yes with, I presume, her boyfriend. You know, the fellow with the Trotsky beard,' she prompted her husband.

Stephen Meadows' eyes lit in recognition. 'Oh, right. Yes, I remember.'

'Do you know their names?' asked Shepherd who had already demolished the slice and wanted to get a run on the board in front of his boss.

'No,' answered Hazel Meadows for both. 'We just, to one another, called him Trotsky and a few of the others picked up on it. I don't think we've seen them at any of the recent rallies.'

'Did you happen to notice their vehicle?'

The Meadows looked at one another then shook their heads.

'Would you know if they are local?' asked Clement. 'Have you seen them around Broome?'

'Not recently,' said Hazel Meadows. 'Not for at least a month and only ever once or twice. They were in town selling t-shirts; animal rights slogans and things. Not in a shop or anything, just on the street.'

'Was this around the time the abattoir workers' cars were set on fire?' asked Shepherd with all the lightness of a Clydesdale. Clement wanted to wrap gaffer tape around his junior's mouth. That was the sort of question you built to after some real rapport had been established. Their hosts almost physically recoiled and Clement wondered if the barometer showed a plunge in air pressure to meet their mood.

'I'm not sure,' said Hazel Meadows and for the first time refused to make eye contact.

'I only remember them at the mangroves and we didn't speak a lot,' said her husband. Clement had the sense that if this wasn't a lie it was at least a prevarication. He tried to retrieve the situation.

'Look, I'm all for peaceful protests but sometimes they cross over ...'

'And sometimes, Inspector, young people get passionate in the cause of those who are unable to speak for themselves. Yes, sometimes they do get frustrated and yes, can make a mistake. Should their lives be ruined for that?'

'We're only trying to find out ...' began Shepherd with far too much heat, and Clement was forced to pointedly widen his eyes as a signal to quit. Fortunately Shepherd read it and halted.

'Perhaps you might be able to give us the names of some of your circle,' said Clement. 'They may have had closer contact with this woman.' He turned attention back to the sketch. 'We can't just abandon a line of inquiry. I'm sure you understand that. Substantial damage was done and I wouldn't want somebody's child to wind up with whooping cough while we stood by.'

The little speech helped.

'We wouldn't want that either,' said Stephen Meadows. 'But we don't want people made an easy target for every crime in the Kimberley.'

Clement said nothing and was relieved that Shepherd remained silent too. A short time later they had extracted a half-dozen names. Many of the other protesters were transient, they explained.

'These are the people we know who live in the area,' said Stephen Meadows as Shepherd jotted notes on an iPad.

Clement thanked them for their time.

'That tea and slice was absolutely delicious,' he said as they stood to go and was pleased to see a smile rise at the corner of Hazel Meadows' mouth. He wasn't playing her. It had refreshed him.

When they were barely outside, Shepherd muttered, 'They could have told us more.'

'They might have,' said Clement opening the car, 'but these kind of interviews are a dance, not a wrestling match. You have to let them get to know and respect you as a person, not just a cop.'

Shepherd yanked his seatbelt with the force he might have liked to have used on the Meadows.

'We never even got a name,' he sulked.

'No, but we found out she has a boyfriend and we got a description. And we got more names you can follow up. We didn't come away completely empty-handed.' Clement drove out slowly. 'See if any of those people can identify the girl or her boyfriend or their vehicle. Then run the descriptions past all police stations in the Kimberley and Pilbara. In fact, I'd go as far south as Geraldton. And try Perth. More protests there, they might pop up.'

Seeing Phoebe on a computer screen was no substitute for the real thing but better than not at all. It was a little after six in the evening, likely not so hot and stifling in Perth as in the small room above the chandler's where Clement sat scooping out his takeaway curry with a plastic spoon. The day had been a disappointment and he'd avoided the supermart in case he bumped into Lucinda again. I don't have to cook for myself every night, he'd told himself.

'How was squad?' he asked.

He had made notes of Phoebe's schedule so that in the times they got to talk he could show he was taking an interest. Today was her swim squad.

'Hard,' she said munching on an apple. They had around twenty minutes before she would have to leave for dinner at her expensive boarding school. While he paid half her school fees, her mother insisted he should not be burdened with the considerable ancillary costs when her grandmother was dying to splash her money out on her only grandchild. Clement never asked if Marilyn's new husband contributed. He hoped he did not have anything to do with paying for the upbringing of Phoebe and did not want to be disappointed by finding out that he did. Phoebe's room looked typically neat although he noted with a pang that the pony poster that had hung on her wall since she was about seven had been replaced by some fresh-faced pop star. At least it wasn't a rapper. Clement himself preferred rap to the kind of music this poster suggested but this was an area where he was quite happy to let his fourteen-year-old daughter wander a different path.

'Vegetarian korma?' she asked as she watched him devour the food.

'Chicken.'

She grunted. For the last few months, she'd been subtly trying to push him away from a meat diet.

'You nailed butterfly?' he asked, distracting her cross-examination.

'Getting better,' she said, chewing. 'But I'm not going to make top two for interschool in anything. Emma and Marnie are way faster.'

'Even breaststroke?'

'Dad, they're like state level at everything. I might be reserve, maybe the relay if I'm lucky.'

Phoebe never seemed neurotic about not being the best. That was reassuring.

Since the incident with Rhys Earle, Clement had found himself feeling uneasy. Was he really devoting enough time to Phoebe? Would their special bond fade swiftly like the image on a TV suddenly unplugged? 'I spoke to Bill Seratono. He said I could borrow his boat for a week for the holidays. It's a ripper. We could check out the islands, camp. That gear I bought for last time is almost new.'

'Mum didn't tell you?'

If the emotion those words engendered was a sound, it would be the metal wheels of a train skidding on rails after its brakes have been slammed on. He tensed for the inevitable carnage.

'Tell me what?'

Even from this distance bouncing off a satellite he sensed his daughter's disappointment that she had been forced into being the bearer of bad news. Her eyes looked down before tilting up and meeting his gaze again.

'Our school band is going on a trip to Boston and Philadelphia first week of December. Two weeks. I'll be back for Christmas. That's alright isn't it?'

What was he going to say? It was the kind of wonderful opportunity that these schools could provide. Phoebe loved her music, and she was very talented at all the woodwinds. Of course, the selfish part of him, the flesh and blood Daniel Clement, wanted to object, and say that sailing around the Kimberley coast with your dad, camping on hard ground and showering with a bucket of cold water was a far more enriching experience. But he allowed the palimpsest Clement to hold sway.

'Of course.'

'We can do the trip in January.'

No, they couldn't. Not with Bill's boat. Bill had his own plans from Christmas on. It might be possible to hire a replacement but the cost would blow a hole in his finances.

'Sure. We'll do something, anyway. Everything is going well there?'

'Uh-huh.'

He missed that poster of the beautiful pony in the wild heather. In a blink, Phoebe would be a woman. He wanted to tell her: a pony never breaks your heart. A cuddly toy never cuts with a cruel word or a lustful glance. But some streams we have to cross for ourselves. He didn't think until that instant that he'd ever regretted not having more children but he spied for a flash of a second, a crevice, and wedged in there a thought: how wonderful it would be to have another child to play dad to.

'If you ever had any problems, you would tell me, right?'

She shrugged. 'Sure.'

He wasn't reassured, reading the response as somewhere between maybe and possibly. Rhys was that little bit older, and further along the crumbling path.

'Graeme Earle is having a few problems with Rhys.'

She knew Rhys, not as a close friend but through the odd get-together they were well and truly acquainted. A couple of weekends, a year or two back, Graeme and Rhys had stayed with Clement and Phoebe in his Derby house.

She didn't ask him to elaborate.

'He was protesting at the abattoir up here.'

'Good for him,' said Phoebe.

'He was pretty resentful of his dad. Being a cop.'

'That's not fair. It's his job.'

'It doesn't bother you what I do?'

She shook her head. 'Some people are just unhappy and want to blame everyone. Like Antigone. She's always blaming the teachers. All of them. I mean, Mrs Schaffer is hopeless, she just tells us to open a book and copy what's in there but most of them are really good.'

'We could talk though, right? If you ever had a problem like that?'

'I don't. I'm good. I should be getting ready for dinner.'

He said he understood. 'I love you,' he said.

'Love you too.'

He killed the feed, then sat there finishing off his curry. I'm lucky, he thought. Phoebe has a good head on her shoulders. She didn't seem to resent him like Rhys did his father. He'd not noticed any obvious bad parenting from Graeme. Whatever 'bad parenting' might entail. Hell, none of us know how to be a great parent, he thought. Solving a murder was simple in comparison. He'd never had any problems with his own parents, but then perhaps that was because he was a shallow person. He didn't question, he just did. The times he'd spent with Rhys didn't equip Clement to be an expert on the kid's psychology. Rhys had seemed like a normal boy. But he didn't live with the kid. Sure, he'd seen him most weeks over the years but those weekends with Phoebe were the only time he'd spent more than a few hours in his company. When was that exactly that they enjoyed those family weekends away? Nearly two years ago. Rhys was just a boy back then. Now hormones were kicking in. Rhys would be stumbling towards manhood like we all do, he thought. We're worried if there will be a place for us in an adult world. How will we fit? How will we survive? It's easier when you're young to focus on macro questions: the environment, equality, freedom. The other questions are too scary. Is there somebody out there for me? Do I have a role in life? At that age Clement hadn't a clue about anything but he had not forgotten his teenage anxiety.

Marilyn should have told him about the music trip. He was pissed off. He resisted the impulse to call her right then. A while back he would have, an opportunity too tempting to pass up, a self-righteous spray on her responsibilities to inform him of their child's plans. Caught dead-to-rights, him the innocent party. But he would not do that yet. He would calm. It wasn't the end of the world. Marilyn didn't know he had organised the boat. She should have considered that but he figured he was a long way down her ladder of concern.

He binned the now empty container which neatly topped off the rubbish bag. He tied it and hauled that downstairs and into the large garbage bin. Then he took a moment to soak himself in the warm air and study the night sky. He would miss this space if he went back to Perth. But the truth was here he was not just in space but in a void, in his personal and professional life. In Perth at least he'd be close to Phoebe. It was a sure sign he needed a challenge when he had to involve himself in a clinic break-in. He needed to keep his brain occupied. He needed a big, juicy case, and though he'd jagged a couple of those in the past up here, logic told him that wasn't going to happen again. Not anytime soon.

3 MEDA, WEST KIMBERLEY

He woke to a powerful throbbing in his head. Like when the drum-major would beat that huge drum with mallets while they all stood at attention. He was disoriented. Pain swirled through him. Reality tried to solidify.

Orientation?

On his back. Darkness above. He smelled the eucalypts, spied a sliver of moon. The throb seemed to be spreading over his body as if being pumped by an unattended hose. Dull, slowly growing more fierce. Stones or rubble poked into his back. Where was he?

As he went to touch his forehead a razor-sharp pain shot through his palms, wrist and arms and the ubiquitous duller throbbing pain increased too. Again he tried, but he could not lift either hand. They were anchored but not numb like when you'd slept on them, for he had a searing sensation all the way from his fingers along his outstretched arms to his shoulders.

He turned his head to the right and looked down to his right hand. A long nail had been driven through the palm.

His scream scissored its way up the dark, silent curtain surrounding him. Panic flushed through him. He turned to his left and screamed anew. That palm too was nailed down. He writhed, able to twist his torso and flail his legs but now the pain in his hands was excruciating. He called out again. Nothing. Like a village in the early hours of the morning being illuminated household by household, his consciousness was increasing.

He was trapped, fixed to the earth.

He heard the catch of an engine after a key is turned.

'Help!' he yelled trying to free his hands but the word was swamped by the revving engine.

Light stabbed his eyes. Now his heart was pumping wildly, terror roaring through his limbs, his mouth desiccated.

'Nooooo,' he screamed.

He heard tyres spinning gravel, knew now that was what was poking into his spine.

His tears might have looked like bright diamonds had he been on the other side of the headlights. Through them he saw a grim, steel monster baring its fangs as it rushed towards him.

4 FRIDAY

Josh Shepherd walked to his door and said, 'Re the clinic break-in, Keeble can't find any prints except staff.'

News Clement half-expected. 'You might want to thank Lalor and di Rivi.'

'Mmm?' Shepherd appeared confused.

'They helped get the artist sketch copied and around the place. Have you sent it out?'

'Perth, Pilbara, Kimberley.'

Shepherd, who as was his way had spoken without first knocking on Clement's door, now rapped his knuckles there in an irritating farewell. Clement had no sooner turned back to his paperwork than Mal Gross swung into view with something on his mind.

Good, a distraction.

'Got Jared on the phone. He says it's urgent.'

Clement took the proffered phone off Gross. Jared Taylor was one of the Indigenous special constables that worked the region. His knowledge and contacts were invaluable.

'Yes, Jared.'

'I was on my way back to Derby when I got a call to go to the big cattle station near Meda.' Clement knew the massive station that covered thousands of k's. 'They said there was a body.'

'And?' Clement had instantly righted himself from a slouch.

'I'm here now. I've never seen anything like it.'

In his days working homicides in Perth, Clement had seen his fair share of gruesome murders. A few years back he'd had one up here too that ranked high on that list. But he had never seen anything to match this. The dead man was in the middle of the gravel road, naked. His arms were outstretched, the hands pointing at ten and two on your typical clock-face. A large spike, like might be used on railway sleepers or for some other industrial purpose, had been driven through each palm.

'Crucified,' said Graeme Earle shaking his head in bewilderment. Though unsure if that was technically correct, seeing as the feet hadn't been nailed down, Clement did not argue the point. To all intents and purposes, yes, a crucifixion.

This part of the massive cattle station was in its south-east, two and a half hours drive east of Broome, forty k or so out of Derby. An unblinking blue sky with a few wisps of white cloud bore down on Clement as the red-brown earth burned up through the soles of his shoes. The heat coming off the road was intense but not as bad as it often got up here. Definitely under forty C.

Lisa Keeble had left Broome ahead of them with her crime-scene team but was only just making a start. Her team was still erecting a tent over the body. The extreme heat could burn off DNA and destroy evidence that would survive much longer in colder climates. Even so, for a short trip, and up here in the Kimberley, two and a half hours was nothing. Keeble preferred to arrive by car with all her testing equipment, rather than try to organise a helicopter or light plane. Keeping their distance, the detectives had already scoped the murder scene. There had been no sign of wounds, bullet or knife, no obvious ligature marks, but the victim's body had been caked in red dirt, some of it ground down into the flesh.

'Tyre treads?' Clement was pointing at the dirt which formed a vague pattern on the dead man's skin.

'I reckon,' said Earle. There was little point asking Keeble for her opinion at this stage. She had enough on her plate but Clement had watched her team carefully taking photographs. He'd be flabbergasted if she hadn't already considered the same possibility. Studying the victim's swollen and bruised face, Clement wondered if he may have been bashed first. Or had all that been done by a vehicle driving over him?

The first thing he noticed about the man was his dark, curly hair. His skin had a very light-chocolate colouring, his build more solid than most of the Indigenous men up here, no leanness in his arms and legs. He was muscular. A fit man, not forty yet, reckoned Clement, racial background indeterminate.

'You think it might be religious?' Earle was gazing around at the vast scrubland as if he expected to find a ring of ancient stones there to support such a theory.

'Could be bikies,' said Clement who was thinking the cruelty of the murder might as easily be explained by payback as any religious motivation. He walked over to where Jared Taylor stood close by a young Aboriginal man who was squatting in the miniscule shade of a ute while waving flies away with his hat. Taylor left the young man and came towards them.

'He's the one who found the body?' Clement studied the young stockman trying to shade himself.

'Yeah. He radioed the station and they called Derby. They knew I was coming back from the gorge.'

'Does he know the dead guy?'

'Nah, never seen him.'

Clement indicated the stockman. 'What's his name?'

'Bryce. The other mob from the station came down with him but I met them on the road and sent them back to the house. I told him to stay.'

'Good.'

Clement walked over and introduced himself. Bryce was in his early twenties, sinewy.

'Tell me what happened.'

'I was driving to make sure the heifers was okay, and I seen something on the road. I hit the anchors. Pulled up just short, you know?'

'What time was this?'

'About ten thirty. I done me other job first.'

'Did you get out of the car?'

'Yeah. Like I stopped, you know. I thought it was somebody just sleeping or something. I couldn't tell through the windscreen.' Clement imagined it could have been covered in red dust. 'And I jumped out and walked over and ... shit.'

'Did you touch the body?'

'No. I spoke to him but I could see he was cactus. I didn't run over him.'

Clement nodded to show he believed him.

Graeme Earle said, 'You ever seen him before?'

The stockman shook his head. 'He's banged up pretty bad but he's not one of the boys here.'

'How many of you?' Clement gazed over to see the tent was up around the body now.

'There's nine of us ringers. Couple of bosses, then Mr and Mrs Garland.'

'How often is this track used?'

'Most days only me when I go to check on the heifers.'

The cattle stations up this way were vast, probably half the size of Manhattan.

'So you travel this road how often?'

'Usually once in the morning and then in the evening.'

'How many ways are there to access this track?'

Bryce considered. 'You mean if you're sticking to the road?'

It was a salient point. Up here a four-wheel drive could easily cut though the low scrub.

'Yes, how many ways if you stick to the road?'

According to Bryce there were two – the way Clement had driven in off a private road that could be accessed from the Gibb River Road, and then a backroad that ran kilometres around the property.

'Is the gate to the main road locked?'

'Not much point. If somebody wants to get in, they can find a way in through the bush.'

'When was the last time you know for sure somebody would have been on this track?'

'I came back after I checked the heifers about five yesterday arvo.'

The sound of a chopper made Clement look up. His first thought was that Keeble had asked for some reinforcements but then he realised it was the station's. They used helicopters to muster.

'Nobody else would be here after that?'

Bryce was certain none of the ringers would have been through. 'It's too far for any of their runs. Anyway, everybody's in by six for dinner.'

So, whoever did this would have had plenty of time, more than twelve hours from when the sun went down last evening right through till this morning, to be here unobserved. Hopefully Keeble could give him a time of death but he was pretty sure it would be wide.

Graeme Earle moved off towards Keeble, seeing if she had even a remote idea of time of death. He'd also get photos of the dead man's face in the hope that somebody here at the station might recognise him. That was the advantage of working with a long-time partner. Saved words and time.

'Would you hear a vehicle down here if you were up at the homestead?'

Bryce smiled, big white teeth. 'No mate, it's too far.'

He thanked Bryce and told him not to talk to anybody other than the police at this stage. Then he walked to the car and took a swig from his water bottle. The water was already unpleasantly warm. So much land, he was thinking, just for cattle. His mind drifted back to the protest at the abattoir and Rhys Earle's attitude, his certainty. Clement wondered if he'd been so certain of his opinions at that age. His youthful attitudes were a fog. Did he care about anything except finding a girlfriend back then? A lot of Madonna on the radio, he seemed to recall. A girl, Tania Wellings, whom he had his heart set on until he found out she was dating one of the boys who'd finished school the previous year. That had been humiliating. He'd been riding his bicycle when she went cruising past in the guy's Commodore.

Clement waited for Earle to come over as he knew he would. Despite the long drive, they had not talked a lot about Rhys. Clement had asked a perfunctory, 'How'd it work out with Rhys?'

43

Earle had confessed that he had no idea how to communicate with the boy. 'It's like we're from different tribes with different languages.'

Clement asked how Rhys' mother handled it.

Earle had looked at the vast clear landscape and said, 'Barb's given up. She wants us to all be one big happy family. I don't mind him being passionate, having his own opinion. But it's not his own opinion. He's hanging out with these losers, reading conspiracy theories and bullshit half-arsed science.'

That had been the extent of the interaction. Father and son schisms were as old as life. Clement couldn't help but wonder how long before he and Phoebe lost touch. It had been over a year since they'd spent time at the house in Derby. And now his summer plans with her had been scuppered.

Earle was heading over. He started speaking when he was still two metres shy of him.

'She has no idea of time of death, other than at least five hours.'

That meant anytime last night.

'You got the photos?'

Earle shoved his phone in front of Clement's face. 'This is interesting. On his back.' The screen showed a tattoo of a sun with a face, bright rays like wavy spokes. He had seen this image before. Was it from some children's picture book?

'Know it?' asked Earle.

'I feel I should.'

'It's the Sun King, Louis Fourteenth.'

'All that SBS viewing paid off.'

They cranked open their car doors.

'I only watch the fishing shows,' said Earle. 'Keeble told me.'

They couldn't interview all the stockmen in one go as four were out at the extremities of the property, but those they could had nothing of value to report. None of them knew the dead man, nor had heard anything in the way of vehicles or arguments. The same went for their two supervisors.

'You get people coming in from time to time, trying to camp, or spending a night and buggering off before we tell 'em to,' said Warbo, one of the supervisors, as he expertly rolled a cigarette for himself with his sun-damaged lips. Clement recalled his grandfather doing that. The world had patience then, he thought. Smokers didn't mind deferring their pleasure, they enjoyed the ritual. It was the same with travel, anything really. Now we want everything instantly, there was no savouring imminent pleasure.

'We get a lot more outsiders and campers up the May River side of the station. Not so many here.'

Clement thanked Warbo and his mate and then he and Earle headed off to the main house where the managers, the Garlands, were waiting. The other four stockmen were on their way back but Clement figured he was better off to keep things moving. It was still hot. There was no wind but the shade of a large gum had been a blessing. Quite a few pindan wattle trees were scattered about but the shade from them was as slim as Warbo's rollie.

The manager's house was large with a wide verandah and low steps. It might have been built in the thirties or forties but it looked like it had been fairly constantly remodelled over the years. Alice Garland had told them to call out when they were at the door, one of those old-fashioned ones with flywire behind a wood-pattern face. Alice Garland came bearing a two-year-old on her hip. She was small, wiry with a tan and pleasant smile.

'It's cooler inside,' she said as she guided them down a hallway into a living room where a big ceiling fan worked overtime. The sofas were well used. Clement and Earle took a seat. A box of kids' toys suggested more little ones somewhere.

'I'll get Ryan.'

She picked up a two-way and called as she moved through into an adjoining room. They heard her side of the conversation and a fridge door opening. A moment later she reappeared, still with the child on her hip but now she had a big jug of icy liquid in her other hand.

'Old-fashioned lemonade,' she said and placed it on the coffee table in front of them. She put the baby on the floor and brought over four tall glasses that had been waiting on a sideboard.

'This, what's happened, it's awful,' she said, pouring them lemonade.

Clement wasted no time gulping his. He felt instantly reinvigorated. 'Thank you.'

'Ryan won't be a moment. He drove down there to the body but the policeman sent him back.'

'We don't have any doubt that it is a murder.'

A door banged somewhere and Ryan Garland entered. He was probably just on forty, sandy hair, thinning, medium build and height. Introductions were done.

Earle said, 'This may be a bit distressing but we'd like you to look at the photo of the dead man and see if you recognise him.'

'Sure,' said Garland.

Earle showed the photo on his phone. Clement studied them for any sign of recognition but there was none. The Garlands looked at one another and shook their heads.

'Sorry.'

Earle showed a photo of the tattoo. That rang no bells either.

Clement asked if they had any previous employees here who may have mixed with a criminal element. No.

'Anybody who was a problem?'

'Not at all. Our guys are great,' said Alice Garland.

Her husband added, 'It is a big property. We have people camping on it from time to time, or sightseeing. They just assume that it's government land. We can't police it. It's too big.'

Tell me about it, thought Clement.

Keeble was still hard at it when they returned to the crime scene. She couldn't give them an exact cause of death but could rule out knives or guns.

'Most likely crush injuries from being run over but I can't be certain.' She had removed the spikes and bagged them. 'They measure one-fifty millimetres in length. Diameter is approximately twenty millimetres.'

Clement noted the end of the spike was not pointed but square.

'I'll leave you to it,' he said.

They'd been driving back towards Broome a half-hour when Earle said, 'You don't know who influences them anymore.' Then he added by way of explanation, 'Rhys.' But Clement had already assumed that. 'When you and I grew up you hung out with your school friends or the kids in the next street, or the kids you played footy with. But now, now they get their ideas from online. Could be in another country, some arsehole who peddles drugs or porn, you wouldn't know. People can write any shit online and some gullible kid somewhere believes it. You have that yet?'

'Not so far as I know.'

'How's Phoebe doing?'

'Pretty good, I think. She seems to like school. She has a circle of friends. But I'm a long way away, who knows?'

'She's level-headed. Rhys has always been a good kid but lately ...' Earle drifted off.

'Maybe it's natural,' said Clement. 'Kids get to that age.' He was trying to remember whether he'd rebelled against what his parents stood for. Guessed he hadn't or what was he doing being a cop?

'You've tried talking with Rhys?' he asked.

'He doesn't want to talk to me. We used to go fishing all the time. It was the best time of my life. Now I wouldn't dare suggest it.'

***

No, she wasn't going to regret what she did. Those kids needed protection from their own mothers. They needed a voice. Okay it was only a temporary reprieve. They'd just send more of the shit out sooner or later but even if one of them stopped and thought about it and changed their mind, then it had been worthwhile. Honestly, people would inject themselves with mouthwash if their doctor said it was good for them. She was in the small supermart and looking up, she saw a couple of female paramedics at the counter chatting with a cop. She wasn't worried. Just act normal. She hadn't left prints, she'd made sure of that. No cameras either and they wouldn't pick out her features in her COVID mask even if they did have them. She wished the fucking cop would clear off but he was too busy flirting with the paramedics. Stuff it, she had nothing to fear. Derby was more than an hour out of Broome. Deep breath now …

Her phone rumbled in her pocket. She extracted it and checked: Lana. Oh, Lana! Wasn't she in Darwin?

She backed away to the rear of the store. 'Hi Lana, how's it going?'

'Sweet. You guys should get up here. Darwin is great. Hey listen, I wanted to warn you. I just had a call from some cop in Broome asking about you.'

Holy shit! How did they … It must have been one of those mothers from the other day.

'What was it about?'

'They didn't say. They sent me a sketch on my phone. It was you. They wondered if I knew your name. I played dumb.'

Her insides were churning. 'Thanks for letting me know.'

Who was to say the cops wouldn't be checking Lana's phone right now? 'I better go.'

'Okay. Keep in touch.'

She ended the call. The cop had gone. Fuck. She pulled her sunhat lower. That had been pretty stupid, to break in when the mothers could describe her. Stupid but she still didn't regret it. People had to be saved from themselves.

***

The first thing Clement did back at the station was brief his boss, Scott Risely.

'Homicide, no doubt. Very cruel and methodical.'

Risely took that in, moved some papers on his desk. 'You think it's bikies?'

Risely had recently had skin cancers burned off, a hazard for this region. His face looked like a stocking after a dash through a rose garden. So far Clement himself was unscathed but that couldn't last, especially having grown up here when sunscreen had been as unknown as a Pritikin diet.

'Bikies is what comes to mind first but if it's not then we have one hell of a sicko out there.'

'No ID on the victim?'

'Keeble has taken fingerprints and uploaded those. Graham's looking at any missing persons that might fit the bill, but unless he's been missing a few days, he won't even be in the system.'

'What are you thinking re media?' Risely swung in his chair, contemplating what his own feelings might be.

'Let's see what we get off the prints, DNA and missing persons. If we draw a blank then we should put it out there. I don't want to scare people but I don't want some maniac out there without people being on their guard. We need to identify this victim.'

'What do you want me to tell Perth?'

The Major Crime unit, including Homicide, was headquartered in Perth, twenty-two hundred kilometres south. Normally they would take charge of any investigation but given Clement was considered by his superiors to be as good a homicide detective as any in the state, they would cut some slack, defer to his request.

'For now, let's liaise, see if they have the dead man in their records.'

The body would be flown to Perth for the autopsy so Clement knew there would be limited lines of investigation just at present. 'We can do the grunt work here. See if we can find witnesses, identify the spikes.'

Risely said he would look after it.

'Body's on the way to Derby,' said Earle as Clement emerged from Risely's office. There was an airstrip at Derby so the body would arrive in Perth without the kind of delay that might occur in more remote parts of the region. 'Keeble is packing up at Meda now.'

Clement called over di Rivi.

'I want you to focus on the spikes. Mal says he's sure they are railway but they can be used for all kinds of heavy anchoring. Let's see if there are many sources around here. Perth can help with who the manufacturer might be and who the distributors are. Don't be frightened to use them.'

Keeble, he knew, would print the spikes and test for DNA. He asked if they had uploaded all the photos from the crime scene yet. Jo di Rivi confirmed they had.

'Get started.'

As she moved off, Earle was back at his shoulder.

'I've done a quick search on crucifixion murders, can't find any in this country.'

Clement contemplated their most fruitful courses of action. How you canvassed witnesses in such a vast, desolate area was always a problem. The only people who might have seen something could be completely out of the loop by now on some outback excursion.

'Mal.' Mal Gross knew everybody who had inhabited the region for the last thirty years. 'I want you to check with all our people, all the rangers too. Derby cops especially. See if they recognise the victim and ask if there were any vehicles acting suspiciously over the last forty-eight hours, around that crime-scene radius. I want every speeding violation checked. I want to know if there were any domestic or public confrontations in the last forty-eight hours that might fit the victim. And I want you to call Pedro and tell him we need to meet him right now.'

The meeting place was ten k out of Broome on a seldom-used track in the middle of nowhere. Clement and Earle arrived first and had been waiting fifteen minutes, hugging narrow shade in airless heat, when the old ute appeared spitting dust over comatose scrub.

''Bout bloody time,' muttered Earle.

The ute flopped to a halt. No birds left in sudden terror, no leaves shook in panic. The only motion was the red cloud that had been created by the vehicle, drifting away slowly like the momentary recognition of an Alzheimer's patient. The man who stepped from the ute had skin that matched the old leather hat he wore. Once upon a time he had favoured a bandana and, maybe because of the high cheekbones and long black hair, had drawn the name Geronimo. In those days he'd been in the hierarchy of a local bikie gang, affiliated with one of the national gangs. But the police had popped him with a large amount of meth and, rather than do serious time, Geronimo had agreed to provide intelligence. That intelligence had been used to secure big drug busts in Perth and Melbourne. With no local busts, Geronimo had never been under suspicion from his gang. A bout of cancer had seen him forced down the gang's ladder. His hair was still long but with grey streaks now. Over fifty, his access to useful intelligence had been greatly reduced. Pedro was their code name for him.

'Got here as fast as I could,' he said.

'Surprised you made it at all,' said Earle. 'There's more rust than metal in that heap of shit.'

'Ha-ha.' The biker stared at Clement. 'Whatever it is, no fucker's told me. I'm almost a pensioner.'

Clement didn't waste time. 'Got a homicide over at Meda. They nailed the victim to the road using what looks like railway spikes.'

Geronimo raised his eyebrows. 'That's a new one on me.'

Earle said, 'You never heard of anything like that?'

'Long time ago heard about, I think it was the Angels in Sydney, tying a bloke up and painting a dartboard on his body, then playing a few games.'

'No one lately? Especially around here,' said Clement.

'No mate, I have not heard of anybody nailing anybody to the floor, ever. I mix in polite circles.'

Earle asked if he'd heard of any wars or disputes.

'Like I said, I'm out of the loop these days but if there was some major war going down, I'd know. And if it was punishment sanctioned by the club, I'd know. It's not us, I can say that for sure.'

'What about this tattoo, ever seen it?'

Geronimo studied the close-up photo on Earle's phone. Clement tried to read if there was any recognition.

'No,' said the biker eventually.

That tallied with his expression. Clement asked him to keep his ears open for anything that might seem relevant.

'What are you paying me?' asked Geronimo.

'If you don't inform us of something you know, a very long visit,' answered Earle.

When the ute had disappeared back the way it had come, Earle said, 'Well, that was a waste of time.'

Though they had nothing to show right now, Clement had done enough investigations to know that sometimes even seemingly fallow ground bore unexpected fruit.

'I'm getting soft,' said Earle squeezing himself into the car. 'I need air-con.'

5 TWO WEEKS EARLIER

Friday 29 October 2021

He stood on the low red rocks above the white sandy cove staring out at the ocean and, not for the first time, was given to thinking of a little book he had read as a boy, about Napoleon, held as a prisoner on St Helena. The irony, he supposed, had been deliberate, the British saying, here you are – emperor of half the world one day and now this is all you have left.

That was something he related to. His whole world had been shrunken that day nearly six years ago. Some days it seemed like yesterday, others it was so faint he might have dreamt it. He and Napoleon, both on islands, both of them islands. Napoleon, he remembered, had been fifty-one when he died, and he had a feeling that was in his sixth year of captivity, although he couldn't swear to that. He might look it up later. Not that the specifics mattered, it was their decline from dizzy heights that marked them as compatriots. That day the dam burst had ended his life as surely as Waterloo had Napoleon's. Officially nineteen people had died but that statistic did not count their unborn child who had perished with Gabrielly.

Nineteen or twenty, it seemed a small figure yet had it been two thousand or twenty thousand, for him the tragedy would have been no greater. The rest of the family had survived. He'd attended the church service with them. Her father stared blankly into space, the boys shuffled and twisted. Her mother brushed tears but had found solace in her faith, over and over declaring Gabrielly was with Jesus now. She probably said something about her daughter being in a better place, his Portuguese was limited, but that's what he was guessing. It was a sentiment he couldn't share. Her place had been with him and she had felt that way too. Though he resented Gabrielly's mother believing Jesus was better for her daughter than him, at the same time he wished he might have been able to find space for such a belief in his own heart. But there was no such space. Grief had flooded to its every border, filled every pore. He gave the family several thousand dollars. Along with the compensation they would get, it ought to be enough for them to live well but he told them to get in touch if they ever needed anything. Perhaps when the boys were bigger, he said, they might visit him in Australia. Not that he believed that day would ever come. Without their big sister trailblazing, he felt sure the boys would likely live and die in the valley. He hugged them all, feeling the warm tears of the quiet father soaking his shoulder. Gabrielly's mother held his face between her hands and cried, but he was crying more. They didn't need to speak.

Then he left Brazil for good.

Probably he should have taken more than two weeks off but he kept telling himself he would be better off working. First, he went to Queensland near Mount Isa. While he'd never been much of a drinker he gave it a good go. Rum, bourbon, vodka, he tried them all. The thing was, they didn't dull the pain one iota, he was achieving absolutely nothing, and so he stopped drinking to excess as easily as he had begun. He was being paid more than ever before. It was obscene. The giant company that had written off the deaths of Gabrielly and her fellow villagers with some empty words in the annual report and a sharp pencil on the debit side of the balance sheet was making money hand over fist. China's appetite for minerals was insatiable. Gabrielly's life was buried not just under tons of sludge and mud but money, and vexingly, he was its recipient. He sent more money to Gabrielly's family, quite large sums to various aid agencies. He needed so little himself to survive, his parents were well enough off. None of it made sense. He wished he was a doctor, something useful like that where you could make a difference, join Médecins Sans Frontières and help others like Gabrielly, but he wasn't smart enough. No profession was more worthless than HR. Human Resources, the very name stank to high heaven of corporate hoo-ha. Humans weren't resources. They were people who loved, got hungry, cried, swore, laughed, fucked, danced, prayed, sang. And now he did none of those things, so perhaps he wasn't human himself?

Looking around, he saw he was no longer on the beach but back in the belly of the massive body of pipes and machinery that had nested on the island like some giant steel lizard. He didn't recall getting back here. These memory gaps had been happening more frequently lately. There were parts of a day that had vanished from his life as Gabrielly had. What he was tasked to do, anything pertaining to his job he remembered just fine though. Perhaps it was an after-effect of the medication they had given him, pills to help him sleep, to filter out despair. He'd taken them for a month. Once he was sleeping okay, he'd stopped. He didn't want to lessen the pain, didn't want to artificially heal, he relished his wounds. The pain he could dedicate to her. After a year at Mount Isa, he'd felt the need for a change, away from open-cut mining with its earthmovers and tailings. And memories. His bosses were sympathetic. They had found him a job at head office and he had stuck it out for two years but under the slate-grey skies of Melbourne he was a foreigner. His family tried to help but what could they do? His married sister was flat out working and managing teenagers, his parents were elderly, and the family home with its increasingly wild garden and louder and louder television, he found depressing. Somehow what had happened in Brazil had not only robbed him of his future happiness but of any joy he might draw from the past. Even going to the football with his brother-in-law, an experience he'd always found enjoyable, left him emotionally flat. It was like he was on a long airport travelator, the world moving past without needing any interaction from him. He'd only ever had two close friends, Ed and Sean. They made an effort, took him to the pub, quizzed him about Brazil. One night they all went to see a band that they used to frequent when they were at uni.

He had actually been enjoying himself a little, the music helping. But then he had this vision of the wall of the pub caving in and a river of sludge pouring into the room and swamping them. He had huddled over the tall beer table and nervously pretended to react to whatever Ed and Sean were saying but he wasn't listening to anything except the wild rhythm of his heart. On the tram on the way home he had started sobbing.

By then he was in a rented flat. One of the neighbours had a cat who would call in on him and he would sit there reading while the cat sat on his lap. Apart from history books he had never read much, a couple of cricketer biographies that was about it, but one day he was walking home and he found a box of books left on the verge and he picked it up and brought it home. Television was just so much crap, well the free-to-air anyway. Ed and Sean and everybody at work now paid for their television content. His parents seemed to be the only people beside him who still watched the old channels, and that made him feel old too. So, he would sit there and read, sometimes with the cat on his lap or beside him. The books were all different and not like any he would have picked, even if he had been more of a reader than he was. There were books on politics, philosophy, a couple of novels, child-rearing theories. He wondered who had left them there, not even bothering to take them to a bookshop. Had somebody died and a relative just dumped them on the verge? The books were pretty old so maybe it was somebody downsizing, being forced to accept that their old way of life was over. One of the books he liked a lot was about men being from Mars and women from Venus, and it made him smile for maybe the first time since that day because it was so like him and Gabrielly. His favourite was a book about the early writings of Karl Marx. He knew nothing of Marx and in truth he found the book hard to grasp but there were passages that resonated, especially about the relationship between our work and humanity.

'The only connection still linking them with their existence, labour, has lost all semblance of self-activity and sustains their life only by stunting it.'

If it was true in Marx's day, that was even more true now, he thought. He began to go on the internet and look at other industrial disasters of which he had been only dimly aware. The Ixtoc oil spill, the San Juanico explosion and Bhopal, my God. They still didn't know how many people had died in that but more than half a million people had been exposed to toxic gas and the effects would be felt for generations. As always, it was the poorest people who suffered the most. The dull log of his grief sharpened into an angry spear.

One day he had found himself over in the inner-western part of the city responding to an ad offering a second-hand bicycle. He had been thinking that cycling might be a suitable activity where he could keep up his fitness but not have to interact too much with others. The idea of a gym was anathema to him, same with any kind of boot camp. The bike was nowhere near as good as had been advertised and he didn't buy it, but on his way to the train station he passed a small restaurant specialising in Brazilian food. This was truly the first time he had felt at home in his old home town. He ate, enjoying the chicken and rice soup just how Gabrielly used to make it. Francisco, the owner, cooked it all himself. Of course, he didn't know this until he became a semi-regular. On his fourth or fifth visit, he had got to talking with Frank, as he insisted on being called, and explained he had worked in Brazil but he didn't go into detail. Frank had invited him to a Brazilian night they held at a local hall every so often and he had actually travelled out there on a rattling tram through the drizzle. But once he arrived, he couldn't take himself up into the hall. He stood outside and every now and again when the doors opened, he would hear laughter and music but he told himself, this is not for you, you don't belong here. The next time he had gone to the restaurant, Frank had asked why he didn't come to the party, and this made him feel uncomfortable so he weaned himself away from the restaurant. It was kind of pathetic really, trying to keep something alive that had died four years earlier.

And it was too cold here.

And so, he had found himself another job in the resources industry, not mining this time but gas, all the way over the other side of the country on a small island in the Indian Ocean.

He missed the cat, however, and felt guilty that he had abandoned it.

***

The food in the canteen was nothing like Frank's but it was a good standard and there was always a lot of seafood, even though it was all flown in. Today he was having a salad.

'Mind if I join you?'

He hadn't noticed her approach. She was the English engineer. He tried to recall her name. Eve? She had placed her tray down but not let go of it yet, in case he said he did mind. Clearly, she didn't expect that, she had a welcoming smile. He wanted to say, yes, he preferred to eat alone like he nearly always did here at the second-last table on the left-hand side.

'Of course,' he said and gestured she sit. He was pleased she sat on the other side near the end, not too close.

'Ingrid Cavendish,' she said, and then before he could answer, 'You're Paul.'

'That's right.'

'I wanted to thank you. You okayed me for the job but I've been on odd weeks and our paths haven't crossed.'

He nodded, sipped his 7 Up. Then felt he needed to say more.

'It wasn't really me. I just ticked a box.'

'Well, I'm glad you did. I really needed this job.' And then as if he might misconstrue and report back to HQ, she added, 'I mean, it's a dream job for me, but it was timely too.' Before he could respond she edged herself off her seat and peered over at his meal.

'Just salad?'

'I don't eat much for lunch,' he said.

She gestured at her plate of fish and salad. 'Can't help myself. I lay off dessert though. Most days.'

'How are you finding it?' he asked, though he really had little interest.

'I love it. The work, I mean. And I like the sun too, after Manchester it's paradise.'

'Same. Melbourne,' he said and was surprised she laughed. He wasn't meaning to be funny. He couldn't think of the last time he made anybody laugh. Well, it would have been Gabrielly, maybe watching him try to dance.

'You live there?' she asked.

'From there,' he said. 'I rent a place in Broome.'

'Broome is gorgeous. I've got a flat in Perth but I'm thinking of ditching it.'

He had finished his salad and felt uncomfortable sitting here but he didn't want to be rude.

'When were you in Broome?' he asked.

'Shinju. I was thinking then, I wonder if I should live up here instead of all the way in Perth.'

She looked about thirty-five.

'You have a partner?' The non-subjective words of governmental forms came easily to him now. When he first started in the job you would have asked 'boyfriend' or 'husband' but those words were all obsolete, like himself.

'Not any more, thank God.' She laughed. 'That's why I came to Australia, true love. Following my man.' She gave a thumbs down. Now she was going to ask him about his family.

'Excuse me,' he said, getting up with his tray.

'Nice meeting you, Paul,' she said.

'You too, Ingrid.'

There was still a third of a can of 7 Up left when he dumped it in the bin.

6 FRIDAY EVENING

By 6.30, Clement was alone in the squad room. He'd let Earle go home for dinner and was waiting for Keeble.

'You should spend as much time with Rhys as you can,' Clement had said.

'Makes no difference. He barely acknowledges his mother or me. He heads off to his room or his phone and he's back on the net. I take it off him, he sulks. He thinks he can butt heads with his old man and win but he's got another think coming.'

That was the last time Clement would bother to offer the kind of dumb advice parents give with good intentions but no expertise. They'd arranged to meet back up in an hour to start the rounds of the local pubs. There was no guarantee the victim had been living in Broome but it was a small place, so chances were that if the victim was living around here somebody would recognise him. Given that he appeared to be a male somewhere between late twenties and early forties, there was a very strong likelihood he would have been a drinker at one of the local watering holes. There weren't that many, and Friday night was a good time to hit. Mal Gross had contacted the Derby police and they would do the same there but so far, they'd turned up nothing either. The arse-end of the afternoon had produced zilch. Earle and he had fruitlessly searched the database for any missing persons in the Kimberley that might fit the description of the dead man. They'd sent emails to Perth to distribute his description statewide for missing persons but he wasn't holding his breath on that. It was likely the dead man hadn't even been reported missing yet.

Even though Earle had already done it, Clement trawled the

internet looking for similar crucifixion style murders. Nothing in Australia. He'd been across most WA homicides of the last decade and knew there was nothing similar in that period. It was not something you'd forget.

The dead man was fit. Clement would get Mal Gross to detail some uniforms to do a round of the local gyms and pools. An environment like that, the tattoo would be on display and might prompt memories. But the fellow may not even be from Broome. Maybe not even from the Kimberley.

Clement rang the two local gyms anyway but drew a blank. Pubs would be their best bet. People crisscrossed the region for work, holidays, adventure. You could bump into somebody from as far afield as Kalgoorlie who remembered having a drink with him in some outback bar, somewhere, sometime. Could be a long night ahead he was thinking as Keeble entered halfway through a carton of fish and chips. She looked grimy and understandably tired.

'Late lunch,' she offered. He didn't even get to pose a question, she anticipated him.

'It's far too early to speculate but I'm ninety-plus percent certain that he was killed by the crush injuries.'

'Someone pegged him out alive and then ran over him?'

'What it looks like. I checked. The body has arrived in Perth and they autopsy him first thing in the morning. I've drawn bloods, they will have done that too. They'll have a full tox screen done, I reckon, day after tomorrow.'

He knew she couldn't match them for timing on the full-screen test but he was thinking –

'I know what you're thinking,' she said.

'What am I thinking?'

'You're thinking how do you get somebody to lie down for you while you drive stakes through their palms. Maybe he was drunk, maybe he was drugged.'

Clement hoped he wasn't so transparent in everything.

'Was he?'

'Come on, give me a break. Soon as I finish my *lunch*,' she emphasised the word to ram home how hard she'd been working, 'I shall run a test for benzodiazepine. That's the most likely drug, right?'

He conceded that it was. Most sleeping tablets had that as their basis.

'Ketamine too?' he asked hopefully.

'Now you're pushing it. Okay, that too. The alcohol test will take longer. I expect Perth will beat me. You want to know about fingerprints?'

'Please.'

'I found partials on the spikes. They match the victim.'

'So he nailed himself down after running over himself,' said Clement facetiously. 'Or maybe we can assume his killer was careful.'

'Hmm, the latter, I'd say. Now let me go. I need to shower.'

There was little more he could do here. They would do the autopsy first thing in the morning and he could organise to watch it live if he wished, but he thought he'd leave them be and get the results as soon as it was over. This time of night there was no chance of making progress on the spikes. What he really needed was the victim's identity. The fingerprints of the victim were in the system, computers doing their work. If there was a match, Clement would be notified immediately. He was resisting the temptation to go to the local media. A homicide victim who had been nailed to the road would be big news for sure, too big. He'd find he was dealing with nationwide media inquiries. He was surprised the story hadn't leaked yet, but so far so good, no phone calls asking him about it and soaking up his energy and time. Once it broke, he would be grateful for any help he could get, but if he could just identify the victim first then he might have a chance of snaring a killer before they'd ditched evidence like the railway spikes or the car.

'Not one of ours,' said Jill the bar-person at the Anglers Club as she scrutinised the photo of the dead man on Clement's phone.

'He had this tattoo on his back.' He showed her the next photo.

'Have to keep their shirts on in here. The beer garden at the

Cleopatra would be a different matter. Or the Picador.'

'I thought you might save me some legwork, give your mates there a call, text them the photos.'

Jill looked over at Bill Seratono standing at a high table waiting patiently with the two untouched beers Clement had just bought.

'What do you reckon, Bill?' she asked cheekily. 'Should I help Columbo?'

Clement had never been sure of Jill's age but that reference put her in the ballpark he'd figured, sixty or not far south. He bet she would not only be able to correctly identify a fax machine but remember how to work it. Bill took a sip of his beer.

'Your civic duty, I reckon.'

Jill smiled, took Clement's phone and set to work. If she came through, he could let Earle have a night at home. Wouldn't do any harm.

'Let you know when I'm done,' she assured Clement, who took the hint and joined pretty much his only friend outside of the department. He and Bill Seratono had gone to school together in Broome. They'd made no attempt to stay in touch when Clement had left with his family for Perth in his last couple of high school years but had re-bonded on his return.

'Bad news for me, good news for you re December,' said Clement. Then, off his mate's look, 'Phoebe is going to the US with the school band. Marilyn never told me.'

Bill took a long sip. There was only one other table occupied in the Anglers: three blokes in shorts and polos almost certainly bought by their wives as birthday gifts. They favoured the short-hair look that gentlemen their age adopted to hide thinning patches. Too neat to be full-time fishermen, Clement guessed they worked at one of the businesses in this small complex, a mix of offices and panel shops.

Bill remained silent.

Clement reassured him. 'It's okay, I know you can't offer the boat in January.'

'I would if I hadn't made plans.'

'Understood. Phoebe and I will still have some fun.'

Clement had called Seratono and arranged to meet here. They convened here every other night as it was, neither man having anything to occupy the space of their lives but work or hobbies. Seratono had sustained a long-term, part-time relationship with a woman, Samantha, but it had run aground nearly a year back. Clement figured Samantha may have wanted more commitment than Seratono had in him but on reflection realised that thinking was dated. Might have been Seratono who wanted more or neither wanted more but both just couldn't be bothered to keep it going. Outwardly Seratono had shown no emotion at the split but then he likely wouldn't. It had been over for more than a month before Clement had twigged.

So far Clement had kept his information as to what was on his phone to a minimum, just asking if Bill had ever come across the fellow in the photo.

'I presume that fellow was cactus,' said Seratono.

'Yeah.'

'You can't say any more.'

'Not really.' Although it was pointless holding out. He was going to have to break the story in the next few hours and Bill wouldn't tell anybody anyway. 'Looks like a homicide, over at the station on the Gibb River Road. They don't know him.'

'Could be from anywhere, Darwin, Adelaide.'

Didn't Clement know it. Seratono didn't pursue the police business.

'Nothing from those two fillies whose hearts you broke?'

Seratono had been the only person he had confided in about his love life. Clement related his previous day's unpleasant experience with Lucinda.

'Live by the sword ...' observed Seratono.

'I've learned my lesson,' said Clement. He watched the cardboard coaster absorb the moisture from the cold heel of his glass, thought, my life is as flat as that coaster.

'Did you ever have any ambition?' he found himself asking before he even thought about it and halfway through realised how patronising he sounded.

'My ambition,' said his friend evenly, 'was to have ambition. I never managed it though. You did.' Seratono tilted his glass at his mate and took a slug of beer.

'Yes, I did.'

He had wanted to be the best detective in the whole world. He had wanted to be the best dad and husband too.

Seratono said, 'I never had a plan beyond forty-eight hours. I saw a car I wanted, so I saved for that. Or a fishing rod. Or a boat. I spent my money each week on beer and fags. I liked women who were too beautiful for me so I got drunk, and of course beautiful women then avoided me like the plague. Now there's a phrase that has a whole new meaning post-COVID. I don't know any single blokes like me who are content, and yet it would be wrong to say we're unhappy. Blokes with wives and kids seem on the whole content and yet much more stressed.'

Clement thought of Graeme Earle.

'And blokes with no wives but kids seem neither happy or content,' added his friend.

Clement was sure that was added directly as a comment to Clement himself.

'I'm happy when I'm with Phoebe.'

Seratono drained his beer and said, 'I'll see what I can do for January.'

Jill bustled over with Clement's phone.

'I've tried my mates at all the pubs. He doesn't ring a bell with any of them. They're not saying they never served him but they don't remember if they did. He's not a regular.'

Shit. Life just got harder, thought Clement. Twenty-four hours earlier he'd been bored, praying for a big case. He should have learned his lesson: be careful what you wish for.

7 SATURDAY

'The spikes are, surprise surprise, manufactured in China. Very commonly used in mining,' di Rivi was sitting with her iPad on her lap and a cup of coffee at the ready. It pleased Clement to see how relaxed she was now with him and Earle and Mal Gross. For the first month or so as a detective she had always set herself up at the outside of the circle like she would be trespassing to join.

It was just after 8.30 a.m. Clement and Earle had turned up nothing on their previous evening pub crawl, leaving Clement going to bed still annoyed at Marilyn and frustrated he'd got nowhere yet on the case. The case he'd wished for. To his great surprise he had slept like a teenager and needed his alarm to hammer him awake. Earle, Mal Gross and di Rivi had joined him for the morning debrief. Brett Manners, the IT guy, was at home on standby. Keeble had arrived but was in the kitchen. He'd not drafted Josh Shepherd to the case but was wondering now if he should have already done so. Shepherd was officially still on the clinic break-in.

Di Rivi said, 'Mal's liaising with Perth about the spikes.'

Mal Gross spoke. 'Most of these supplies will be sold by a national distributor. Perth didn't have that information yet but they had a list of possibles so I'm getting requests out this morning to those. Hopefully I'll get all the relevant information from China but my mate in Perth warned it can be two steps forward and one back.'

'I thought it might be quickest to get on the phone and chase up every local mining or railway company I could find listed for the Kimberley,' said di Rivi.

'Good idea,' said Clement and swivelled to see Keeble with some kind of yoghurt and fruit bowl. 'Still nothing on the prints?' he called. First thing he'd checked when he had arrived was whether there'd been a match yet on the victim's prints.

'Nope. But just in – the autopsy confirms he was crushed to death. Traces of potato chips, bread and cheese in the stomach.'

That was not going to help much.

'However ...'

They all hung on her next words. Clement knew Keeble enjoyed toying with them.

'... bingo on the benzodiazepine.'

Earle spoke for them all. 'It was planned. The Sun King was drugged, driven out to Meda, nailed down with his own spikes and driven over by a ...'

He threw to Keeble.

'Don't have the likely vehicle yet,' she said.

Clement's phone vibrated. The name on the display was that of the chief crime reporter for the *West Australian* newspaper. The story was already beyond local then, but Clement would have to pick up to find out how much they knew. Clement ignored it. The paper would call Scott Risely next and he would deal with it.

'Still sounds like bikies,' said Mal Gross.

'Except there's been no hit on the fingerprints,' countered Clement. He didn't need to elaborate that were Sun King a bikie, he would likely have some criminal history.

'Maybe he wasn't a bikie himself. Maybe Sun King was clean till he got involved with the wrong crowd?' said Earle.

Emma Parentich, a new constable who was training under Gross, poked her head around the corner.

'There is a woman on the phone, says her boyfriend never came home last night.'

Clement's first thought was that Emma would learn to screen better. Even in a small town like Broome, there must have been thirty men who hadn't made it home. Mal Gross had already dealt with two such calls before joining the meeting and had swiftly established the men's whereabouts. One had been picked up drunk and passed out and was safely in the holding cells, the other was still playing cards at a mate's house.

'Did they give a name?' asked Gross, debating whether he should break to take the call.

Constable Parentich said, 'Her name is Lauren. The boyfriend is Jean-Claude Seydoux.'

Earle locked eyes with Clement who threw to Keeble. She flipped out her spoon as if taking a bow.

'French,' she said, and scooped her yoghurt.

The flat photo sat in a small plastic frame on top of a small, flat loudspeaker that in turn squatted on one end of a low, rectangular, black entertainment unit, a flat-screen TV in the middle. The photographic image of the late Jean-Claude was the apex of a pyramid, and it occurred macabrely to Clement that the last time he'd seen Jean-Claude, he too had been flat. There was no doubting the man in the photo was him.

The policeman made this assessment from the vantage of a rectangular black sofa of indeterminate fabric. He and Graeme Earle were on the first floor of Unit 8 in a rectangular block in Bilingurr, a northern suburb. Through the lounge room's glass sliding doors, across the narrow balcony, Clement had a view of the surrounding brown countryside. It was just as flat as the floor, the table, the speaker and the photo.

Lauren Bagot was still dabbing tears that had started nine minutes previous. Clement felt very sorry for her, although he forced himself to remain neutral as to her potential involvement. There was a Ford ute sitting out the front that could have been the instrument that turned Jean-Claude into a human wafer. Forensics had suggested a four-wheel drive or small truck, so it was in the market. Keeble was already on her way here to test it.

'Meda?' Lauren Bagot said, red eyes puffed.

'You know where it is?'

'Yeah.'

When they had arrived, they had told her that a body, possibly that of Jean-Claude, had been found. When she had confirmed the tattoo marking, they had shown her a photo of his face only. Her lip had trembled and she'd had to sit while she absorbed the horror. Since then, Clement had been releasing information in dribs and drabs in the lulls between her sobs. When she had asked how he had died, Clement had told her that it appeared he had been crushed by some vehicle but there were no witnesses and the death was suspicious. He had not mentioned the crucifixion. As she fetched his passport, Clement had added more detail.

'Jean-Claude's body was actually on a gravel service road of the cattle station,' he had explained. Lauren Bagot had not been able to offer any explanation of what her boyfriend might have been doing there. As far as she knew, he had no friends out there or association with the station.

'Sometimes he would head off for the day,' she had offered weakly as she passed over the passport to Earle. Bagot was wearing shorts and an aqua-coloured blouse, sandals on her feet, bright pink nail polish.

'Did he have a car?' asked Graeme Earle.

'A motorcycle.' The reply was muffled by a fistful of damp tissues squeezed tight against her face.

At motorcycle, Earle and Clement swapped a knowing look.

'It wasn't there?' she asked looking up. Her eyes were now a shade darker than her nails.

'No,' said Clement. He wanted to take his time on this, first get to know Lauren Bagot before he got into the technical details of vehicles and bank accounts.

'Can you tell us a little about yourselves? Have you been together long?' asked Clement.

'Just over a year.' Bagot sniffed. 'We met in Port Hedland.'

She had an accent, English, north maybe but Clement didn't consider himself an expert. She was small and had a toned body that suggested a regular workout routine.

'How did you meet?' Clement continued to take it slow. Experience had taught him that way you caught bigger fish.

'The gym. He was hitching his way around Australia.'

Clement gave himself a tick on the workout observation. Earle passed over the passport. Clement studied it. Jean-Claude Seydoux was a French citizen born 1989.

'And what were you doing at the time?' he asked.

'Back then I was working for Rio.'

'And now?'

'Hardcastle Minerals. Mining site out at Fitzroy Crossing. I'm the cook. I work Monday to Friday.'

'And come back here for the weekend?' Clement surmised.

She bit her lip and nodded. Clement understood how she would know Meda. She would pass the turn-off on the way to Fitzroy Crossing, which was about a four-hour drive from here.

'I take it that's your ute out front?' asked Graeme Earle.

'Yes. Well, company car.'

'We'll have to examine it,' said Clement. 'You won't be able to drive it for now. We'll likely tow it to our garage. As soon as it's clear we'll let you know.'

She barely reacted.

'You're English?' said Earle, saving Clement the trouble.

'Lancastrian. Grew up in Leyland, the town where they made the buses. I came out here when I was nineteen. I'm a citizen now. I never wanted to go back. Can't stand the cold. You don't have any idea what happened?'

'Not at this time,' said Clement hating the stock answer but there was nothing else he could offer.

She just sat there slumped like a rock with waves breaking over it.

'Did Jean-Claude have a job?' Clement cast about for a clue as to what it might be.

'A couple, but not full-time. He works for a diving outfit sometimes when they need somebody. And he is a personal trainer.'

The world constantly disappointed Clement. Not even Broome was safe from personal trainers. Clement got the name of the diving business and a contact.

'Did he have regular clients in his training group?' asked Earle.

'Some of them. He usually had a class of about five or six down at Cable Beach most days. He'd put fliers up at the holiday lodges, so a few regulars but casuals too.'

'Would you have a list of his clients?' All potential suspects, Clement was thinking.

'It'll be on his phone.'

'Unfortunately we didn't find a phone,' said Clement. 'A computer?'

'No. He did everything on his phone.'

Clement got Jean-Claude's phone number off her. She wasn't sure who his provider was.

'I think Vodafone. A lot of time he wouldn't have coverage and they are probably the weakest up here.'

Clement remembered from when he'd let Phoebe have a mobile phone. He was pleased to have one with poor coverage. Not that he needed to worry. She was responsible. Graeme Earle got Bagot's own phone details from her. If she realised that they'd be checking her records, she was able to cover skilfully. It seemed she was still drifting through fog.

'By the way, do you use a logbook with the company car?'

'No.'

Pity. If she was involved, that might have told them if she had diverted on her run home.

'What about social media?' asked Earle. 'Did Jean-Claude engage in that?'

'He didn't do Twitter or Snapchat or Facebook, but Instagram, yes. He'd put up photos of his class.'

'What was his handle?' asked Clement.

'Sunsetsunking.' She spelled it out for them.

'What about you?' asked Clement.

'Facebook but just with a few old school and work friends.'

'Under your name?'

'Yes.'

Something for Manners to check. Clement had already texted him on the way over and told him he would be needed at the station.

'When was the last time you saw Jean-Claude?'

Clement had held off on that big question. He wanted to build some rapport first, not frighten the young woman into thinking she was prime suspect, though of course for now she was their only 'person of interest'.

'Last Monday morning. I leave about three and drive straight to work to get the breakfasts going. He was asleep.'

'And the last time you spoke to him?'

She sighed, trembling still, cast her mind back. 'That would have been Thursday night. Well, evening.'

'What time exactly?' asked Earle.

'Just after his class. So, a bit after six. Normally he would text me again and then call me Friday before his morning class, and then he'd be here when I got home.'

She ebbed away. Clement sensed her thinking that by then he would have already been dead. Clement heard vehicles arriving outside. That was likely Keeble.

'So, you waited for him?'

'For a little while. I thought he had gone for a Friday catch up. Then I texted him and when he didn't reply I rang but only got his voicemail. I thought probably he'd taken his bike for a long run and was out of range. He does that sometimes. You said his bike wasn't there?'

Clement could see she was starting to work the logic, maybe discarding her first assumption that it had been a hit-and-run. Or she could be playing them. But if she was, she was damn good.

'Somebody took his bike and his phone. Was that why he was killed? It wasn't an accident?'

Clement felt she was asking the question more of herself than them.

'It definitely wasn't an accident. We hope we can find out what happened as soon as possible. Would you know the registration number of his bike? Have a photo of it?'

She didn't answer. Her eyes were faraway. Graeme Earle was poised with a notebook.

'What sort of bike?' he asked gently.

'It was a Honda tourer.' She came back to reality and began searching her phone. 'I don't know much about bikes. I think the licence is here.'

Lauren Bagot got up and rummaged through a kitchen drawer still checking her phone with one hand. 'This is a photo of the old one.'

'Old one? Asked Clement as she handed across the phone. He passed the phone onto Earle.

'He bought a new one about three weeks ago.' She stood peering at two printed documents, making a judgement.

'This one is the new one,' she said, handing them the licence.

'If that's the old licence, may we have that too?' Clement pointed at the other piece of paper. She handed them both across. She was still searching her phone, wiping tears.

'He took heaps of photos of the new bike on his phone. He probably sent me one. I'll check my texts.'

Clement studied the date of the licence transfer. Just over two weeks. Clement passed the licences to Earle who had a much better grasp of cars and cycles than he ever would.

'Any receipts?' asked Clement.

'Don't think there are any receipts. The guy wanted cash.'

She had a cursory look in the drawer. 'Not in here.' She was exasperated, still trying to find a photo of the new bike on her phone. 'Sorry. I'm sure he sent me a photo of him and the new bike.'

Studying the licences, Earle said, 'The new bike is a two thousand and nine model, a tourer. Cost him what, ten grand?'

'He got it for just under nine. Said it was a great deal.'

'So, he sold his old one?' asked Clement.

'Yes. The dealer near the airport.'

Clement knew the one she meant. There were only four in town. He would be able to chase that down.

'Here, this is the only photo I can find.'

Clement and Earle took a look. Jean-Claude was sitting proudly astride the motorcycle. It was very similar to the previous one but newer.

'What did he get for the old one?' Earle buying back into the conversation.

'I think about six thousand.'

'And the balance?' Earle again. 'Did he have that much saved?'

'His parents sent him the money.' A whole new swirl of ideas seemed to suffocate Bagot. She spoke in a kind of trance. 'Who is going to tell them? I don't even know their phone numbers. He had all that on his phone.'

Clement said, 'Perth will notify the consulate and they will let them know. Have you ever met his family or spoken to them over the phone?'

She grabbed for another tissue. 'Well, I've sort of said hello when Jean-Claude held the phone out to me a couple of times but that's it.'

'He didn't have any relatives in Australia?'

'I don't think so. He never mentioned any. A brother and sister in France.'

'Had he ever been married?'

'No.'

She looked anxious. Clement took her answer to mean that Seydoux had never mentioned having been married. But he could have been. He helped her out of the mire.

'His family will likely want to speak to us, and I presume you. When we get it, we can forward their number if you like?'

She nodded but she only had one foot in reality.

'Was he in regular contact with any of his family?'

'I don't think so. He phoned his mum for her birthday back in August. I think he texted his brother a bit but not very much. They weren't close.'

They would have to check up on all this. Clement allowed himself a moment to think about the motorcycle purchase. These days dealing in cash from people you met online could get you targeted by some very bad individuals. It wouldn't be out of the question that some arsehole could sell his bike for the cash then kill Jean-Claude and take back his bike. But the manner of the death was so savage … Clement couldn't help feeling it was more personal.

'The guy he bought the bike from, that wasn't the dealer?' Clement doubted a dealer would insist on cash.

'No, a private sale. He went to Port Hedland for it.'

Port Hedland was six hundred k south, give or take. If he'd already sold his bike …

'How did he get there? Did you drive him?'

'No. I was working. He said one of his clients, Rex, was heading there and would give him a lift.'

'Do you know Rex's second name?'

'No. I've met him once or twice.'

She described a man about thirty, tall and slim with prematurely thinning hair.

'And you don't recall him mentioning the name of the person who sold him the bike?'

She shook her head.

'Are there any bank statements?' he asked, not hopeful.

'No. He did that on his phone too.'

'Do you know what bank?'

'Commonwealth. I don't know the branch.'

'You too?'

'No. ANZ.'

'Has he ever transferred money to you for anything?'

She thought about it, indicated the entertainment unit. 'Yes. When I paid for that.'

Good. They could trace back from that. Earle took her bank account details and asked if she would mind forwarding statements to them. The quicker they could look at all these things, the better. Bagot didn't ask why they needed the information. Either she was sharp enough to have figured that out already or was still in shock.

'Did Jean-Claude have any enemies?' asked Clement casually. 'People who might wish to do him harm?'

Bagot shook her head and grabbed more tissues from the Homebrand box.

'Was he part of a ... motorcycle group? Anything like that?'

'No. He didn't mix with bikies. He just liked to ride.'

'Do you ride too?' asked Clement.

'I didn't even like riding pillion.'

'He looked very fit,' said Earle.

'He worked out all the time. He was in the French equivalent of the SAS.'

Clement wondered if that was a tale. Mind you, if Jean-Claude was a diver, maybe he had been.

'Does he have any friends here?'

'Not really, not close ones. Just me. Some of his clients like Rex he might spend time with. He didn't drink much at all, so he never went to bars. He liked to swim and hike, that kind of stuff. He'd go out for a ride for the day and get back for his sunset class, that was usually his biggest.'

'And you can't think of anybody with whom he might have recently had some run-in?'

She shook her head, moaned and started crying once more.

'Drugs?' asked Earle.

'A bit of pot.' Because she was crying, the words came out strangled and she had to swallow, take a breath and try again. 'A bit of grass.'

'That's okay, we're not drug police, we just need to know if he could have come across the wrong people that way.'

She wilted a little. 'He might have had eccies now and again but nothing ... you know he wasn't involved in drugs. He was fit and loved nature.'

'How long have you been in Broome?' asked Earle.

'About three months. He wanted to keep travelling so I quit my job at Rio and then we came up here and he loved it and we decided we'd stay. After a couple of temporary stints, I applied for the job at Fitzroy Crossing.'

Clement had to ask, 'Could you tell us where you were yesterday and last night?'

'I left the mine at about four and got here close to eight. I just waited in all night getting more and more worried when Jean-Claude wasn't answering my texts. I couldn't sleep. I drifted off, I don't know, about three in the morning. Woke again before six. I knew something had happened. I thought maybe he'd had an accident. I called the hospital but they had no record of him. So then I called the police.'

Perhaps she was clever enough to pretend she didn't know about the body at Meda. Perhaps she was genuine and completely engulfed now by the darkness of sudden death. That's how she looked.

'What are the sleeping arrangements at the camp?'

'We have our own units in the dongas.'

'Can anybody confirm you were at the camp all of Thursday night?' Before she could react, he said, 'I'm sorry but we have to ask this.'

'There are two other girls on the site and we were up chatting till about eleven thirty. Then I went to bed. I would never hurt Jean-Claude. I don't know how anybody could. And he could fight, I mean self-defence, all that, from the army.'

It would have been possible for her to have driven to Meda. If she was lying about riding the bike, perhaps she could have ridden it up a ramp into the ute. But if she didn't ride, how would she get it into the ute? Maybe there was another bloke on the scene, an accomplice. Her phone records would help in that regard.

'We won't take up more of your time,' said Clement and made as if to stand. 'Did Jean-Claude ever show you anything like this?' Clement handed over his phone with a close up of one of the spikes.

'They use those in mining.' Her voice betrayed confusion.

'Found near Jean-Claude's body,' said Clement watching her closely. Her face was blank as a cricket sightboard.

'I've never seen him with those.'

'Do you have these at your camp?'

'Maybe. I haven't seen any. But I'm just the cook there.'

Then Clement stood and thanked her for her patience. 'Could I have the car keys please?'

With trembling fingers, she removed the house keys from the keyring and handed him the car key.

'Can I see him?' she asked.

'I'm sorry, Lauren, but the body had to be flown to Perth for an autopsy. I'll get somebody to call you about arrangements you may wish to make. In cases like this it can take some time before a body is released.'

Earle bagged a toothbrush and pillowslip for DNA comparisons. They left the woman whose whole life had been shattered and walked down the outside staircase in silence. The sun blazed on.

***

Keeble was already suited up with her team. The trailer that would be taking the car hadn't yet arrived.

'Was out of town but it's on its way,' she explained. 'I'd have to do this anyway.' She pointed at her team taking samples of scrub by the driveway. 'This won't be the same as Meda, so best to eliminate it.'

Clement knew Keeble would leave any detailed internal examination of the car till the garage.

'We couldn't see any blood in the cabin or tray,' said Clement. They'd only looked through the window of the car at the interior before they had called on Bagot.

'Me either. And there's no smell of disinfectant in the tray.'

Clement used the electronic key to pop the door.

'Would you?' he asked Keeble, indicating he wanted her gloved hand to open the door. He wasn't going to poke around in there, he just wanted that first whiff.

Earle knew exactly what Clement was up to and he stood close behind. Clement nodded and Keeble pulled open the door. Clement stuck his snout in and sniffed. The smell of warming plastic in a newish car, a faint odour of sweaty feet or boots and a half-thimble smell of pizza. No remains though. Lauren Bagot was clean enough to remove any from the car. Clement guessed she grabbed a slice or two for the drive back from Fitzroy Crossing. If she'd murdered her boyfriend, she was brutally cold. But then you'd have to be to nail your lover to the road. She worked in a mining camp, Clement reminded himself, she potentially had access to spikes and could have reached the murder scene at the time of death.

He pulled out his head and indicated Earle take a whiff too. The tow truck was just arriving.

'No bleach. If he was killed beforehand and then pegged out, there's not a chance in hell his body was transported in there,' said Clement. 'Tyres?'

'I'll do comparisons when we get it in the garage.'

Earle said, 'Well, if she did run over him, she might have used one of the other vehicles from the mine site. She wouldn't be stupid enough to have come home in the one she used.'

A good point, thought Clement. She could have killed her boyfriend and driven back to camp while the rest slept. Taken a car from the pool, returned it and brought this one home. Keeble looked at him knowingly.

'You want me to check all those too, don't you?'

Clement smiled. 'I'll phone ahead, ask them to cease using all the possible vehicles.'

He was about to ask Earle to remind him of the name of the company but his partner was already there.

'Hardcastle Minerals.'

Clement put on his most sympathetic voice for Keeble. 'You better head there first, eliminate what you can, then come back and do this one.'

'There goes my weekend,' she said.

As Earle and Clement reached their car Earle said, 'Bikes and cash.'

'Yeah,' said Clement, anything more being unnecessary. Clement turned and looked back at the rectangular block. He had one word to describe how he felt: flat.

8 TEN DAYS EARLIER

Wednesday 3 November 2021

As he did most days, Paul walked his chosen path to the shore. Passing the fat termite mound of orange clay, he found himself wondering what there was for termites to eat here on this sparse rocky island. There were so few trees. Somehow, they found enough physical nourishment. If humans had the same limited demands, he'd be fine here. There was always plenty to eat. Some days he would look at the crayfish boats out there in the distance, just outside the permitted zone. How interconnected we all are, he thought. Me, standing on this rocky finger surrounded by ocean, scanning for boats who hunt creatures in deep, lonely waters that will be plucked out of their world, snap-frozen and sent to kitchens in the neon-lit alleys of a loud, hurtling Asian city, there to meet their doom at the end of a fork. Interconnected, yes, but only as an image, a theory his bored mind had momentarily conjured. The truth was, once that special connection to the one and only person who ever mattered in your life was severed you were nothing but a satellite dish, transmitting and receiving data that meant bugger all to you really. There was no emotional kick, just dots and dashes. So, he was under no illusion. There was nothing profound about him standing here dreaming of the interconnectedness of all things, it was cheap whimsy.

His life should have been different. He could have been nursing their child. Greed, slackness, the worst traits of our human nature had robbed him of all that he cherished. His life was as inconsequential as a sapling crushed under a tank. That's what these corporations were – mechanical, relentless soulless things, each as bad as the other. What did they put back into the world? They stripped dirt, rock, earth, gas, oil, they mixed it up in some alchemy and replaced it with what? Traffic, exhaust fumes, stress, wide-screen TVs for teens to play virtual games where they killed each other, leaf-blowers, constant noise and glaring light, scooters delivering unhealthy meals that people had grown too lazy to prepare themselves. And the fumes melted the ice and made the world hotter, and places like this dryer, till only termites could survive.

But we put up with it because it gives us a job. Every time a government announced it would be bulldozing more trees or digging out more earth, what was the spin? It will create two hundred jobs. Don't worry that these little rodents or lizards or birds will be wiped out, that the workers will need most of their money to live in a concrete and glass box so hot and uncomfortable they require air-conditioning, which means more gas and coal and oil, and more melting ice, and respiratory infections, and more bored, dumb people leaving their boxes more often to visit parts of the world that still held some semblance of nature and humanity, thereby accelerating the process to inevitably degrade those too.

The young Karl Marx might have thought our alienation had peaked in his day, but a hundred and fifty years on the process was far more advanced. Perhaps the physical labour was reduced but the leeching of our humanity was almost complete. Now giant trucks laden with ore didn't even have a driver at the wheel but instead a youngster at the end of a computer stick in faraway Perth munching on their latest Uber Eats. Man truly was alienated from his essence. You couldn't blame religion now. Nobody went to church and yet the situation still declined. The corporations had all the power of the old religious institutions and were even less accountable. They threw out phrases like 'diversity' and 'conservation' as if these were some guiding ethos but they were nothing but catchphrases, the contemporary equivalent of 'Peace, man.'

He dropped down off the low ledge of spare grass to the thin strip of sandy beach and stood, hands in the pockets of his shorts studying the fairy terns. There were so many birds here still, thank God. Different species picked one part of the island for their own kind, like little countries. Others were daytrippers, nesting on one of the other hundreds of small islands out there and flying in to the big smoke for something that only an ornithologist might know. Paul didn't mind. He just liked to immerse himself in the sound of the ocean and birds. Here it was still almost untouched. For now. To be fair, the company here worked hard to preserve the native habitats. Anyone coming onto the island was rigorously checked they weren't bringing on some environmental pest. But that was the exception. You'd not find that rigour in Africa or South America.

Nothing good will last, he thought, not while people are infected by apathy. Better than anybody, he understood this truth.

Something made him look down to his right. The beach was only short, no more than about sixty metres before it ended in a low, rocky bulb. A blurry shape was moving his way. He needed glasses for that kind of distance but never bothered with the pair he'd bought in Melbourne. He'd noticed it had been hard to decipher the names on street signs when he was walking around the suburbs by himself. The optometrist had dispassionately tested him and told him at the end of it he would need glasses.

'What are you, mid-forties?' the optometrist had said.

Yes, he had confirmed.

'That's when most people start to notice it.'

He wondered what Gabrielly would have said had he walked into their house wearing a pair of glasses. She might have laughed, gently mocked him, called him 'Mr Professor' or something similar, and then she would have hugged him and told him she thought he looked great.

Whoever it was heading towards him waved. The blur settled into the recognisable shape of a cotton frock and just a few seconds later he realised it was the English woman, Ingrid.

'I thought that was you,' she said as she drew closer.

They had bumped into one another a few times since meeting in the canteen. He was surprised that he actually had enjoyed the brief encounters, and even now that she was intruding on his special little nook, he was not at all annoyed.

'A dress,' he heard himself say.

'Yes,' she seemed a little embarrassed and he worried he might have been impolite in commenting on her outfit. 'I couldn't face jeans in this heat and my legs aren't up to shorts.'

She was wearing one of the company caps with a long bill. He didn't think she was fishing for a compliment about her legs. They seemed okay to him. People often worry about their physical features when others don't give a damn. Gabrielly thought she had knock-knees and she probably did, he realised once she pointed that out, but it never bothered him. In fact, the opposite, he thought it was cute. He wondered what about his own appearance did he place too much store in? He always thought his general shape was unattractive, like a solid block, his thighs too big, his legs shapeless as a Lego piece.

Ingrid said, 'You talked about the birds, so I thought I should check them out.'

Had he? He didn't remember doing so. He didn't think he'd mentioned his pleasure in these birds to anyone.

'What ones are these?' she pointed.

'These are fairy terns. They've only started to arrive again this last week or so.'

'They are very pretty.'

'Yes. Sometimes I think of them as one big family.'

And the family that he might have had, brushed past him in spirit form like a gust of wind.

'Have you seen the osprey?' he asked.

'The eagles?'

More like hawks, but he went with it. 'Yes. They're quite something when they dive for fish.'

'I have seen one occasionally out there.'

She gestured loosely to the sky over the ocean.

'They fancy the north side more.'

'You do know your birds, then.'

He shrugged. He was a long way from being an expert. 'You spend enough time on the island, you get to notice things.'

'Not most of that lot back there,' she laughed jerking a thumb at the residential blocks.

He found himself smiling. Her laugh had a nice ring about it, it was natural and light but still a real laugh.

'You'll have to show me,' she said, still smiling. And then perhaps feeling she might be being too forward said, 'If you have time.'

'Sure.' He didn't want her feeling self-conscious about it. He liked her company. She dug into her pocket and brought out something wrapped in an absorbent paper towel.

'Do you do biscuits? I made these myself.'

He didn't tend to eat biscuits. It had been a long time since he'd had homemade baking. Gabrielly and her mother didn't bake much, and he'd never himself baked anything.

His fingers hovered over the small stash. There were only three.

'Please, have one. Or two if you like. I have plenty back in my room.'

He gave in and took one. It was pale and sweet but not too sweet.

'Good,' he tried to say, and felt embarrassed that he was spitting crumbs.

'I like baking,' she said. 'It relaxes me. Shall we walk?'

What could he say to that? They began walking up the strip of sand. It was a very long time since he had walked with anybody for pleasure and now with the breeze in his face and the sweet taste of biscuit in his mouth, there was almost a spring in his step.

9 SATURDAY

'He wanted six and a half, kept saying it was worth it. I said it probably is if you sell it privately but I have to get my margin when I resell, so six tops. He took it.'

Wendell Croft made a bobbing motion with his jaw as if giving himself a tick. The used-car salesman didn't look anything like the image city people would have in their head for somebody in his occupation. Instead of a wide-lapelled suit with a garish tie, he wore shorts, sandals and open-neck polo. With a haystack of blond hair on his tanned face, he put Clement in mind of one of those Aussie cricketers from the eighties. Early forties, thought Clement, where I was not all that long ago when I felt I could still make a good fist of social sport. Not that Clement had actually bothered with social sport, just that he thought that at that age it had still been within his grasp.

They had stopped in at the car yard on the way back from interviewing Lauren Bagot. Now Wendell was flipping through a physical ledger in a cramped office so flimsy a decent cyclone would smash it to smithereens. A small fan was battling and rattling.

'I've got it on file on the computer but this is easier. Yeah, here.'

Croft put his finger on the transaction. Monday 25 October.

'How did you pay him?' asked Graeme Earle.

'Deposit to his account.'

'Did you see the bike he was buying?' Earle again.

'Didn't see it but he talked about it. If my memory serves, he said it was a Honda VFR800, can't recall the year, two thousand and nine or ten, I think. Reckoned it was worth nine-nine and he was getting ten percent off. I remember that because I said, "See, what you save on

that you don't need to get six-five for this one. You're still in front."'
Again, the salesman smirked, drawing a thrill from his own craftiness.

As soon as he got back to the station, Clement turned the passport
over to Risely, who had been enjoying the start of the weekend until
Clement called him en route from Bagot's.

'What do you think of the girl?' asked Risely as he examined
Seydoux's passport.

'Too early to form an opinion but she seemed genuine.'

'I'll get onto Perth now to chase up the consulate and Seydoux's
family in France.'

The fact that it was the weekend wouldn't help. All down the line
you'd be getting part-timers, people who weren't that familiar with
the job. But this was serious enough Clement hoped they'd go straight
to their big guns, even if it was a weekend. Clement expected that the
family would be as eager to hear from him as he was them.

'I'd also like to get his service record, and if possible, speak to his
old commanding officer just in case there is something relevant.'

'You think somebody from his past might have turned up here?'

On his relocation from Perth seven years earlier, Clement had been
faced with the case of a former German policeman. The tentacles of
that case had gone all the way back. Risely hadn't forgotten and wasn't
dismissing the notion out of hand.

'It's highly unlikely but let's face it, the manner of the death is pretty
damn violent, almost like torture. And it seems personal. So, it could
be somebody from his past. I'd like to know if his unit was involved
in anything untoward. Or if there were rumours of it.'

In recent times, Australia had been rocked by findings of an inquiry
that had shown some Australian service personnel while overseas in
Afghanistan had committed murder and other illegal acts against the
civilian population.

Risely saw where Clement was coming from. 'He could have been
a whistleblower and had old army cronies after him, or the opposite.
He might have had a hand in some atrocity and somebody close to a
victim has tracked him down.'

'Like I say, unlikely but we need to be sure. I'd like Perth to also check recent French nationals arriving in Australia and see if any might have a connection to the French commandos.'

'That will take time,' said Risely, dubious.

'I know, and I don't think we can pursue it as a priority but if Perth could chase it up, or the Feds. Anyway, if I can talk to the family and CO that might be a start.'

'I'll get the wheels in motion.' Risely took his leave.

The case was spreading outwards like a big puddle, but like a puddle it was shallow. For now, Clement had no recourse but to splash around willy-nilly.

Clement found di Rivi still working on the rail spikes.

'No luck yet,' she said.

'We've identified the victim.' He told her about Jean-Claude Seydoux and Lauren Bagot and asked her to call Hardcastle Minerals at Fitzroy Crossing and see if they stocked the stakes.

'Pretty sure I already did,' she said and consulted her list. 'Here, Hardcastle. No, they didn't think so but were getting back to me.'

'Good work. Park the stakes for now. I'd like you to get over to the apartments and speak to every neighbour you can find. We want to know when was the last time they saw Seydoux or his motorcycle and what, if anything, they know about the relationship with Lauren Bagot. Were there other visitors to the flat, were there other motorcycles, wild parties. Any unusual activity Thursday night. And did they ever see Lauren Bagot riding the bike herself.'

Di Rivi began to get her things together. I need Shepherd, too, he thought, annoyed he hadn't contacted him earlier. Saturday, Shepherd would be playing cricket. Clement rang but got only voicemail. He left a message for Shepherd to get to the station as soon as. After a quick dash to the deli for sandwiches for him and Earle, and an even quicker demolition of them, Clement hustled to Manners' office. Manners had only had Seydoux's bank details for little more than an hour. Clement stood looking over Manners' shoulder, his attention momentarily seized by the multicoloured flashing lights on the IT man's keyboard. Clement would have found it distracting but Manners seemed to think it gave him some élan.

'This is Seydoux's bank statement. There's the six-grand deposit from the dealer.' Manners highlighted the entries.

Up until then there had been a total of four hundred and fifty dollars in the account. A few days later, the six thousand was withdrawn again in cash. No sign of any international transfer. Lauren Bagot might have lied to them about Seydoux's parents sending him the money, or her boyfriend might have lied to her. Speaking with the parents would be a start.

'What about phone records?'

Manners momentarily seemed peeved. 'I'm still waiting for his. They said we should have them by the end of business today. The girlfriend's I have requested too. And of course, I tried his phone but there's no signal anywhere.'

'Facebook and Instagram?' Clement had got Manners to check. Again, Lauren Bagot may have lied or her boyfriend could have been hiding stuff from her, although it would seem pretty lame to try and hide something from your girlfriend that was accessible to others.

'Couldn't find anything on Facebook from Seydoux but there are a few Instagram posts. Not that many, mainly just photos of the beach giving time and place for his personal training classes. I've Drop-boxed them to you. Just a few personal messages too that I've also sent to you.'

Preferring to look at any photos on his computer screen, Clement headed to his office. Earle was at his desk just clearing a phone call.

'That was Alex Christos, the guy who sold the tourer to Seydoux. I got his details from the licence transfer. Works for BHP in Hedland. Says Seydoux paid nine grand in cash. Here's the interesting thing, Christos says he did not insist on cash, that direct deposit was fine with him but that Seydoux wanted to do it all in cash.'

'What do we know about Christos?'

'No criminal record, has been working for BHP for three years. I called our police brothers in Hedland and they have no flags on Christos, twenty-nine, single.'

'What was your vibe on Christos?'

Earle pursed his lips. 'Genuine, but you never know. He says he took a ride up to here about two weeks before and got talking with Seydoux in a carpark at the beach because they both had similar bikes. He says Seydoux was looking to trade up. Christos says he was keen to sell and get a cheap car, reckons he just doesn't get the time to make use of his bike.'

'And did he buy a car?'

'Yes, second-hand Hyundai hatchback. So, if he was involved, I think he would have used a different vehicle. That would've only tickled. Previously Christos lived in Perth. I have a call in to the gang squad just in case he may have crossed their radar. He says he was with friends drinking from Thursday late afternoon till nearly two Friday morning and he's supplied names for me to check. Of course, he could have organised somebody else yadda yadda but I'm not getting a vibe.'

'So why would Seydoux insist on cash?'

The question was pretty much rhetorical. They both seized the same answer but Clement let Earle say it.

'He wanted to hide the cash payment. Maybe he was worried about tax or maybe it was dirty money. Maybe his parents sent the money via PayPal or something,' said Earle. 'But even then, to access it, he would have to get it into his account.'

Clement's mind was working overtime. 'The guy's a diver. Is it possible he was diving for drug shipments, something like that?'

Earle pushed out his lips as he considered. 'It's not the silliest suggestion.'

'What was the name of the outfit he worked for?'

Earle consulted his notes. 'Deep Adventures.'

'You know anything about them?'

'They've been around for a while, big tourist trade.'

On an impulse, Clement pulled out his phone and dialled.

'Deep Adventures,' said the voice of a middle-aged woman.

'Good afternoon. This is Detective Inspector Clement from the Major Crime Squad.' He looked at the contact Lauren Bagot had given them. 'Is Mark Coleman available?'

No, the woman explained, he wasn't. Mark Coleman was the owner and skipper and was currently out with a party on a tour. The boat typically did a three-day, two-night run around the coast for diving tourists and was currently due back 'tomorrow afternoon'.

Could she confirm that Jean-Claude Seydoux worked for them?

She confirmed he was a casual employee but had not worked for them recently, though he did pop in from time to time.

'Does Mr Coleman have a personal phone number I could contact him on?'

She warned that reaching him by phone would be problematic while at sea but that he did radio in from time to time. Clement took Coleman's phone details and got the woman to take his own. He asked she get in touch with him as soon as possible. Then he tried Coleman but got no response. Earle had followed it all.

'Instead of my worthless opinion on the bona fides of Deep Adventures, why don't we ask the expert?'

'Good reliable dive business. Been around close to ten years or more. Why?' Mal Gross sat back in his comfortable office chair. Gross had also foregone his typical Saturday to come in; well almost. A marked form guide was open on his desk and a low-volume race call coming from his phone beside it.

'Seydoux had unaccounted cash,' said Graeme Earle who stood with Clement. Mal Gross addressed both of them with a single barrel.

'You're thinking drug-smuggling. It'd be more likely I actually back a winner. My nephew worked their boats for a couple of years too. Totally clean. I'd be more than shocked, I'd be electrocuted so bad I'd be blacker than one of Scott Risely's barbecue sausages.'

'I'll take that as a no then,' said Clement.

'There might be a more fruitful course of your labour,' opined Mal Gross as Clement went to move off. Clement waited for the oracle's insight.

'Wildlife smuggling,' said Gross.

Earle mulled it over. 'Seydoux had done stints overseas. That might provide him with dodgy contacts.'

Clement didn't dismiss it.

Mal Gross said, 'I've put that motorcycle rego out statewide. I'll ask Darwin and Adelaide to keep an eye out too.'

'Cameras?'

'I'm pulling all the camera vision we have for the twentieth and twenty-first: town, highway, servos. See if he turns up on anything: shops, red-light. We've drawn a blank on any speeding tickets for last Thursday night.'

That had always been a longshot but sometimes the longshots came in.

Clement wondered how big a timeframe was plausible. 'I'd like you to go back to October twenty through to twenty-five. I'd like to know if we can place him meeting with any likely sorts. He got money from somewhere around then.'

Scott Risely appeared. 'We're on for a call with the parents at four. They don't speak English but the vice-consul in Sydney has offered to translate for us both. They got the news a little over an hour ago so it will be very raw still.'

'Your office at four,' said Clement. Risely vanished as silently as he had appeared. Clement turned to Earle.

'Why don't you follow up the wildlife smuggling?'

Earle said he would. Mal Gross offered to help.

'I've got good contacts in Parks and Wildlife, and the Feds. Mind you, Saturday arvo ...'

Clement sat down at his office desk and began flipping through the photos that Jean-Claude had posted on Instagram. Lauren Bagot had been accurate when she said her boyfriend didn't post a lot. There were a number of shots of Cable Beach, mainly at sunset, with a line of people doing sit-ups or stretching out with small weights. **Just turn up at 5.15 PM**, exhorted the caption. **One hour, $20 casual, discount for five sessions or more. Look for the yellow balloon.**

A photo showed a tethered gold party balloon overseeing the action. Over the weeks there were a half-dozen close-up shots of the group, a fairly even spread between male and female. Three faces were in nearly all of them, one likely Rex of the thinning hair. A small, dark-haired woman in an athletic singlet and another, a blonde, hefty with a vivacious smile in a t-shirt. Sometimes there would be a group of young Asians in designer sportswear. Clement guessed these might have been the casuals, likely staying at the Mimosa or one of the other luxury places around. The only non-beach post went back three weeks, a happy Jean-Claude sitting side-on towards camera on what must have been his new touring bike. **My new ride!** declared the post, and from the red dirt in the foreground and blue-green sea behind but mostly from the sign that said Walkabout Hotel, Clement knew it had been taken in Port Hedland.

He looked up to see Josh Shepherd limping still in his cricket whites. Josh always limped after a sporting day, whether it was footy in winter or cricket in summer.

'Had them on toast. Both openers gone in the first session. I was first change. Only got the one over in before lunch. Then I saw your message. I followed up on those names we got from the ageing greenies. Got onto half of them. Of course, they know nothing about the chick in the sketch.'

He said it with exaggerated surprise in his voice to show he didn't believe them.

'You can put that on ice for now. I need you on the murder.'

The limp seemed to instantly vanish from Shepherd's body.

'What do you want me to do, Skip?'

Shepherd referred to everybody in sporting parlance.

'We have the identity of the Meda victim.' He explained what they knew so far, which was very little. 'I want you to cover town. As many shops as you can. Show them this photo.' Clement sent one of Seydoux when he was healthy and alive to Josh's phone. 'Ask if they know him.'

The disillusionment hung off Shepherd like sweat after a hard bowling spell.

'Isn't that a job for the uniforms?'

Patience, Clement told himself.

'No, because if you find somebody who knows him, you will follow up with detective-like questions. When did you last see him? What was he like? Who did you see him with? If somebody knows Lauren Bagot ask if they argue or are love birds.'

'Got it, Skip.'

Clement doubted that he did and wondered if Beck Lalor would have been better.

He checked in with Earle who was still waiting for a call back from Wildlife, and then phoned di Rivi. She'd got through the neighbours in the apartment block and was starting on other dwellings in the area.

'So far nobody recalls the motorcycle after Thursday around lunch. One neighbour heard it leave as she was putting her baby down. She says the rumbling bike drives her nuts because it often wakes the baby. That was Thursday around one p.m. One of the men recalls seeing Bagot arrive home Friday about eight p.m., just as she said. The neighbours next door say they have little interaction with either Bagot or Seydoux but they are quiet, no fights or parties. Nobody has seen Bagot driving the bike.'

Clement thanked her and told her to continue. So far everything fitted with what Bagot had told them.

He checked back in with Manners and asked he liaise with Mal Gross to see if they could pick up any movements of the motorcycle from Thursday afternoon. It was now 3.55. Time for the phone call to France. Risely was waiting in his office.

'I thought they might want a video conference,' said Clement. Risely explained that the parents apparently weren't very technologically savvy and the vice-consul thought a phone call was the simplest solution for now. As the seconds ticked by, Clement prayed that he would never find himself in anything remotely resembling their situation: trying to find out how your child, whom you had nurtured and loved, had perished violently in a faraway continent. The phone rang right on time. Risely answered and then listened.

'Yes, we're ready for Monsieur and Madame Seydoux,' explained Risely. 'I have Detective Inspector Clement, the lead detective on the case, with me.'

Risely clicked on the speaker. The vice-consul, a woman, who was handling the Sydney end of things, said that Mr and Mrs Seydoux could now hear them. She explained that in Nîmes it was 9.00 a.m. Risely wrote down the vice-consul's name on a pad for Clement's benefit. *Madame Charaud.*

She began. 'It is with great sadness that we are all gathered for this call. Superintendent Risely, would you like to begin? Just leave me a moment to translate after each sentence.'

Risely expressed his sympathy to the Seydoux parents and Charaud translated. Weak, fraught voices came back thanking him. Clement didn't need the translation for that. He figured they were likely still in shock. Risely informed them that he had Detective Inspector Clement with him and he would let them know what the police had ascertained so far. No doubt, Inspector Clement would have questions of his own for them. He then turned it over to Clement who began with his own expression of regret.

'I am very sorry for your loss. We are doing everything we can to find out what happened to your son.'

After this was translated, Clement asked them what they knew of the case so far. The answer came back: very little. They had been told via a phone call from the consulate just a couple of hours ago that their son had been killed in Australia in a place called Broome and that police were investigating and believed the death was suspicious.

Slowly Clement told them that there was no doubt their son had been murdered. It seemed, he explained, he had been incapacitated and then run over by a vehicle sometime in the early hours of Friday morning local time. At this stage the perpetrator or perpetrators were unknown but he had several leads they were following up.

This, Clement knew, was a bare-knuckles delivery of the situation but he felt that if he were the parent on the other end of the line, he would want facts, no soft-soaping. Even so, he did not tell them about Jean-Claude being nailed into the ground. He asked them what questions they had for him. Naturally they wanted more detail. And of course, did Jean-Claude suffer? Clement and Risely swapped glances. They would get the real story later so Clement warned them it was likely that Jean-Claude had been drugged first, thus incapacitating him before he was run over. He deflected questions on further detail except to say there was no evidence of sexual assault and that the body was intact. Then he asked if he could ask them some questions that would help with the investigation. They gave permission.

'When did you last speak with Jean-Claude?'

About five weeks ago.

'Did anybody else from the family speak with him?'

No, his mother was the last to speak with him. Jean-Claude seemed normal. He did not seem worried about anything.

'Is it true he was in the commandos?'

Yes indeed, a marine. He had been in the commandos for six years and done tours of duty in Africa and the Middle East. He could dive, handle explosives, weapons of all kind. He was a specialist in extraction. With Seydoux's background confirmed, Clement found himself wondering if it were possible, however unlikely, that it was his past catching up with him.

'Did he have any enemies at all? Even going way back? Anybody who might want to do him harm?'

No, he had never received any threats that they knew of.

'Has he ever been married or engaged or had a long-term relationship with anyone?'

He had a local girl when he was a teenager. They were sweethearts for a couple of his teenage years but that had broken up a long time ago and there had been no complications. Other than that, he had various girlfriends but none seemed that serious or long-lasting. He had not married, been engaged or lived in a de facto relationship.

'And no problems from his military life? No enemies from within or outside the service?'

No, Jean-Claude was popular and never said he had any problem.

Clement asked if the parents could give him a brief run-through of their son's life.

Jean-Claude had been an average student at school. Not an academic but not a poor student. He had liked sport and been good at it. As a teenager he had enjoyed going on long runs, swimming and parkour.

He had not been in trouble with the police for anything major although he and his friends had got up to a few things. He had never had a drug problem and, so far as they knew, had never sold drugs.

Clement made a note to speak to the brother. Maybe he would have more of an idea.

According to his parents, Jean-Claude had been fascinated with military things from the time he was fifteen and by seventeen had been talking about joining the armed services after school. He finished school and spent a few months working in a café but then applied for and was accepted into the navy. He did basic training and spent some time as a navy diver before applying for the commandos. You had to be elite to make them, but he set his sights on doing that and accomplished his goal. For around six years he was a commando but then he grew restless. His tours of duty made him want to see more of the world while he was still young so he left the commandos and returned to civilian life when he was twenty-six. For a short time, he came back home and worked again for a little while at a café but soon he landed a job in Portugal helping to teach diving to tourists and novices. From then until now he had cruised around the world doing this and that. They listed some of the places he had lived in: most of Europe, Bangkok, Vietnam, then Australia. He had not been to the Americas. He had wanted to go to Australia because it was a long way away and he liked to be out in the open with nature.

Clement felt he had at least some idea of Jean-Claude now. It was time to get specific.

'Did you or any members of the family send him a large amount of cash recently?'

There was silence, then what may have been quiet interrogation of each other.

The parents had certainly not sent him any money. They doubted his sister or brother would have but they would check. Why?

Clement explained that Jean-Claude had bought a motorcycle and used a large amount of cash. So far, the police had been unable to trace the source of that cash.

From his girlfriend? they had suggested.

'No, she thought the money came from you. Do you know Lauren?' he asked.

They had spoken to her a little on the phone, just a couple of words. Jean-Claude seemed very happy with her. They asked how she was coping. Clement told them she was extremely upset and that she had expressed a desire to speak with them. He promised he would send contact details.

She was not there when he was killed? asked Mr Seydoux.

Clement cautiously replied that there were no witnesses, that the place this happened was very isolated and that the police were trying to construct how Jean-Claude had ended up out there. Lauren Bagot was working at the time some two-hour drive away; however, the police had not been able to rule anybody out of the inquiry just yet. He repeated he was following a number of leads. For the time being, Clement had exhausted his questions and so he said that if they had no further questions for him, he would return to the investigation and turn them back over to Superintendent Risely. He asked if they could let Jean-Claude's brother and sister know he would like to speak with them, and extracted the contact phone number of Jean-Claude's closest old friend from Nîmes. They did not have contacts on any of his friends from the commandos. Clement left the room with their sobs sounding like hail on a concrete path.

He went to the kitchen and made himself a coffee. Somebody had arranged a pod machine and the younger staff raved about the quality but Clement hated people who rated coffee quality as if they were ranking something worthwhile like Springsteen albums. To him it was just a beverage. The fiddly pods annoyed him and nobody ever emptied the bin.

'You have to feel for the parents,' said Risely joining him and shaking his head at the proffered coffee.

Clement agreed. 'At least we know the cash didn't come from them but I'd like to speak to the brother and sister, and his old friend to be certain.'

Risely said the consul was working on that and added, 'And I've asked to see Seydoux's service record, and for you to speak to his old

CO just in case there is something relevant.'

'I know it's unlikely but let's face it, the manner of the death is pretty damn violent, almost like torture. And it seems personal. It could be somebody from his past, somebody military.'

Risely's phone buzzed. He checked it with a grunt. 'Media. I have to give them something. I'm saying it's a murder inquiry but keeping quiet on the crucifixion. Sooner or later somebody at Meda will talk.'

Clement agreed Risely's strategy was the best they could pursue. Leaving Risely to deal with the media, he joined Earle and brought him up to speed on the conversation with the family.

'So the cash is still unaccounted for,' mused Earle. He explained he had made contact with Parks and Wildlife, and Mal Gross was tapping friends in the Feds to see if Seydoux or any other ex-French commando had crossed their path.

It was going on for 5.00 p.m. and sunset was only thirty minutes away.

'I thought we should try the beach,' said Clement. 'See if any of Seydoux's class turn up.'

'Better than me sitting on my arse waiting for Wildlife or the Feds to call,' said Earle as his phone began to ring. Both men's hopes rose momentarily but then Earle read the ID.

'Barb,' he said. 'What's up?' Earle's face rippled as he listened.

'Shit.' He didn't look happy. 'Yeah, I'll call them, don't worry. I'll call you back.'

Earle sighed, stabbed a gaze at Clement. 'Rhys never showed up at his mate's barbecue and he's not answering his phone. Barb's freaking out. I said I'd call the hospital just in case.'

'I'll be okay at the beach by myself. See how you go.'

'Sorry. Barb is checking to see if any of his mates are missing too but I doubt it. Lately he seems to have cut himself off from even them.'

'Listen, you know ninety-nine percent of the time it's nothing. They just want space.'

'I know,' said Earle. But it was that other one percent that burned like acid through your guts.

And both men knew it.

10

Clement stood on Cable Beach staring out to sea. It was only about fifteen minutes since he'd left the station but he'd not heard from Graeme Earle to say he'd found Rhys. In spite of himself, that made him uneasy. It shouldn't even be on their radar that something bad had happened. It was just a few hours, for goodness sake. Even Clement himself had done that as a kid, ridden his bike to a bush point and stared at the ocean wishing a girl would fall in love with him or that a sailing ship would appear on the horizon and whisk him to another time. But back then fourteen-year-old boys didn't suicide, girls didn't cut themselves. Or maybe they did in the city but not out here. He turned back to the ocean for solace, wondered what it was about the sea that soothed us. Or the desert. Was it just that it was free of us? Whatever it was, it was more than just a notion, it was physical. He was sure most people felt it.

As a younger person he would wonder what old people could find so interesting about sitting in one place for hours and staring into a void. Now he understood: nothing, that was what enticed them, the void itself. They had learned a simple wisdom: there are too few moments in our adult lives where we allow ourselves the very special pleasure of being in nature and doing absolutely nothing about it. Somewhere along the line it becomes all about our work, or exercise, or kids.

It had been a lifetime since he'd prayed. Actually, that wasn't true. He'd begged for Marilyn to come back to him. Please universe, just let it be, he'd asked to no avail. Perhaps because he didn't believe enough in anything. Perhaps because he didn't believe enough in Marilyn and himself. Regardless, he put that disappointment aside, aimed his gaze at the golden sun and whatever spirit might listen, and said a quick, 'Please, let Rhys be safe.' Maybe because he wasn't asking so much for himself, this time it might work.

Work. There was that word again.

No escape from it.

There would be no balloon on the beach today to mark Seydoux's fitness class, so Clement's idea was pretty much to stand around in the middle of the beach and look about seeing if others were doing the same. He felt overdressed in his suit pants, had sought to dilute the image with a short-sleeved white shirt but it just made him look like a US college basketball coach. Shorts unfortunately, while comfortable, just wouldn't be right in public during a murder investigation. Clement toyed with the idea that he might get lucky, that one of the regulars would not turn up and that would mark them as the killer. Clement caught sight of a likely group of Seydoux's clients swivelling around, scanning, rolled exercise mats under their arms. They were about eighty metres north, four of them, three women and a man, tall with thinning hair. Clement trudged over through the white-grey sand. When he was about thirty metres away, they noticed. They were all facing him as he approached, no doubt wondering what on earth he was doing dressed as he was.

'You here for Jean-Claude's class?'

They seemed genuinely puzzled.

'Yes.' The small brunette answering.

'Is he coming?' asked the blonde.

'No. He's dead.'

It looked like genuine shock on their faces. Clement introduced himself. The blonde began comforting the dark-haired girl.

'You're Rex, aren't you?'

Clement saw even more confusion on the man's face. His Adam's apple bobbed.

'Yes,' and his voice sounded weak.

'What's your second name, Rex?'

'Cairncross.'

'And you ladies are?' If he didn't say 'ladies' and left it at 'you' he sounded, to his ear, curt and brutish. If he said 'women' it came out as authoritarian. 'Ladies' could be deemed patronising but it was his best option. Modern etiquette was a broken bottle for middle-aged men in bare feet.

The blonde spoke. 'Jacinta Richmond.'

'Catherine Khoury,' managed the smaller girl through tears. The girl he'd not seen in any photos who had that raw-boned fit look of an A-grade netballer announced she was Gemma Young.

'What happened to him?' asked Richmond. Clement did not answer her.

'You are all regulars here?'

'Not Gemma,' said Khoury.

'My first time,' Young volunteered.

'Do you have your phones on you? Could you send me your details? Name, address.'

He gave them his number and they obliged. Catherine Khoury did not have her phone with her but Jacinta Richmond took charge of that. No sooner was that done than she seemed to suddenly twig.

'That wasn't Jean-Claude who was found out Derby way?'

'I'm afraid it was,' said Clement. There was a point where obfuscation was of no value.

Only Catherine Khoury appeared ignorant of the news of the body. Clement allowed a moment of babble, then cut in.

'When was the last time you saw him?'

He addressed it generally but looked at each of the regular three in turn.

'Thursday session, here,' said Rex Cairncross. Richmond was self-appointed spokesperson though and she took up the running.

'We all turned up last night but there was no sign of him.'

'I dm'd him,' said Cairncross just getting in ahead of Richmond, who overlapped.

'Rex messaged him.'

'Did you speak to him?'

'I don't have his phone number,' said Cairncross.

'Then how –?'

'Instagram,' explained Jacinta for him, and added, 'I have his phone number,' trumping Cairncross, 'but I usually don't bother with it.'

'Same,' said Khoury. 'But I don't like to bring my phone to the beach.'

Jacinta Richmond rolled on. 'We thought maybe his new bike had broken down or something so we arranged to turn up tonight anyway. We thought if he didn't turn up, we'd just do our own thing like last night.'

'I bumped into Gemma and told her to come along,' explained Khoury.

Clement was getting the information straight in his head: according to them, none of them had seen Seydoux since the Thursday.

'What time did you last see him on the Thursday?'

'The session finished about six thirty.' Richmond again. 'We chatted for about ten minutes.'

'I asked if he wanted to come for a juice,' said Cairncross, 'but he said "not tonight".'

Jacinta Richmond looked at him as if she was mildly put out that she hadn't been across this.

'Was he anxious? Worried?'

Cairncross and Richmond shook their heads but Khoury nodded.

'Really?' Jacinta Richmond was affronted yet again. 'I didn't think so.'

'He seemed ... distracted,' said Khoury. 'To me, he wasn't his normal self. I can't say why but I felt it.' Sticking to her guns.

'You didn't see him leave with anybody?'

Blank stares.

'There's a girl who turns up sometimes after the class on a bicycle,' said Richmond.

'Dark-haired girl,' said Khoury. 'But I haven't seen her for a while.'

'Pretty sure I saw her Thursday after class. As I was leaving,' said Richmond, getting the last word. Apparently, this young woman, slim, black hair, medium height, had not attended classes and they had not socialised with her. Clement made a note. He turned to Cairncross.

'I believe you drove him to Port Hedland when he bought his new bike?'

Cairncross pulled a face. 'Me?'

'About three weeks ago?'

'No, wrong information, wasn't me.'

'He didn't ask you and then something stopped you from taking him?'

'No, he didn't. And I work. I couldn't take a day off. Except for Sunday.'

The sunset was magnificent but Clement was not looking as he leaned on his car in the carpark and banged the sand from his loafers. He was thinking about Rex Cairncross, who apparently was an accountant and had been living in Broome for three years. He was thinking Cairncross was a very credible man. They were all credible, the four of them. So, if they were to be believed, then either Lauren Bagot had lied to him, or Seydoux had lied to her. He slipped his shoe back on and was about to call Graeme Earle when his phone rang. Keeble.

'I've checked out the Hardcastle fleet. There are five possible vehicles but none with obvious bloodstains or recent bleach. I've checked their tread and taken tyre casts and done the interiors and trays. I told the foreman you would be in touch to ask the questions, I'm just the science graduate. I'm texting you his details.'

'Thank you.'

'Big of you, Dan. Now I have to drive back to Broome and supervise the garage. Oh, and check through the search results of Bagot's apartment that my guys did. Thank you so much.'

'Don't mention it.'

'You owe me big time.'

'Kahlua?'

'Just for starters. See you.'

He tried Earle but the phone rang out and the tension in his body wound higher. He fired up the car and swung out of the carpark and forced his thoughts from Rhys Earle to Lauren Bagot. If you assumed that she was innocent, she'd just had her whole life turned upside down. No family, no obvious friends, not even a car to get around in and the body of your loved one snatched away from you. Murder was cruel to so many.

None of the newer cars these days had a CD player. Some had a USB port. This one was radio only. Sometimes for a long drive Clement took an old portable CD player with him and reminded himself of his youth by listening to what was left of his once thriving collection. He'd thrown a bundle of CDs into a small suitcase when he'd come back from Perth. He hadn't brought the player with him today so it was mere speculation what he might have dredged up to suit his mood. Something bittersweet. Maybe a little of the underrated Mike Nesmith, maybe Wolfmother or go local with Steve Tallis, a Perth guy he'd discovered who apparently had been around for years, toured Europe and had this eclectic rep. The radio was throwing up a so-called classic, 'Born to Be Alive'. No. He turned it off, preferring silence, and cruised back to the station trying to discern some shape in the lines the investigation was squirting out. All he saw were unrelated squiggles.

11

Earle was beside himself. He had checked the school, all the sportsgrounds, the skate park and the beach. Rhys hadn't taken his bicycle. So, he'd either gone on foot or arranged to be picked up by somebody in a car. That thought terrified Graeme Earle. Now he was trying desperately to slow without skinning rubber outside the house of Dylan, Rhys' oldest and closest mate. He dashed out of the car and up the side path. He could hear the pop of a tennis ball off a cricket bat as he emerged onto the patio out back. Dylan and half a dozen other boys whom he recognised were playing backyard cricket on the well-tended lawn. Earle felt embarrassed and awkward at blundering into the game.

'Sorry fellas. Happy birthday, Dylan. Just wondered if any of you might know where Rhys might be. He's not answering his phone.'

To go public on his ignorance of where his son might be was humiliating. He felt like the walls had come down around him and left his parenting naked and exposed but he would suffer that a thousand times over to be reassured. None of the boys had the faintest idea where Rhys might be. Dylan was the most worrying when he almost apologetically confided, 'We hardly ever see him. He had a go at Jamie for eating a meat pie. Lunchtime he just sits on his phone. I invited him but I didn't think he would come, barbecue and all, you know.'

Graeme was beginning to.

'Does he have other friends?'

'Not our age. Weirdos. Sorry.'

'What do you mean, weirdos?'

'Antis.'

A new term for Earle. 'Antis?'

'Yeah, anti-this, anti-that, anti-everything.'

'Do you know their names?'

'No. I've seen him in town, in the distance speaking with them, but I didn't get close. I didn't want to get roped in to that shit.'

'Was this in a coffee shop or –'

'No, just on the street. I asked who they were but Rhys wouldn't talk about them.'

According to Dylan, there were about three or four, a mix of men and women probably in their mid-twenties. Asking for the boys to call him should they learn anything about where Rhys might be, he exited with a curt greeting-cum-farewell to Dylan's dad who had emerged from the house with the offer of a cold beer. He'd already asked Mal Gross to send out an alert to all the uniforms to keep an eye out for Rhys. Back in the car, he called Gross as he blasted off.

'Nothing so far,' said Gross. 'Try not to worry too much. It's early days.'

'I know. Could you let Dan know I'm still looking.'

Gross said he would and Earle found himself driving north to the edge of town with no clear plan.

Shit. If Rhys was in a car, how would he ever find him?

Despair was running across his skin in spikes. He rang Barb, knowing she would have messaged him if she had news. Barb was a total mess.

'It's alright, love. He'll be okay,' he tried to reassure her but to him his reassurances sounded hollow. For now, he kept to himself the more worrying details of what Dylan had said, diluted it down to, 'Dylan said he didn't think he'd show up but wasn't sure what he had planned.'

'There's a psycho out there right now.'

He could have argued the point: we don't know they're a psycho. Maybe there was some obscure logic to driving stakes through a man's hands and running over him. He didn't bother to dissuade his wife because that same fear was already camping in his own paddock.

'I'm just going to keep driving. Mal has every cop in the Kimberley looking out for him and it's only been a few hours.'

'He's always answered his phone before,' said Barb.

But now he's pissed off at me because I stuck my chest out and bumped him backwards like a big old kangaroo, thought Earle.

'We'll find him,' he said, told her to stay calm and ended the call. How could you stay calm? Rhys had cut himself off from friends and was hanging out with this older crowd who might well be druggies. The sun was petering out. Darkness rushed across the sky, sudden like a flock of scared bats. He put on his headlights.

Rhys is a young boy becoming a man, he told himself. Lots of kids struggling through this go AWOL for short periods.

And some of them top themselves, came the reply in this internal dialogue. He was riven by guilt. Had he been too strict or too lenient?

Twice he slowed to get a closer look at boys who resembled Rhys. They probably think I'm a pervert, he thought, but he didn't care. He cut across the northern border of town east and started south. He couldn't think where Rhys may have gone.

His phone rang, a number showed that he did not recognise.

He snatched at it, answered on a hair trigger, 'Graeme Earle.'

'Mr Earle, this is Hazel Meadows.'

She sounded English, that quaver in her voice that people get once they are north of sixty. 'We wanted to let you know that Rhys is at our place.'

The small house was near Cable Beach. Earle reached it quickly but took a moment to sit in the car to compose himself. He'd already called Barb to say Rhys was fine and he was going to pick him up.

'Don't go off at him,' she urged.

And he hadn't planned to but knew he might, just to vent the terror he'd felt. He took a deep breath and walked up the short gravel driveway. The front garden was fragrant and lush. The flywire door swung open as if they'd been keeping an ear out for him. A man, mid-to-late sixties, stood there in shorts and sandals.

'Rhys is inside. I'm Stephen Meadows.' He was standing back with the door open. Earle hadn't expected this, he'd been thinking

Rhys would be waiting outside and he would just pick him up. He considered standing his ground refusing the invitation but that would be truculent so he stepped inside the cool, dark house. A silver-haired woman sat next to Rhys on a patterned sofa, talking quietly. Rhys' gaze was directed not at his father but at the ground.

'Tea?'

Stephen Meadows was already moving towards the kettle.

'I'm good, thank you. I'll just grab Rhys.'

Meadows looked like he was about to say something but held his tongue and then moved to the electric kettle anyway and clicked it on. His wife came over with her hand extended.

'I'm Hazel. Rhys was going through some issues and felt he needed somebody to talk with.'

Why not me? thought Earle as he shook her hand. Rhys still wasn't meeting his gaze.

'I'm sorry, where do you know Rhys from?'

Earle was thinking they looked too old to be parents of his friends. Grandparents maybe?

'We met at the live sheep export protest, and then again at the abattoir protest.'

Animal activists. Earle forced down a knee-jerk reaction.

'I believe we met your colleagues the other day. Inspector Clement and the younger detective.'

That rang a dull bell. Shepherd chasing down leads on the break-in at the early childhood clinic.

'Oh, right.'

Hazel Meadows smiled over at Rhys who was still studying his trainers.

'We've become good friends.'

'He's not half bad at chess,' added Stephen Meadows.

Chess? Since when had Rhys been interested in chess? It had always been a chore to prize the Xbox control out of his hand.

'Rhys had asked to stay here,' said Meadows aloud so that Rhys knew he was included. 'We told him he needed to call his parents and reassure them he was okay. Of course, he's welcome, any time.'

Earle's panic was subsiding now. 'Well, thank you. His mother and I were very worried.' Now Earle found himself imitating Meadows by talking aloud to include Rhys.

Everybody stood awkwardly. While Earle did not want to appear ungrateful, there was too much he needed to say to Rhys and he would not do that publicly. These people seemed normal but no way was he letting Rhys remain here.

'You ready, champ?'

Rhys got to his feet and then finally met his eyes with the look of a slave being called to work.

'Bye,' said Rhys to the Meadows and Hazel gave a little wave. Rhys started through the door and headed towards the car. Earle turned back.

'Thank you. We were very worried.'

'It's a very confusing time for him,' said Hazel.

It suddenly popped into Graeme Earle's head that Rhys might be gay. He'd never shown any obvious indication. But that was the kind of thing he might find trouble talking to his parents about.

'Is there something specific ...' Earle let the words hang there like smoke from a bush ceremony.

'It's everything,' said Hazel and her eyes seemed full of compassion, as much for Earle as for Rhys. 'He feels powerless. We all do, don't we? But at his age, well ...' It was her turn to leave her thought unfinished. 'You two need to talk,' she finally said.

Earle might have said 'Yes, I know' but he was annoyed at being lectured to even if they were on the same page, so he just left. Stephen Meadows made good time beating him to the door and politely opening it for him.

Outside, Rhys stood sullenly at the car. The air seemed warmer, friendlier now.

'Fancy a milkshake?' Earle said moving towards the driver door. Rhys had always loved his milkshakes.

'I'm vegan.'

That's right. No milk.

'You can talk to us, mate.'

Graeme Earle had parked by the beach, thinking it might be better to have a heart-to-heart with his son before heading into the cauldron at home. There was only a rim of moon out. The sea was shiny black satin. You heard it and smelled it more than saw it.

'You say that, but you don't mean it.'

It was the first real sentence Rhys had said since they had been in the car.

Earle sat and listened to the gentle roll of waves.

'Well, I mean it now,' he said. 'I want us to be friends. I'll listen to you, and you listen to me. Please don't go off without letting your mum and me know. We were very worried.'

'The Meadows are nice people. They wouldn't hurt me.'

'But there's no harm in letting us know. And sometimes you might think people are nice and they aren't at all. I'm not saying the Meadows,' he hastily emphasised. 'Some of those people have pretty extreme views.'

Rhys made a disparaging sound.

'Come on, mate, be fair. Some do. Somebody vandalised the abattoir workers' cars a few months ago. That's not the right way of going about changing people's opinions. And the early childhood clinic has been smashed up probably by anti-vaxxers. You don't think that's right do you?'

'Not the clinic.'

As if the abattoir workers' cars were fair game. Earle didn't want to push too hard.

'All I'm saying is, if you want to talk about this stuff with your mum and me, we'd be happy to listen. Nothing in the world is more precious to us than you kids.'

He wondered if he should go further. He wasn't exactly frightened to raise the question of sexuality but he had trepidation.

'I mean, your mum and me, you can talk to us about anything. If anything was worrying you, thinking we might, you know, disapprove.'

'You did, before, when I was at the protest.'

'And I give you my word we'll talk more. I'll handle it better. Parents get short with their kids sometimes because they are worried for them. That's all.' Rhys was staring straight ahead. 'I mean, whatever it was. If you were gay, say, we're totally okay with that. It's your life.'

Rhys turned towards him registering that.

'Are you saying you'll accept me if I'm gay?'

'Of course.'

Rhys said, 'I'm not gay.'

Earle did not feel relief. He might be an old-fashioned type Aussie bloke but he'd meant what he'd said. He just wanted his kids to be happy, and to make good decisions.

'Are we good?' he said.

Rhys nodded and Earle took that as a positive and started the car. Small steps, he told himself.

12 SATURDAY NIGHT

Clement thought he owed his colleagues better than takeaway in the station house so they were now ensconced in the dining room of the Cleopatra Tavern. While the front bar had all the class of a ute's tray, the food out the back was pretty good. The surrounds were budget – plastic tables and furniture – but the green tablecloths were crisp and clean and the staff polite. The dining room was fairly full. Some pop music Clement didn't like was playing but fortunately not so loud they had to raise their voices.

Graeme Earle was going to join them when he could. It had been with great relief that Clement had taken his phone call to say the boy had turned up at the Meadows' house. For now, it was di Rivi, Shepherd and Keeble. Josh Shepherd was going the pork-belly burger – with chips of course. Jo di Rivi had selected calamari, Lisa Keeble a mushroom risotto and Clement grilled fish.

'Where's Manners?' asked Keeble.

'I think Saturday is his Dungeons and Dragons night,' said di Rivi. Shepherd chuckled.

'No seriously,' said di Rivi, swirling her coke and ice. 'He invited me once.'

'He fancies you,' said Keeble.

'No, he has a girlfriend,' said di Rivi with authority.

Clement did not want to admit it but that surprised him. Manners seemed the perpetually single guy, but there was the irony, Clement was the solo man now.

'I let him off because he's done a good job,' said Clement and tapped the folder filled with the fruits of Manners' labour. 'He's still waiting on some things but he's not dragging his feet. So, tonight I thought we could kick around where we are at, look at the gaps and see which of those we could close. Jo, where are we at with the stakes?'

Di Rivi said, 'I've emailed or spoken to WA railways and every mining and energy company in the state I could find. Three have confirmed they had stocks of that stake, two in Perth and one in Kalgoorlie. Seydoux has never been an employee of any of them. I'm still waiting on more than half of them to get back to me, the weekend and all. They did say that they are the sort of thing that companies could swap if somebody gave them a mate's call. In that case there would be no paper trail. Monarch Minerals don't have them.'

Clement explained for the others' sakes that was where Lauren Bagot worked.

'So she's our prime focus?' asked Shepherd stretching his long legs.

'For now. Mainly because we have nobody else. Jo interviewed the neighbours.'

She took her cue. 'Nobody recalled any arguments or affray from the apartment, or between Bagot and Seydoux in public. Nobody recalls strangers frequenting the apartment or other motorcycles being there. At least two witnesses from different households can swear that Bagot arrived when she said she did Friday evening. But I did find something very interesting. Something you don't know yet.' She looked here at Clement. His interest was piqued. Their meals arrived.

'I told you one of the neighbours heard the bike leaving Thursday around lunchtime.' Jo di Rivi forked calamari. She was primarily addressing Clement but the others were included although Josh Shepherd seemed preoccupied with how much of his burger he could consume in one go.

'That's right. She remembered because it woke the baby.'

'Correct. More on that in a second.'

'Did she actually see the bike and Seydoux or just hear it?'

'Only heard it but she says she knows the sound of that bike. Here's the thing though. She was certain the bike wasn't there Wednesday night at all. I asked all the other residents. I got a guy in one of the other flats who says the bike isn't there lots of nights, in fact he was thinking Seydoux must be a shiftworker. I went back to the nursing mother and got more specifics. Usually, the bike leaves around four p.m. That's not a problem because the baby is awake.'

Seydoux going to the beach to prepare for his class, thought Clement.

'But Thursday it left earlier, at one p.m., and that woke the baby. "But," I said to her, "you said it *normally* wakes the baby." See, I was confused. She said, "Oh, that's just lately the bike started leaving around one and waking her up. Before that the problem has always been when the bike came home, around one p.m. At least on weekdays. That would wake the baby. The bike would head out at four but that wasn't a problem." I asked her if she knew what time it got in Thursday. She said she didn't know but it wasn't there when she did the bins the night before, or first thing in the morning when she took the dog for a walk. She went out shopping around ten a.m. and guessed it might have come back then but she couldn't be sure if it was back when she got home. The baby is awake at that time.'

It was then that Graeme Earle entered the room and made his way to join them.

'Sorry for all the drama,' he said. Clement tried to reassure him there was nothing to forgive. He knew Earle wouldn't want to say more in front of the others anyway. Earle begged off food and Clement recapped what di Rivi had just told them.

'The witnesses are all over the place, like they often are, but it seems,' says Clement, 'there are nights when Seydoux isn't at home.'

Earle reminded him, 'Lauren Bagot said he likes to go for long drives on the bike and sometimes camps out.'

He could be doing that, thought Clement.

'Recently his routine seems to have changed. He'd normally leave about four, I'm guessing to go to the beach. Lately though, he was leaving around lunchtime. What was he doing?'

Blank faces stared back at him. Josh Shepherd licked his fingers clean.

'He could just have been testing out his new ride,' said Shepherd.

That was true, thought Clement. Maybe he was overthinking but it would at least be nice to know where Seydoux spent Wednesday night. He moved on.

'Josh, how did you go?'

'Stuff all,' said Shepherd leaning back in his plastic chair. 'I got through about a third of the shops but a lot closed up early for Saturday. A few people said he looked familiar but I didn't get one bloody hit of any use until I got to Squeeze.'

That was a juice shop.

'The girl there remembered him as a Pineapple Express, that's the juice he always ordered. She said he had an accent, Spanish she thought, durr, and he often came in with two or three other people who looked like they did Pilates or something together.'

That would likely be the crew I've just met at the beach, thought Clement. He turned to Lisa Keeble.

'Fill us in.'

'As for the flat, no large sums of cash, no flunitrazepam – otherwise known as Rohypnol – no blood stains, no railway spikes. Nothing there to suggest a violent struggle recent or past. On the vehicle that killed Seydoux, some progress. Perth reckons their best guess is it's a standard four-wheel drive that crushed Seydoux, went over him, then backed up, then went over him again. The tyre marks were only partial but they say the weight looks right. We took various other photos and casts of tyre marks in the vicinity. If we believe the ringers at the station, then some tyre marks we found about fifty metres south of the body could be better versions of the vehicle's. That's why it's Perth's best guess but they won't commit to an exact make of tyre even.'

Earle asked, 'How about the vehicles at the Meda station?'

'Two four-wheel drives. I've run tests inside and out and there's nothing that says either is the one used.'

Clement said, 'And nothing that rules them out?'

'Correct.'

Clement then spoke his own thoughts aloud. 'If this was a crime in the heat of the moment then maybe somebody at the station could be involved, but Seydoux was drugged. I think that's premeditation. It's planned, and in some way personal. So why, if I work and live at the station do I shit in my own nest? Much more likely somebody drove or met Seydoux somewhere in the middle of nowhere.'

'Although not too far from where Lauren Bagot works at Hardcastle Minerals.'

Shepherd was vigorous on his burger.

'Indeed,' said Clement and looked back at Keeble, bidding her to continue.

'Three possible vehicles at Hardcastle but two we think we can rule out. The keys were in the locked office in a locked cabinet and the site manager keeps the key to that on his person. You can't rule out that somebody made a copy of the key to the cabinet but the office is alarmed and only the site manager and his assistant have the code.'

'Mal checked them out,' volunteered di Rivi, 'and there are no flags on either the site manager or the assistant.'

Keeble went on. 'The third vehicle was being used by a Kevin Atkinson. He says the key was in his room with him when he went to sleep and right there when he woke up. His room was unlocked so it's possible that somebody could take it and return it while he slept. We've tested the vehicle and there is no sign of blood, Seydoux's prints or anything nasty. There is also no indication at all of it being bleached. The soil around Hardcastle is near identical to Meda so any match in the tyres means nothing really. I know I'm not a detective but speaking as a woman, there is no way Lauren Bagot is having it off with Atkinson rather than Seydoux.'

'He's like me, fat and old?' said Earle.

'You're George Clooney compared to him.'

Clement knew, however, there could be myriad reasons why Bagot might work in concert with Atkinson.

'Jo, I want you to drive there tomorrow first thing and make some inquiries at Hardcastle about what Lauren Bagot might have said about her relationship with Seydoux. She mentioned two other women who work there, they might be a good starting point but, you know, a mining camp is a very limited space. If Lauren was close to anybody up there, somebody will know. I can tell you guys that Manners has done a good job and there is nothing in the phone records of Lauren Bagot that indicates any other relationship. Her texts to Seydoux are not angry. Her bank statements are exactly what you'd expect. As for Seydoux, no activity on his phone after he received a call from Bagot at six twenty p.m. Thursday.'

Earle deduced, 'He knew where he was going. If Bagot is involved, that phone call might have set the arrangement. But it could have been organised beforehand or he met somebody right off after the class.'

Clement agreed. 'Manners is sorting through Seydoux's phone calls and messages. There is a young woman with dark hair whom he sometimes meets after his class. A witness says she was there around six forty. I'd like to find her, so I'll get Mal Gross to get a couple of our better uniforms out to the beach to ask around.'

Everybody had finished their meals and Clement did not want to keep anybody, particularly Graeme Earle, longer than necessary. It had been a gruelling day.

'So what do we think about Lauren Bagot?'

Earle ventured, 'So far what she told us has no holes in it. She had possible access to the vehicle and the murder site but it would not be easy. It would take a deal of planning and a bit of luck, and I reckon she'd need an accomplice.'

'I agree,' said Clement. 'We'll see what Jo can find out but I'm inclined to rate her very low. We can't rule out that somebody simply killed Seydoux for the bike but why they would peg him out like a claim ... that seems personal.'

'Unless they are trying to throw us off the scent,' said Shepherd.

Keeble wrinkled her nose. 'Still seems a very complicated way to go about it if all you're after is the bike.'

Clement said, 'I agree, but I don't think we can discard any theory yet. The key to this is who Jean-Claude really is. Where did he get that money? Was it from something illegal?'

'He's not on the radar of the Feds or Wildlife,' said Earle. 'I got a message about an hour ago from Mal Gross.'

'Like I said, we can't rule anything out,' repeated Clement. 'Tomorrow morning, Jo, Hardcastle. It's a Sunday, so some workers might be offsite. Any who aren't at work might be in Derby or Fitzroy Crossing, so chase them up. Some could be in Perth or interstate. Josh, continue with the shops.' Josh looked downwards and dropped his serviette to the table like a kid pretending his bomber was unleashing a payload. He was sulking but too bad.

Clement ran on. 'Lisa, everything and anything.'

When the others had gone, Clement and Earle leaned back against Clement's car.

'Josh was underwhelmed,' chuckled Earle.

Clement smiled. 'I think Lauren is genuine.'

'Me too.' Earle scuffed loose stones on the bitumen. 'Rhys was with those protest people. The Meadows.'

Earle gave Clement a short version of events. Told him about the heart-to-heart.

'I mean maybe I have been deaf to him. You expect, you know, when they're eighteen or something they will go their own way. You don't think it's going to happen this soon.'

And Clement felt it then rising up, that buried fear that Phoebe might feel the same, like he was an intrusion on her life. And where would that leave him? A lonely, middle-aged man with his best years adrift.

'You best get back,' said Clement, and watched as his friend drove away.

The air was a warm flannel. Over the last several years rain seemed to be coming earlier in November than what Clement remembered as a kid but so far this year it had been as dry as Marilyn's quips. A thunderstorm would be welcome.

Clement sat on his bed. Even with the window open and the fan on, it was still oppressive. He'd not long got off the phone from Seydoux's sister who had called him direct. She spoke reasonable English and had already talked things through with her other brother who did not. Unfortunately, she had been able to shed no light on her brother's killing, other than to say that he had seemed happy in his relationship with Lauren. His brother, who had also spoken to Jean-Claude's best friends, had passed on that Jean-Claude did not appear to be troubled in any way when he'd last spoken with him.

Dead end. Clement was frustrated.

The phone he discovered still in his hands might as surely have been the apple the serpent tempted Eve with. It whispered to him. He dialled. The phone rang, three long burrs. On the fourth it was answered.

'Yes, Dan.' Marilyn's world-weary voice like he'd been calling every day for a week when in actual fact they'd not have spoken more than twice in the month.

'You didn't tell me about the band tour.' It came out like a spray from an *Untouchable*'s Tommy gun and even as he pulled the trigger, he regretted that he had not fought the impulse harder. There was a pause. A breath, the passive-aggressive, I'm-being-patient kind.

'No. I should have. I'm sorry.'

'Well, I appreciate your deep and obvious concern but I went to a lot of trouble to organise a boat and plan out a schedule.'

'I doubt that. I'm guessing you walked into the Anglers one night and asked if anybody, or maybe it was your mate Bill, had a boat free. Now,' she added hastily, like ointment after a burn, 'I know that doesn't excuse me and I know you're a good dad and you love your time with Phoebe ...'

'Damn right.'

'... but I only found out myself a week ago. Maybe just over. And I meant to tell you. I did.'

'I guess you were too busy arranging the champagne in the fridge by size.' It was a poor comeback and she duly smashed it across his bow.

'I thought you would have remembered I hardly drink champagne.' Another sigh. 'One of the reasons I probably put off the call is because in the back of my mind I knew it would devolve into this bickering.'

'It wouldn't have if you had let me know.'

'You sure about that?'

Why did she always manage to make it like it was his fault? He never should have called. He had squandered the high ground to plunge headlong down the slope and find only a stalking-horse waiting.

She kept on. 'You have my apology. If you'd like me to refund the hire or find another boat later, I can pay.'

'I can manage, thank you.'

'If there's nothing further then ...'

He stabbed the button to end the call and cursed himself. She'd almost been out of his system. Almost. And now she was right back in there.

When he turned out the lights it would only be her face he saw.

13 FIFTY-TWO HOURS EARLIER

Thursday November 11 2021

Ingrid and he had taken a walk to the west side of the island where he had shown her some of the bird habitats. They had fallen into step side-by-side but they had not held hands. At one point he'd gone to reach out for hers as a reflex because the only time he'd ever had any woman walking to match his step had been Gabrielly and it just came naturally to him. He had caught himself in time and didn't think Ingrid had realised but he had panicked after that, becoming aware for the first time that he was *not* holding her hand. That had been disconcerting but eventually the feeling had faded. She'd had some rounds to do and he had a few spreadsheets to fill out but when those were done, they had met up in the cafeteria again and then Ingrid had invited him into her unit.

She had pulled a bottle of beer for herself and one for him from the bar fridge and he had not refused. She had a bunch of DVDs and had offered him the choice.

'You pick,' he'd said, self-conscious because he hardly ever watched any movies and wouldn't have a clue what to suggest.

'Most of them are girl things you'll probably hate.'

'I don't care,' he'd said.

'Funny or sad?' Before he could answer, she said, 'Actually I've only got funny.'

And it made him laugh. Not a belly laugh but a chuckle.

The movie she picked was *Fun With Dick And Jane* with Jim Carrey and a woman he remembered from TV who was really good. Attractive too. He'd never seen a Jim Carrey movie although he had heard of him.

It was an interesting movie. Dick and Jane were ordinary, good people but they lost everything because of others' greed. That was a story Paul was all too familiar with.They decide to do robberies. They break the law and we can all see they are only doing this because it has been forced on them. And all that is well and good but it raises the question of the innocent people who might suffer because of them.

That point resonated with him. It's not just about you, it was saying. And there it was again, that ... well not so much panic, as rising dread.

Ingrid laughed a lot throughout the movie and he enjoyed her laughing, and even he, despite his muddle of thoughts, couldn't help himself, especially when Jim Carrey got brain freeze from the icy drink. There he was, laughing, getting pleasure from life.

Everything had seemed so settled just a few weeks ago. He had been so certain that life was a desolate wasteland, that life was non-life. For sure, the corporate forces didn't care about the little man. They were a juggernaut whose goal was to grow bigger and fatter by feeding on the misery of the peasants. And this unformed, shapeless idea that he'd sensed but not been able discern fully had coalesced when he'd found the Marx book on the verge. He was sure there had been a purpose in him finding that. He was sure a hand was guiding him, maybe Gabrielly's. Yet he had felt alone, isolated from everybody he knew. His new knowledge hadn't helped one iota, if anything it was salt to his wounds. The inexorable path he was on might be certain but it offered no rescue. It led to the edge of a cliff and he was going over it. Until one night you are wandering under the pleasant early-spring night sky of Broome and boom! You collide with destiny. And you say, well I'm going over the cliff but why be a lemming, why not make Gabrielly's death and that of my unborn child count for something?

It seemed that he was being channelled by some universal plan.

Except now he had to ask himself, was that really destiny or was that nothing but a false trail? Was this, could this possibly be, destiny? The warm body of another human being beside you? What made more sense, Gabrielly as the avenger, or Gabrielly as one who forgave? She was compassion itself. So this, this with Ingrid was confusing. Since that day when Ingrid had met him on his walk and they had talked about the birds, he had felt something in his universe shift. He cared for her. Not as a lover, not yet at any rate. Here they were fully clothed watching a movie, that was all. But the big point was that he had found himself able to care about somebody at all. What was important in the movie is what Dick and Jane feel for one another. Yes, they get the bad guy, give him a satisfying comeuppance, though that probably wouldn't ever happen in real life, but it's their love that is important.

After the movie, Ingrid had had another beer. One had been enough for him. They had sat on her bed to watch the movie, that was the most comfortable way but it was a tight space and they had been squeezed together.

'Want to try another one?' she had asked.

'Sure,' he said. This time it was *Pirates of the Caribbean*.

'It's kind of silly but I like Johnny Depp.'

And it was silly but that was a good thing because his head was still spinning from the first movie.

Halfway through, she had fallen asleep resting on his chest. It was the most intimate thing that had happened in his life since that day. He should feel guilty, disgusted with himself for his treachery to Gabrielly but he did not. In fact, he imagined Gabrielly smiling at him with those dimpled cheeks as if saying, 'Go on, there's nothing wrong.'

But then he was worried that might just be his own self-serving projection. He'd never seen Gabrielly jealous. Not that he had ever given her reason to be. He wondered if the situation had been reversed and it was him who had perished, whether he would want Gabrielly to be lying with her head on some stranger's chest. No. That was the answer that jumped out at him. But once you are dead what is it to you? It should be a simple question shouldn't it? Do you want your lover happy or not? He supposed you wanted to give them that opportunity but only if you knew that they weren't going to take it up because then what if they were happier with the new person? What did that say about the life you'd had together? That it hadn't been that special after all? That time healed? That worse, the first instalment was but an illusion. For a long time, he just lay there watching the movie but not really taking it in. Instead, he kept wondering about Gabrielly and destiny. Loyalty.

When she had been lost to him, it was as if he was the one who had been shipwrecked, life disappearing in full sail over the horizon. He felt totally alone, and that isolation became his status quo, it defined him. Until that night in Broome wandering along the beach, he had heard voices and spied the glow of a campfire. He had stopped and stood in the shadows listening, catching the words, expressing, incredibly, the very sentiments he had been mulling over. Yes, in a different way, but the same sense.

'Humankind is fractured,' this man's voice was saying. 'And it is no accident. Globalisation has deprived us of everything: our nationalities, yes but that could have been a good thing if it had rid the world of jingoism. But has it? No. That's worse than ever but it is allowed to play out on sports fields. Games to distract the masses, while our humanity is leeched from us, keystroke by keystroke. A man or woman is no more than a digitised stroke that exists in cyberspace. We are an algorithm's DNA, that's what we are. The multinationals are a bunch of cleverly adapting viruses working in concert. Each attempt to rid us of them is absorbed and mutated so that the virus gets even stronger and humanity weaker. We are replaceable, interchangeable. We trade our souls for something as useless as this.'

Something appeared in his hand like a magician. It was hard to see from back there but as the palm moved past the fire, Paul saw it was a shiny black rock.

'Souls for coals,' said the speaker. 'You think that's a good bargain?'

And then as he stood there craning in to hear every word, the voice had called out, 'Don't be afraid, you over there in the shadows, come and join us. We won't bite.' Like the voice of a great spirit or god seeking him through the darkness.

His feet sinking into the sand, he trudged over, the effort evoking pilgrimage, the glow of the fire reinforcing the spiritual nature of the moment. He had taken his seat. The voice had asked, 'What's your name ...'

'Paul?' Ingrid woke dozy. 'Did I sleep on you? Sorry.'

'That's okay. I didn't want to get up and wake you.'

She smiled. 'You are very sweet, Paul Isegar.'

The electric clock said it was a little after 2.00 a.m. The movie was nearly finished.

'I had better go,' he heard himself saying.

'You can watch to the end if you want?'

'No, I'll let you get some sleep. You have the early shift.'

She smiled, 'You know my routine?'

He felt himself blushing. 'I looked it up.'

They stood and he thanked her for the beer and the movies.

'Anytime,' she said and stood on tiptoes and kissed him on the cheek.

'I'll see you tomorrow ... today,' he hastily corrected.

'Don't forget you're going to show me the ospreys, sometime.'

He hadn't forgotten. 'Of course,' he said and stepped out.

The night air seemed to vibrate with the hum of the plant. It didn't stop because it was two in the morning. It was a funny thing being the HR manager. While it was a totally pathetic position, you got to know all the workers and where they would be, or ought to be at any given time. He gazed out towards dark sea. How long had this rocky island been here under these stars? He was still, not even breathing so far as he could tell, like he was a fossil and part of this place too.

The night with Ingrid had been very pleasurable in many ways but now it left him horribly confused. Automatically he pulled the phone from his pocket and was going to call then and there but he restrained himself. He needed to think things through better before he did that. But one thing in his breast beat with certainty: Ingrid was precious and so was the earth on which he stood under the unfathomable sky.

14 SUNDAY

Jared Taylor had been camped at the roadhouse all morning asking anybody who straggled through if they had seen a touring motorcycle since Thursday afternoon. Mal Gross had asked him to check the stretch between Broome and Fitzroy Crossing. It was a long shot. Yes, there were so few vehicles on the road that somebody might remember seeing the motorcycle and any cars that seemed to be with it but the trouble was finding that person because almost everybody on the road was coming from a long way away and going to somewhere a long way away. By now that witness could be in Halls Creek or Port Hedland or Adelaide. The best chance of course had been the roadhouse people themselves but they didn't recall a motorcycle coming through Thursday night. They said that somebody from Broome police had already requested the CCTV of the cameras by the bowsers. Taylor guessed that would be the funny bloke Manners. Taylor thought the ringers and bosses at Meda might be a chance but according to Mal they couldn't help. The police at Derby had canvassed the town with no luck so Taylor had decided to hang here, a hundred and sixty-five k from Broome. Every red-dirt-encrusted vehicle that stopped Taylor took a note of the number plate and asked his questions. It was 11.00 a.m. now and the air-conditioning was pleasant. He sat with his Coke, conversation with Cheryl, who was serving, pretty much exhausted.

A sedan rolled in from the east. Jared didn't rush to get up. Nobody ever just filled up and drove off, everybody came in for a refreshment or the toilet. It was a couple. While the man went to the tank to get that out of the way, the woman, who looked maybe thirties, came into the shop. Jared let her get her order underway before he stirred.

'Long trip?' he asked.

'Came from Fitzroy Crossing,' she said. 'We're going to Derby, then onto Broome.'

'Don't suppose you were on the road last Thursday anywhere near here?' he asked.

She looked mildly concerned.

'Thursday we did come through here on our way to Fitzroy Crossing.'

Taylor felt a stirring of hope. 'What time of day?'

'About lunchtime.'

Damn, too early. He went through the routine of asking about the touring bike. No, they hadn't seen it. The fella came in then. Taylor introduced himself and told them what it was all about. They didn't seem to have heard about the murder and were sorry they couldn't help. They sat and ate their burgers and drank water. They were from Albany in the south of the state and had put aside three weeks to travel all the way up the coast and around the Kimberley. The next thing, their car was heading off, leaving Taylor alone again with Cheryl and Jack, who divided his time between the kitchen and sitting at one of his own tables reading some kind of manual. Looking through the window, Jared caught a glimpse of what seemed at first to be a crow flying low. But when he focussed, he realised it was a man on a bicycle rolling in. Seeing a cyclist all the way up here might have caused some people to doubt their sanity but Taylor didn't blink. He knew who it was, old Martin, who might or might not be some kind of relative of Taylor. Martin declared he was but nobody from Taylor's family would confirm it. Martin was a fixture up here, drifting usually between Derby and Fitzroy Crossing but sometimes getting across to Broome. On the long hauls he would try and hitch a ride with a kindly motorist who could take his bike too. Taylor hoped for their sake they had plenty of air-freshener, Martin could get pretty ripe. It was something of a miracle that Martin could pedal his bike at all with his swag strapped to the back of it. He camped out, lived off the land mostly, but in the towns he would bunk in with his relatives. Taylor had only ever thought of him as 'old Martin' but he likely wasn't over fifty. He only had a few of his teeth and it was probably the sight of his gummy mouth that piled on the years.

Taylor watched him place his bicycle carefully in the shade, and dust himself off before pushing through the door. No doubt he'd already spied Jared's car.

'Hey nephew, they let you out!'

He laughed and that turned into a wheezing sputter.

'G'day, Uncle.' Taylor went with it. Martin greeted Cheryl and Jack, who knew him of course. Cheryl asked him if he wanted anything to eat but he wrinkled up his nose.

'Just a Sprite,' he said and felt around his pocket for change.

'I'll get it,' said Taylor. Martin smiled and pulled up a chair. They chatted about the heat and Martin asked after Taylor's family.

'What about that Irene?' His eyes always twinkled when he got to inquiring after Taylor's aunt. Taylor suspected this was the real origin of Martin's claim they were related. Martin *wished* they were, through him and Irene being a unit. Irene had waved off that suggestion with a one-word comment, 'Never.'

Cheryl delivered Martin's cold Sprite and he sipped it gently, holding the dewy aluminium skin to his cheek for a second or two.

'Oh, that's good,' he said. Then he finally got around to asking. 'So what are you doing here sitting on your arse?'

Taylor told him about the murder. It was all news to Martin.

'A white fella?' The story was getting juicier by the minute.

Taylor told him the fella rode a motorcycle and he was trying to see if anybody had seen it late at night.

'I seen a motorcycle, one night, late, real late.'

'When?'

Martin had to rummage his memory. 'I think three nights or four nights back. I'm not sure. But it was real late, nobody else around.'

'Where was this?'

'May River. I can show you.'

Taylor's mind was racing. May River was on the western border of the vast Meda station. The murder had happened in the south-east.

'Can you draw the spot for me?'

Cheryl came good with an exercise book. Martin painstakingly drew his map.

'I can just come with you,' he said again but Taylor was thinking that might cause a whole lot of problems. On the other hand, he wasn't all that familiar with the area by the May River.

'Okay, but draw it anyway,' said the police aide. At some point he was going to need to explain it to somebody and the map would be useful.

'I was camped in here,' Martin stabbed a position with Taylor's pen. 'Having a little drink. Then I hear this...' Here Martin imitated the sound of a motorcycle. 'I was about from here to the other side of the road away. I seen the motorcycle drive through the trees heading towards the creeks. You won't catch me down there with those big crocs. Then next thing. I hear a car and see lights.'

'A car as well?'

'Yeah. Four-wheel drive. There's a dirt track. They must have come down it, then turned off.' Martin drew the track and made an arrow to show what he meant. 'I hear them turning this way towards them creeks.'

'Could you see what sort of car it was?'

'Too dark. But it was a four-wheeler, the lights up high.'

Martin couldn't get the time exactly but weighing the probabilities Taylor reckoned if it was Seydoux's motorcycle it was more likely after the killing at Meda than before. This could be a big breakthrough.

'Come on then,' he said. 'Show me whereabouts.'

***

Once he'd finally got to bed, Clement's night had been all Swiss cheese. He regretted that call to Marilyn almost instantly. He'd moved on. Now he was back where he'd started. Sleep had been furtive. He'd cornered it a few times but never for any length. The air in the room had felt heavy, the walls sweaty. So, he was pleasantly surprised the workday started well. Risely called as Clement was driving in to the station to tell him Seydoux's former CO would call Clement on Risely's line at 11.00 a.m. Apparently he spoke very good English so there was no need for a translator. He would call on Risely's line. Risely himself was planning a morning round of golf but was ready to abandon at a moment's notice should anything break. So far so good with the media. Nobody yet had leaked the gruesome nature of the murder.

The first hour and a half consisted mainly of Clement checklisting every possible line of inquiry he could think of with Seydoux. Was there something he was missing?

Manners was slowly identifying the phonecallers to Seydoux, Mal Gross coordinating the continuing search for the motorcycle.

As Clement ticked off the lines of inquiry they needed to follow, Graeme Earle sat with him checking Clement's double-checking. Jo di Rivi was already at Hardcastle. Only one of the women co-workers whom Lauren Bagot had mentioned was on duty but di Rivi had chased up contact details for the other.

At 10.55, having achieved no apocalyptic insight on the case, Clement and Earle took themselves off to Risely's office. The phone rang at 11.02. Clement put the call on speaker. Colonel Phillipe Locard possessed excellent English.

He wasted no time in coming to the point. 'How can I help you, Inspector?'

Clement confirmed that Locard was aware of the death of his former soldier.

'It was a very violent murder,' explained Clement who had debated whether he needed to go into detail and had decided not at this stage. 'We have no suspects at this point and we are trying to get a picture of Jean-Claude as a person. How would you describe him?'

Locard took his time. 'A very professional and adequate soldier. Commandos must be extremely fit and disciplined. I was not surprised he left the service though. It wasn't ...' Clement assumed he was searching for the words, '... his life total.'

His whole life. Clement understood.

'Did he have any problems with his superiors or colleagues?'

'Not with his superiors. As for his colleagues, I am not aware of any feud. Certainly nothing ever came to our attention. There may have been minor things. That is common in any profession.'

'Drugs?'

'No.'

'As far as you are aware have any of his former colleagues met with violent death? Apart from in action,' Clement hastily added.

'No.'

'Was Jean-Claude involved in any conflicts that could engender lasting bitterness?'

'War always creates lasting bitterness, Inspector. Especially for the losing faction.'

Clement felt he may have to tread delicately. 'Was there any conflict though that could lead to the pursuit of an individual soldier as revenge?'

'I don't think so.'

'Was Jean-Claude a whistleblower or himself the subject of any inquiry for failure to act as a soldier should?'

He had to explain whistleblower for the colonel.

'No, he was not. He joined. He served his time well. He left.'

'What were his particular areas of expertise?'

The colonel explained that his regiment were marine specialists but experts in many fields.

'Jean-Claude was a very good diver. He could act as an engineer and improvise too very quickly. He was competent with weapons, martial arts and explosives, as are all my people. His English was very good.'

'Would you be surprised if he was involved in any kind of illegal activity?'

There was a substantial pause and Clement was about to prompt him when the colonel came back on.

'For our people when they return to civilian life, there are few areas where their services are in high demand. Security, yes. The divers for oil rigs. Some become mercenaries but a few do play with the margins of society. I would say it is possible Jean-Claude could be in that category. I would be surprised but not ... it would not be impossible.'

Clement wondered if the colonel knew if Seydoux had been in close contact with any of his former colleagues.

'I do not know that. I can ask some of those still in the service if they hear from him. The family is more likely to be of aid.'

Clement thanked him for his time and rang off, little the wiser.

'Between the lines,' said Earle, 'he said Seydoux could get into something shady.'

But was that really any help? So far, Seydoux remained an enigma.

In spite of the potential for chaos and the smell that emanated from Martin, Taylor was glad he had brought him along. The map he had drawn was fairly detailed but even so it was hard to be certain you were in exactly the right place out here. He had called through to Mal Gross and let him know that he was pursuing a lead on the motorcycle and Mal had said he would pass the news to Clement as soon as he was free. The plan was for Taylor to see if he could establish that the vehicles and camp were still there near the May River. If so, backup from Derby would be sent. Taylor assumed that if whoever Martin had heard that night was still in the area, they would be either in a campervan, tent or bunking in their car. There were no huts for weary travellers out here. From what Martin had described, it seemed that where he had been camping was on or near the north-west fringe of Meda station. It may have been just outside it but people fished and even, foolishly in Taylor's opinion, swam at the river crossings. The station people allowed this. The property was so big. The Frenchman had been killed to the south-east of the massive station so it was possible his killer or killers had simply come back onto the main road heading back towards Derby and then cut back up again on the track Martin had taken. They may have been in the area the whole time but, even if the Derby cops had been looking there, it would have been hard to find people who didn't want to be found.

Taylor was driving with his window down, catching fresh warm air in preference to being trapped in the air-conditioning with the odour.

Aunty was going to kill herself laughing at this. Given that Martin could be pretty exact about where he had been camping but could not say where the motorcycle had ultimately finished up, Taylor decided it was best to get to Martin's old camp. He could leave him there while he went off to explore.

'Track is coming up here,' said Martin pointing and Taylor eased the car down the rutted dirt track.

'You ride your bike down here?' He couldn't imagine how uncomfortable that would be.

'I don't carry it,' laughed Martin. 'Well, sometimes I do. Sometimes I just ride through the bush. It's easier a lot of the time but you get a lot of punctures.'

'You eating good?' Taylor gave him the once-over, trying to divine how healthy he was. He looked in pretty good shape and the cycling had to help.

'Eating fine. Drinking good too,' Martin cackled. 'That radio work?'

He was talking about the car radio not the police one. The policeman got the hint and turned it on. Martin sat back like a king on his throne. He bopped along to the country tune and smiled over at Taylor. Martin began to half sing and half hum the tune. Taylor couldn't distinguish much similarity with either half to the actual song that was playing.

'Turn right coming up. Slow down.'

Taylor did as he was commanded.

'Here.' Martin pointed and Taylor turned off the track and into the bush proper. The bigger trees were widely enough spaced that the car could mostly go straight but every now and again Taylor had to perform a zigzag. About three minutes in, Martin called a halt and Taylor stopped.

'I was camped right there.'

The men climbed out onto a carpet of twigs and leaves. It was hot, the air sticky as the sap you could smell when you got up close to the bark. It was near silent. The flutter of leaves above helped substantiate this wasn't a dream. The invisible wings of an insect buzzed close by. Martin took a dozen or so steps and pointed to the earth that had been casually swept clear of twigs in a small semicircle.

'See, that's where I was.'

'The vehicles?'

Martin swivelled back to his left, pointed about forty-five degrees. 'Over there somewhere.'

That would be north-west of this spot.

'You stay here. I'm going to take a look.'

'I'll come too.'

'No. You stay here.'

Jared Taylor checked his phone. It looked like there was a weak signal. 'I could be a while.'

'I got nowhere special to be,' said Martin without a trace of irony.

Jared Taylor moved in the direction that Martin had indicated. Knowing it was at least three hundred metres where Martin had last seen the vehicles he didn't bother to walk softly yet. It was still hot and he had brought a quarter-filled water bottle with him just in case, as well as his police radio. Every now and again he heard a bird chatter but any of them with sense would be resting up. When he reached the imaginary line where the vehicles had turned from Martin's sight, Taylor grew more cautious. He paused for a moment listening keenly but couldn't hear anything. Martin had roughly drawn the layout of a couple of creeks nearby and Taylor figured they had to be the most likely spots where anybody might camp. It was possible though that they had kept going closer to the banks of the river but not too close if they had any sense, because the crocs here were plentiful and dangerous. Even the creeks could be dicey, although without any rain lately it was unlikely crocs would venture in. He moved cautiously through the bush, pausing each couple of strides on the ball of his feet to listen. Still nothing. He continued for a few minutes like this, his eyes sweeping left to right and back. He saw a glint, nothing more than that but a metallic glint, fractionally to his right. He approached very carefully now.

It took him around five minutes to reach the spot where the reflection of the sun had caught his eye. Even though they had pulled branches over it and spread dry leaves on top, the wind had scattered enough leaves to allow the sun to penetrate through the gum leaves above and strike metal. From five metres away, Jared Taylor knew he was looking at a motorcycle.

He heard the tread behind him and swung around, his arm rising instantly though it would be futile in fending off the inevitable whack from a thick branch.

Martin stood there.

'Looks like they buggered off, eh?'

***

This really was the pits. Josh Shepherd was well and truly pissed off. This was like being a uniform all over again. Or a detective constable. Going from shop to shop, asking 'Do you know this man?' He wasn't supposed to identify him yet apparently. Another two hours so far. Okay, he'd stopped for half an hour for a bacon-and-egg roll and a hot chocolate, but let's say ninety minutes of wasted time while Jo di Rivi got to drive out to Fitzroy Crossing and do some real police work. Oh yeah, she was the chosen one. It had been a huge struggle to ignore Amy's phone calls. His finger had hovered over the Accept button. How grateful would she be to know that the fellow at Meda had been crucified? That could make the relationship right there. But there would be blowback. Yesterday when she'd called, just before he walked onto the cricket field, he had assumed she might want to invite him over for dinner, or a friend's barbecue or something, and he'd answered cock-a-hoop, dropping in how he was just about to start his cricket match.

'Won't keep you, then. I just wondered ...' she'd started and he was getting ready to fist-pump, '... what you could tell me about the Meda murder?'

Bang. Like he'd stepped into a bouncer, right there.

'Nothing, sorry. I'm out of the loop.'

Which, at that stage he had been. Although of course he shouldn't have owned up to that. What did that make him look like?

'But you must know something. Like how exactly he died. Do you have a name?'

'Not yet.' He had one eye on his teammates already jogging onto the field.

'You don't have a name because you're out of the loop, or the police don't know.'

'Nobody knows,' he'd said defiantly and then cursed himself for giving that away. 'Look I have to go.'

'Okay, but please call me if you hear anything.'

And then just as he was about to hang up, she'd said, 'We should get together sometime.'

'I'd like that,' he'd said. Then, 'Gotta go.'

And then while he was having his hot chocolate twenty minutes back, there was her name lighting up on his phone. He forced himself to ignore it and was now in an even worse mood. Maybe that was his big chance. Well, he'd just do this shop, then he'd call. Why should he stay loyal anyway when Jo di Rivi got all the cream jobs?

It was in one of those gift boutiques that was full of scented candles and soaps and herbs in small stiff gift boxes that cost you, well, not an arm and a leg maybe but several fingers. Brightly coloured prints hung on the wall. A few of the cheaper things for kids on holiday like keyrings and plastic turtles and a bottle opener but overall, you felt like you were a fly inside an air-freshener. There was some compensation however. The sales girl was slim with smooth olive skin, big brown eyes and jet-black hair. She wore a sexy black frock, silver jewellery. If Amy fell over, well …

'Can I help you?' asked the girl. She had some sort of accent. Italian maybe.

'I hope so,' he smiled and leaned into the counter. Then he placed his phone down so the screen faced her.

'Do you know this man?'

The wide eyes went wider. 'Why?' she asked breathlessly.

Shepherd took a punt. 'How do you know him, miss?'

'That's Jean-Claude. He's my boyfriend.'

15

Number 17 Lawrence Street was in the main part of town, a townhouse built probably in the 1990s but hanging baskets of coloured flowers and a Balinese fountain in the small courtyard made it seem exotic, a world away from the flat space and right angles of the Bilingurr place.

Clement and Earle had been half an hour into their drive to the May River site when they got the call from Mal Gross and had to turn back. Keeble's team would process the site, they didn't need the detectives for that. This lead was more important. He'd already warned Keeble the townhouse would have to be processed as soon as possible.

A woman's bicycle was propped against the wall half covered by ivy. An aluminium flyscreen door greeted Clement and Earle, the wooden door behind open and revealing a small entrance space. There was music coming from within, soft, a Latin feel. Clement rang the bell. He heard the light bounce of feet approaching on faux marble tiles. A young woman appeared behind the door. She had light brown wavy hair, a pale complexion and was wearing a tank top and shorts. She had red eyes from crying but didn't quite seem to fit the house or the name Valentina Gomez that Gross had given them.

'I'm Inspector Clement and this is Sergeant Earle, Broome Police.'

'I'm Wanda, the neighbour,' said the girl and opened the door.

That explained why she didn't quite fit. They followed her down the short entrance hall, their wide shoulders brushing against the brims of three different hats on an old style hatstand, making them dance. The narrow hallway gave onto a small sitting room of cane furniture with bright floral coverings. Exotic coloured mats were postage stamps across an envelope of cool white tiles. A coffee table snoozed under a batik sarong. The smell of incense engulfed Clement. Small brass and stone knick-knacks that might have been Buddhist were scattered around the room without any conscious attempt to style it but ironically did just that.

The woman he presumed was Gomez sat on an ottoman, slim legs tucked elegantly to the side. In front of her was a low carved Balinese-style coffee table, on it a bottle of tequila, a third gone, two tumbler glasses and some lemon rind.

'Valentina?' asked Clement, then repeated his official introduction. She had been crying but seemed in control. 'I wonder if we could talk?'

'Sure. I'll be fine, Wanda,' she said. 'Thank you.'

'I'll just be next door if you need me,' said Wanda and took herself off.

Valentina got to her feet and gestured at the two bar stools at the short breakfast island.

'Would you like a drink?' She spoke with an accent.

'Water please,' said Earle and Clement seconded. There was a fan spinning overhead and the tiles cooled the room effectively but Clement knew in this weather you were sweating fluids even if you didn't feel it anywhere except your dry mouth.

'What have you been told so far?' asked Clement as Gomez filled glasses with water from a pitcher that had been in the fridge.

'That Jean-Claude is dead. He was the man they found.'

'Do you know where Meda is?' asked Clement.

'The policeman said it's over past Derby.' Like she hadn't known. Perhaps she hadn't. 'He told me it looked like somebody had deliberately run over Jean-Claude.'

Good, Shepherd hadn't elaborated on the press reports.

'That's right,' said Clement. He did not mention the stakes through the palms. All the clichés about hot-tempered Latins being so furious they would kill a lover swarmed but he shut the door on them.

'We believe he was killed Thursday night or early Friday morning. When did you last see him?'

'Thursday morning when I left for work.'

But Jacinta Richmond had been fairly certain she'd seen her at the beach that evening.

'You didn't go to the beach?'

Gomez's eyes darted. 'No. I worked till six then I ride home.' She was hiding something. Gomez rested her chin on her hand and shook her head like she was struggling to believe all this was true. 'You sure it's –?'

'Yes, we are.'

Clement felt odd sitting while Gomez stood the other side of the bench. He offered his seat but she held up a hand.

'I'm used to being on my feet. I work Thursday to Sunday at the gift shop.'

'So you expected him home Thursday night?'

'Late. In the morning he told me he has to see his boss with the boat and he will be home late so not to wait for dinner with him. I went to bed about eleven and he still wasn't home.'

'Did you text him?' asked Earle.

'I didn't want to bother him if he was doing business. But when I woke up in the night and he wasn't there, I worry. Then I text him Friday morning and call him but I don't get him. I was thinking maybe he has to go out on a charter or something, maybe that's why the boss called him and he is out at sea. He can hardly ever text from out there. But when he still doesn't even text me, well ...'

She started to cry. Not as gushing as Lauren Bagot, restrained.

'But you didn't contact the police.' Clement floated it like a kid a bubble, curious as to where it would land.

'We don't speak much on the weekend. He likes his space.'

And the way she shrugged, the clipped way she said it even through tears, Clement sensed a different emotion for the first time. Annoyance, anger.

'Do you have a vehicle?'

'Just my pushbike.'

But did that mean she could not have got to Meda? She could have had an accomplice, or could have borrowed a car.

'Did you travel on the motorcycle much?' asked Earle.

'Sometimes we go places.'

'Have you driven it?' Earle again.

'Only in the bush, you know for fun. I don't have a licence. Why?'

It was going to occur to her any minute she was a suspect.

'We can't find his motorcycle,' said Clement.

'It wasn't with him?' She muttered a stream of Spanish. 'Someone killed him for his motorcycle?'

'Possibly. You said you were here Thursday evening.'

'Yes.'

'Alone?'

That did it. She got it now.

'I didn't kill him okay? I love Jean-Claude.' More tears flowed.

Clement waited, then explained he was sorry but he had to ask these questions to eliminate her from suspicion of involvement.

'I wasn't alone anyway,' she snapped back. 'Not the whole time. Wanda came over.'

However, from the times she gave Clement, it seemed Wanda was there for no more than forty minutes and back home by ten o'clock. Plenty of time for Valentina to get to Meda in a vehicle. Maybe even with Jean-Claude on his motorcycle. She could have slipped the drug anytime. For that matter Jean-Claude could have been flat on his back upstairs, drugged. But if his bike was here, somebody might have seen it.

'How long have you known Jean-Claude?'

'About six weeks. I met him down the beach.'

'You started dating right away?'

'Pretty much.'

'How serious was it with him and you?'

'Look, I love him, okay, he's fun but I don't need to be with him all the time. I come to Broome, I like it, I meet Jean-Claude, we get on but that's it. Not *serious* serious.'

'Could you tell us a little about yourself? I'm guessing you weren't born here.'

She was originally Colombian and had immigrated with her family to Australia five years earlier.

'I was seventeen.'

The family had settled in Sydney. According to Valentina, she had finished school and done a year of university before opting out to tour the country.

'It took me about a year and a half to wind up here.'

'Was that when you met Jean-Claude?' asked Clement.

'I'm here about a month when we met.' She liked Broome, she liked casual places and warm weather. Previously she had stayed and worked a few months in Noosa. Jean-Claude was a bonus but she hadn't made any decision about whether to stay in Broome long-term. 'I haven't been to Darwin yet. I hear good things. Now ...' she opened her hands up as if to say who can tell.

'Do you know if Jean-Claude had any enemies?'

'No,' she shook her head with certainty.

'Was he involved in drugs? Not necessarily selling them, just using?'

Her chin jutted. 'No way.'

Clement took it with a big grain of salt.

'Did he ever hang around with bikies?'

'Never.'

'How has he seemed lately?'

A moment where her eyes showed she was scanning some memory. 'Okay. Fine.'

'How about Thursday?'

'I told you. He say he is going to see his boss. Normal.'

But after years of interviewing people in these situations Clement felt she wasn't telling him everything.

'Where is he now?' she asked and looked about for a tissue as she teared up.

Clement had one handy for her. 'His body had to be flown to Perth for an autopsy.'

Valentina Gomez didn't say anything. Clement decided it was on him to continue.

'We believe he had a lot of cash recently.'

'I don't know,' she shrugged.

'Did you drive him to Port Hedland when he picked up his new bike?'

'Me? No. I have to work.'

'Not Monday to Wednesday.'

'I didn't drive him to Port Hedland.'

Clement made a note in his pad to remind himself to check with Alex Christos, the man who sold the motorcycle to Jean-Claude.

'Could you take me through last Thursday? Did Jean-Claude spend Wednesday night here?'

She seemed to be thinking. 'Thursday morning we went for an early swim, come back, have breakfast. Then he said he is seeing his boss that evening and might be late. I left for work. That was the last I saw him.'

'You didn't go out to the beach Thursday afternoon when he finished class?'

'No. I used to ride out there on my bike, even do his classes early on but then he said it was better I don't. He did better if the women think he is single.'

'You didn't care?'

'No. He came back here right after. But not last Thursday.'

'So, normally Monday through Thursday, Jean-Claude came back here after his class and slept here?'

'Mostly, not always. Sometimes he went home.'

'If he spent the night here, when would he go home?'

'Tuesday and Wednesday when I have days off, usually about four p.m. to get ready for his class. Sometimes he goes straight to his class from here. Mondays he gets here in the morning and mostly stays till his class. Thursday, I work. He is here still when I leave for work, so I don't know exactly how long he stayed here but I think not that long.'

'Did he recently start leaving earlier?'

She looked at him with curiosity. Clement took that as a yes.

'The last week he said he had stuff to do so he was leaving earlier. More like midday instead of four.'

'Did you ask him what stuff?'

'Yes. He just said "stuff". I guess with the bike. He always cleans it.' She gestured dismissively.

'Did you ever go to his place?'

'No. He shared. He said it was not clean.'

'You didn't mind he liked his weekends to himself?'

'Why would I?' But she looked away as she said it and Clement wasn't so sure he believed her.

'I like my weekends to myself too. Sometimes I miss him but also, I work, and Jean-Claude doesn't like to go out anywhere much at night, so I can go to the pub, dance. Anyway, a lot of weekends he was on the dive tours.' She started crying again.

Certainly, Gomez was acting like she had no idea about Lauren Bagot. Clement decided to hold off on directly confronting her on that.

'Jean-Claude recently bought that new motorcycle. Did you loan him the money?'

'I don't have that much. His parents sent it.'

Clement signalled to Earle it was time to go. 'I'm very sorry, Valentina. We'll leave you be for now but we will likely have more questions soon. I'm afraid we'll have to get our science people to come down and look over your place. And we will need phone and bank records. Please do not clean in the meantime.'

Keeble was going to kill him. So too from the look of it was Gomez.

When they were alone outside, Clement asked Earle what he thought.

'She could have known about Lauren Bagot, got so angry she crucified him. If she had a vehicle, she could have arranged to meet him. She dopes him up, kills him, dumps the bike and returns the car.'

'The old fella camping at May River saw a bike and a car.'

'That means help,' said Earle.

So, who might have helped Gomez? Clement's eyes strayed to the next-door neighbour's, Wanda's. There was a ute in the carport.

'I'll speak to the neighbour. How about you check with everybody close and ask if they remember the bike being here anytime Thursday? Maybe ask if they remember the ute there too.' He indicated the neighbouring carport.

Earle went off to do his thing and Clement headed next door, passing the ute. He'd need Keeble on that. This townhouse had none of the character of Gomez's. The garden was minimal, clinging to life. There was a carton of empty beer bottles by the rubbish bin.

Clement couldn't find a bell so he opened the unlocked flywire door and knocked on the wooden one behind it. A few seconds later, Wanda opened it. He'd expected she might be on the phone to Gomez but she wasn't. The look on her face suggested she probably thought it was Gomez who had knocked.

'Oh, hi.'

'I wonder if I could come in and talk to you. I just need to ask some questions, confirm some things.'

'Sure.' She opened the door and stepped back. Under normal circumstances, Clement thought she would likely be a bubbly fun person. In layout, the townhouse was the same as its neighbour but it was not furnished with anywhere near so much flair. 'Australian rental' might be the title if it were a living art exhibit. It was neat enough though. In the living room area, an out-of-shape young man in a blue singlet and shorts sat back on a sofa sucking a beer and watching some sport on TV. He had dark curly hair and eyes like on roadkill. Clement cut him some slack. This weather flogged the life out of anybody.

'This is my partner, Barton. This is the detective I told you about.'

Barton stood and mumbled a greeting. He pointed at his beer.

'Don't suppose …?'

'I'm fine,' said Clement, though he would have loved one. The room felt hotter, cheaper than next door. The overhead fan clattered loudly.

'The maximum speed doesn't work anymore,' said Wanda apologetically. She grabbed the remote, turned off the TV and sat on the sofa next to Barton.

Clement took the armchair. 'I wonder if you could both take me through last Thursday. Starting with you, Wanda. Run through the whole day if that's okay.'

Wanda, a hairdresser, left for work as usual around 8.40. She could walk to work from here. Nothing special happened at work. Sometimes she would catch up with Valentina for a quick lunch because she worked not that far away at the gift shop but Wanda was pretty busy. Being a Thursday, she worked till six forty.

'I made a quick dinner for us –'

Clement cut in. 'Sorry, but when you came home do you remember if Valentina was home? Did you speak? Was her bicycle there?'

Wanda's brow furrowed. 'We didn't speak, I'm pretty sure. But I think the bicycle was there. Valentina usually beats me home by ten minutes or so. I think I would have noticed.'

Maybe not, thought Clement. Most of the time when we think we are perceiving something real-time we are accessing memory. You expect to see a bicycle there, and that's what you see.

'Sorry, please. You made dinner …'

Wanda took up the story. She made a quick dinner for her and Barton and then he went upstairs to game and she went next door to Valentina's for a drink. She confirmed she had spent 'just under an hour' with Valentina. Wanda believed she'd headed back to her place around 9.30.

'Did she mention that Jean-Claude was coming home late?'

'Yes. He told her he had to see the dive boss. She wasn't all that happy about it. You know, he expected her to be there whenever it suited him.'

'Did you find it odd that he didn't spend weekends here?'

'I think he worked a lot of weekends,' said Wanda.

'He was a bit of an odd dude,' said Barton.

'In what way?'

'Like not unfriendly, but he wouldn't come to the pub much. Didn't want to game. I offered. He liked to hike and ride his bike. Nature stuff.'

Clement asked if Jean-Claude normally parked his bike at Valentina's.

'Yes, all the time,' Wanda said. Barton nodded affirmatively. But when asked if it had been there on Thursday night, Wanda couldn't be certain.

'It wasn't there when I called in, obviously. I don't think I heard it coming back. And I didn't go out after I came back here. Thursday's a killer on my feet.'

Clement looked at Barton.

'Same.'

'Did they argue much?' Clement asked and could see at once that Wanda was conflicted.

'No more than me and Barton.'

'They always seemed to get on,' said Barton.

Clement asked how Valentina had seemed on the Thursday night. Wanda was torn but responsible.

'She said she thought Jean-Claude might have somebody else.'

'Really?' said Barton.

'Yeah. She didn't want me saying anything.'

Barton didn't seem particularly miffed that he'd been excluded. Wanda took up her account.

'She'd seen something. She wouldn't give details. I think, you know, that's what she was thinking when he said he would be home late.'

'That he was with this other woman?'

'Yes.'

Clement said, 'Was Valentina upset or angry or both?'

Wanda considered. 'More upset. Valentina wouldn't hurt Jean-Claude. She couldn't. He's built like a brick.'

'Ever see Valentina with other men?'

Sometimes at the pub when Valentina joined Wanda for a drink on the weekend she would hang with other men. Maybe a bit of dancing, flirting but harmless stuff.

Barton said, 'Once or twice she came with us but didn't leave when we did. I mean I never saw her carrying on or anything but she didn't come home with us.'

Wanda said, 'I think she was just having a good time. She likes to drink and dance.'

Clement picked up the tiniest hint of regret in Wanda's voice that life with Barton was not so exciting.

'Drugs? Either of them?' Clement assured them he was not interested in illegal drug use except where it may relate to Jean-Claude's death.

'No,' said Wanda, and Barton echoed it.

But Clement knew that no matter how much he might reassure somebody, many would just deny, deny. He also struck out on any bikie connection with Jean-Claude.

Next, he got Barton to run through his day.

Barton worked at a smash repairs place on the edge of town. Thursday he'd worked all day with only a lunch break. He'd got back home about 6.00 p.m. and stayed in, exactly as Wanda had said. They'd gone to bed fairly early, about 10.30.

Clement thanked them for their time. He mentioned that if they should think of anything that might be pertinent, even the slightest bit odd, they should contact him.

As he was leaving, he asked if Valentina ever rode the bike.

'No. I don't think Jean-Claude would have let her,' said Barton.

'She's a bit scared of that motorcycle,' said Wanda.

He returned to the car and tried Jacinta Richmond's number. He wanted to confirm her account of Gomez being at the beach on the Thursday evening. Richmond didn't answer so he left a message asking her to return his call. Graeme Earle joined him.

'I got about half of them at home. One guy across the road knew the motorcycle and declared it had been there on the Thursday night but when I pushed, it was obvious the guy wasn't certain. It was likely Wednesday night. Most of the others knew the motorcycle but none of them remembered seeing it Thursday. Nobody claimed the ute wasn't in the carport all night, for what that's worth.'

Back in his office, Clement got a curt message from Keeble that she had a team at Valentina Gomez's house. He had seen that flash of anger in Gomez, no matter how much she made out things with Jean-Claude were relatively casual. Could you honestly love somebody and not be possessive? He hadn't managed it with Marilyn, not that he should be judging the whole world on his insecurities. Had Gomez found out about Lauren Bagot, realised she'd been lied to and gone over the edge? Had Bagot found out about Gomez? He reflected on his brief Don Juan stint. It hadn't taken long for trouble to flare. He pictured his own dead body sprawled on the floor and knew he could quickly write three suspects on the board: Lucinda, Melissa and Marilyn. Jo di Rivi was due back any minute from Fitzroy Crossing.

Josh Shepherd entered the squad room, not limping. No sport, see.

'How did it go with the Spanish chick?'

Clement ran him through the salient points then checked to see if Shepherd had thought to confirm Gomez's movements Thursday with her boss.

'Yes, I did. She said Valentina arrived as usual in the morning and worked through till six thirty. She didn't recall any conversation between Gomez and the boyfriend. Also said that Gomez was head over heels for him and as far as she knows there were no problems.'

That was good work and Clement complimented him.

Shepherd said, 'I was going to ask Gomez a few questions but I thought you'd want me to leave it.'

'It was a good call in this case. Anybody else recognise Seydoux?'

'Four altogether but none claimed to know him that well. Two coffee places recognised him as a customer and two others said they had taken a class with him but that was it.'

'Why don't you head home and get some dinner? I'll call you back in if we get a break.'

Shepherd was happy to oblige.

Clement walked over to Earle. His sergeant was getting off the phone.

'I've left a message for the bloke who sold the bike to Seydoux.'

Earle and Clement had discussed that they still had no indication on who had actually driven Seydoux to Port Hedland. 'I also ran a check on our database. No driver or vehicle licence is registered to Valentina Gomez in WA. Thought I'd check New South Wales just in case.'

'Good idea,' said Clement who then took himself off to Manners' office to see how he was going. Manners was, as usual, hunched over a bank of computers. He wore a polo shirt and neat shorts. Clement fought against the image of Manners in a wizard hat, though whether players dressed the part for Dungeons and Dragons he had no idea.

'How are you going with Seydoux's phone?'

'I have identified all the phone numbers that called him or he called in the last month. There aren't that many. Mostly he communicated via Instagram messages. As you'd expect, a lot of his phone messages are from Lauren Bagot and the Gomez woman. There are also a few from Deep Adventures. There were others that I think were from his personal training clients because I identified the accounts the Instagram messages came from and matched them up against the phone calls. There is a summary on your sheet. I called every number personally and I have made a note as to who they said they were.' He slid across a typed sheet. 'There are six I haven't been able to speak with yet.'

'Could you look at the calls from Wednesday, Thursday and Friday specifically?'

'Done,' said Manners proud to be a step ahead. 'Page two. There were only five all up, apart from Gomez and Bagot. I've got through to three. Two were people who sometimes take his class, one was a motorcycle parts dealer. There are two numbers who have not called me back.'

Clement studied the list on page two. Manners had broken the numbers down into those that had called Wednesday, Thursday and Friday. It occurred to Clement that the killer would have known Seydoux was dead and would not have called his phone on the Friday, unless they were being exceedingly clever and duplicitous.

'It looks like there are a few numbers who called Wednesday or Thursday but not Friday,' he said.

'Three,' said Manners and pointed them out. 'Two of those are the ones that haven't called me back. One had a message from two young women that they were travelling the Gibb River Road and would be in touch when they received any messages. One rang out. That one, I'll need to get details from the phone company.'

'Good work. Make it a priority.'

The Kimberley was a vast region, bigger than many an American state, and while coverage these days was pretty good along the coast there was little in between. It was unfair to expect Manners to do a whole lot of detective work, he'd already exceeded his job description. He'd get Shepherd to help out.

'How about Gomez?'

'I've requested her phone records. Keeble's lot just uploaded her bank records a few minutes ago. I'll get onto those next.'

'And the servo cameras?'

Manners said he had requested all the footage of all servos in the region for Thursday afternoon through to Friday. He said, 'I've already got Willare's and there is no motorcycle.'

Willare was the key stop, as it was between Broome and Meda. Clement thought about that.

'When you get a minute let's see if any of those who called or messaged Seydoux are owners of four-wheel drive vehicles.'

'That's going to be about sixty percent,' said Manners.

As if Clement didn't know that himself. Up here an off-road vehicle was near essential. He was a model of restraint.

'I know. Then check the servo footage and see if any of those vehicles were filling up at Willare, Derby, Broome or Fitzroy Crossing between Wednesday and Friday. If our killer was driving out to Meda, maybe they needed fuel. And of course, check the list of those phone numbers against any known criminals. If Seydoux was in touch with bikies or drug dealers, we might get lucky.'

Clement's phone rang.

'Mark Coleman,' said a man's voice. 'Base told me to call Inspector Clement.'

Base? Ah, Deep Adventures, the skipper.

Starting back to his office, Clement confirmed it was him and asked if it was a good time for Coleman to talk. Nobody likes getting a call from a Major Crime Squad detective and there was a wariness now in Coleman's tone.

'Sure. We're anchored quite close off the coast and I've got reception. What's it about?'

'I believe Jean-Claude Seydoux works for you on occasion.'

'Froggy, yeh.'

Clement could sense Coleman's brain whirring.

'I'm afraid Jean-Claude has been killed and I'm heading up a homicide investigation.'

There was a short silence.

'That's terrible. What happened?'

Clement painted a very brief picture about Seydoux having been found at Meda, apparently run over. He omitted the grisly details.

'Could I ask when was the last time you spoke with him?'

Coleman thought it would have been around ten days previous. 'He'd asked me to get hold of a dive boat for him for some private clients for next week. Every now and again he gets some tourists. I was just reconfirming with him. I've been flat out since. Ever since COVID, Australians have rediscovered their own country.'

'You didn't speak to him Wednesday or Thursday? Ask to see him Thursday evening?'

'No. Thursday I had a day tour. I didn't get back till about seven. I went out to the Cleo with the clients for dinner and drinks, then went back to base and got stuff ready for this weekend haul.'

'What time did you finish up Thursday?'

'Just before midnight. Then I went home and I was up at five thirty.'

Coleman assured Clement his wife could confirm all that. Clement took details on the Thursday clients and Coleman's wife's mobile number in order to verify Coleman's account.

'Seydoux's phone records said there were some recent calls from Deep Adventures.'

'Like I said, I haven't spoken to Jean-Claude for more than a week but I think Safavi at the office said he called up about bringing his motorcycle over to work on it. He has a space in the workshop I let him use as long as it's clear.'

'Last time you did speak how did he seem to you?'

'Normal. But we only chatted by phone. It's been bedlam here.'

'He didn't seem worried about anything.'

'No, he had a new bike he was rapt with but he was always tinkering with it.'

Clement remembered the phone call to a motorcycle spare parts dealer. Perhaps his change in routine was simply down to tuning his new bike. But if he wasn't meeting with Coleman on Thursday evening, who was he meeting with?

Clement asked if Coleman knew how Jean-Claude was able to afford his new ride.

'He told me he'd got some money from home.'

Same as he'd told everybody else. Clement took Coleman through all the usual questions: Bikies? No. Drugs? No.

We are absolutely strict on that,' said Coleman. 'It could cost lives and me everything I've worked for.'

'Jean-Claude was a good diver?'

'Excellent. He could have worked full-time but he liked to do his own thing. Shit, I'm sorry I just can't believe it. You know who did it?'

'We're looking into that. What about with women?'

There was a hesitation.

'He was running two races, Lauren and a South American girl.'

'Nobody else?'

'Two was enough even for him.'

Clement told him he may need to speak further with him when he returned.

'We'll get in about eleven tonight,' Coleman said.

When he finished the call, Clement immediately rang Coleman's wife. She confirmed her husband was with her from midnight till 5.30 a.m. Next, Clement tried the daytrippers who had been out with Coleman on Thursday. They too confirmed Coleman's accounts. Clement sat thinking. He had no reason to disbelieve Coleman. What's more, a consistent picture was emerging of Seydoux lying to near everybody. The cash bugged him. It was such a drugs signpost. But so far, they'd turned up nothing on drugs or wildlife smuggling. Recently Seydoux had changed his routine. It seemed he was spending less time with Gomez during the day, 'Doing other stuff.' Just what though? Clement rang back Safavi, the woman at Deep Adventures, and she confirmed that Jean-Claude had been in a few times over the last week working on his bike. The more Clement found out, the more questions the case threw up. What was Seydoux up to that got him killed? Keeble and di Rivi were due back soon and would likely be starving. Clement knew he was. He'd spring for dinner. Burgers and chips. He went over to where Graeme Earle was sitting back in his chair.

Earle smiled. 'Bingo. Valentina Gomez has a New South Wales driver's licence for a car, but not a motorcycle.'

Technically she hadn't lied to them. She hadn't said she did not have a driver's licence, just that she didn't have one for a motorcycle.

'I checked,' said Earle. 'She can legally ride a motorcycle. Not of the power of Seydoux's, she'd need a motorcycle licence for that. But she could easily know how to ride one.'

'Let's get everybody together and discuss over a burger.' Clement handed over his credit card but Earle refused to take it.

'This one's on me. And I get twenty percent discount from Jago. Leave it with me.'

Earle took himself off to organise the orders. Clement was about to turn back to the office when he saw Earle's phone light up with the name Alex Christos. The bike guy. He answered.

'Alex, this is Detective Inspector Dan Clement from Broome police. Sergeant Earle isn't here at the moment.'

'Yeah, sorry, I was at a mate's, I didn't see the message till just then.'

'That's okay. We had a quick question for you. Did you see how Mr Seydoux arrived in Port Hedland.'

'He drove.'

'Did you see what car?'

'I did but I don't remember. I'm pretty sure he mentioned hiring one for the day.'

'Did you happen to see who he was with, who might have driven it back?'

'Sure did. Very hot-looking tanned woman with a hat and sunglasses.'

'Did you hear him talk to her, mention her name?'

There was a short silence.

'Probably, I'm trying to think. Something Italian maybe.'

Clement ventured, 'Valentina?'

'Yeah, yeah, that's right. Like Valentine.'

16

The sun was down, the air softer now but not much cooler and certainly just as oppressive. A greasy cardboard box sat before Clement, a few chips clinging to the corners.

Clement's team, minus Josh Shepherd, was seated at the small outdoor setting at the end of the station carpark that abutted the kitchen.

'Let's deal with Lauren Bagot first. Jo?'

Di Rivi neatly closed her burger box. 'Everybody at Monarch loves her. I managed to speak to both the other female employees there and both said she wouldn't glance sideways at another man. Certainly, they saw nothing at the camp.'

Lisa Keeble reiterated that there was nothing in Bagot's apartment or vehicle in the least suspicious. Manners seconded that on phone records and bank statements.

'And Graeme and I didn't pick up on anything phony, so let's park her for now. Valentina Gomez on the other hand, well we can give her an out on saying she had no licence – for a big bike she didn't – but she lied to us about driving Seydoux to Port Hedland.'

'Early days on the apartment,' said Keeble, 'but nothing obvious like cash, drugs or medications that were used on Seydoux.'

'She had time to dispose of them by now,' said Earle.

Manners said that, like Keeble, it was early days for him checking her phone and social media records, 'But there's no repetitive phone number there other than her work, Seydoux and her next-door neighbour.'

'Nothing on the neighbour's ute,' said Keeble. 'The car doesn't match the profile of what we're looking for and the tyres and underside revealed nothing like the Meda soil.'

'So if she did it,' summarised Clement, 'she needed help. If her neighbours helped her, they needed yet another car. But she did have a motive. And it would fit the personal nature of the killing.'

'Same goes for Lauren Bagot,' opined di Rivi.

'That's true.'

'Perhaps they could both have been in on it,' said Keeble. 'Hell hath no fury and all that. We can't absolutely rule out a vehicle from Monarch being the murder weapon. Bagot could have met Gomez at Meda.'

Clement appreciated the lateral thinking.

'We should have you working this side of the fence,' he said.

'The hours are shorter,' quipped Keeble. 'What I can do is check Bagot's apartment for Gomez's prints and vice versa. I mean, we have them both now so it won't be hard. There's no guarantee of course that if they plotted anything together it would be in their homes.'

'However,' said Clement, 'if we find Gomez's prints in Bagot's apartment it would mean she at least knew about her. With or without Bagot helping her, that's motive.'

Keeble made a note.

'What about the motorcycle?' asked di Rivi who, stuck at Fitzroy Crossing, had been out of the loop.

'Wiped clean,' said Keeble. 'They tried to hide it but the bush there is not dense. Looks to me like they had a tent there. Preliminary, and I repeat preliminary testing, tells me that it was the same vehicle that ran over Seydoux. We've grabbed some litter from nearby but it's too early to have results back on processing, and at a guess I would say the litter is much older. I think this guy is careful.'

Clement took up the running. 'Jared says the old boy last heard them in the early hours of Thursday or Friday morning. Given the bike has now been confirmed as Seydoux's, that means Friday morning.

'Why not leave the motorcycle where the body was?' asked Manners.

Di Rivi answered. 'Obvious reason is they didn't want us to identify Seydoux too quickly. Soon as we have the cycle, we have the rego, we get his name and that leads us to them.'

'So, in that case they would know him,' said Manners.

'Or at the very least have some link to him,' qualified di Rivi.

The more experienced Earle reined them in. 'It might still be an opportunist killing. Some arseholes meet Seydoux with his new bike, kill him and plan to steal the bike. Maybe they peg him out purely to make it look like some ritual or something. By the time they sober up and think about it they realise the bike is too hot, so they dump it and clear out.'

'However,' said Clement, 'he was drugged first. So, there was some premeditation. And that five grand. He was doing something to be able to afford that cycle. He was up to something.'

'He's a diver,' said di Rivi. 'Maybe he found somebody's stash, you know ditched off a boat to be retrieved later but he found the drugs, got rid of them for cash and they traced him?'

Clement raised an eyebrow at Earle.

'That's the best theory yet,' said Earle.

It could explain near everything, even the vicious nature of the killing. Clement's phone hummed. Jacinta Richmond's name appeared on the display.

'Thanks for calling back,' said Clement. 'About last Thursday. You mentioned you saw that dark-haired girl talking with Jean-Claude after his class.'

'That's right.'

'Are you sure it was Thursday?'

'Definitely.'

'On her bicycle?'

'No. Well, that's why I said I thought it was her. I couldn't see her properly because she was in a car.'

Clement's eyes found Earle's to signal this was important. 'Was she driving or passenger?'

'Driving. A Landcruiser. Needed a good wash.'

Clement and Earle arrived in the carport, rang the little brass bells and knocked. The porchlight was on but nobody came to the door and there was no Latin music this time. Clement pointed to the next townhouse and Earle followed. After Clement's knock there was a shuffling and then a shadow behind the door. It opened on Barton in the same blue work singlet and shorts as earlier.

'G'day,' he said.

Clement said, 'I wondered if Valentina was here?'

A pinprick of light came into Barton's eyes, a spelunker's lamp in a dark cavern.

'She and Wanda went up to the Roey for a drink.'

'You didn't join them?'

'I got a fridge full of beer and Xbox.'

Half an hour later, Valentina sat across from Clement and Earle in the interview room. They had found her with Wanda on the verandah of the Roebuck Bay Hotel and asked her to accompany them for more questioning. She looked miserable.

'Why did you lie to me?' asked Clement.

Her eyes refused to meet his, sliding around the room as if there might be some crevice through which they could initiate an escape. Thwarted, they settled on him. She folded her arms and shrugged in her habitual style.

'You know.'

'No, we don't.'

Her arms stretched out and her fingertips played with one another.

'I'm his girlfriend. I don't have an alibi. You will say I did it.'

'You did drive to Port Hedland?' It was the first time Graeme Earle had spoken to her. She toyed with a denial then spat out.

'Who else will do that? You have to be finding the one who killed him.'

'We're doing our best.' Clement's sympathy had started thin and was now see-through. 'Where did the car come from that you drove?'

'One of his mates. Jean-Claude buy him a case of beer. It was a piece of crap.'

'What was this mate's name?'

She scanned her memory. 'Jacob or Jason.' She described where he lived. 'I have to follow Jean-Claude to drop the car back.'

Clement made notes, then said, 'You also lied about where you were last Thursday.'

'What? I did not lie. I worked, I come home, I waited for Jean-Claude.'

Earle said, 'We have a witness who saw you at the beach talking to ...'

'No. They're lying!' anger flashed in her dark eyes. She jabbed a finger at Earle. 'Or you're lying. I never see him since that morning.'

'You were in a car,' said Clement.

'What car?' She did the full-shouldered shrug, palms open. 'I don't have no car. I have a bicycle.'

Her denial, after she had so readily admitted having lied about driving Seydoux to Port Hedland, surprised Clement. He kept his voice neutral, unthreatening.

Jacinta Richmond had been certain the car she'd seen on Thursday at the beach carpark was a Toyota Sahara. She'd had an ex-boyfriend with one and for a minute she had been tantalised by the idea that he had found her in Broome and come to declare his foolishness for busting up with her. It was not to be.

'Do you know anybody with a tan-coloured Toyota Sahara?' he asked Gomez, careful as a man edging along a windowsill high above a city street. Gomez folded her arms, fuming. Clement started to prompt. 'Landcr–'

'Yes! Yes! You bet I do. Her.'

The 'her' was harsh and loud as the slap of a barista's milk jug on a marble bench.

Finally, thought Clement, a crack. 'Who is her?'

'The woman I see him with last week in the carpark after his class.'

Clement checked that Earle was taking notes and of course he was. A video tape was fine but the old-fashioned notebook couldn't be underestimated.

'You saw him with a woman after one of his classes?' Clement wanted to tease the information apart.

'Friday.'

The week before.

'Let me get this right. You went to the beach Friday before last after Jean-Claude finished and saw him with a woman.'

'That's right.'

'You don't normally see him Friday evening, do you?'

She rubbed a tear from her eye. 'I finished early. It wasn't night-time. I got on my bike and I was riding and I just think I will ride down and see him.'

Clement made a mental note to come back to that point. He said, 'How do you know the woman wasn't one of his class just having a chat?'

'She wasn't. I know what they wear and what they would look like and she got out of her car and walked over to him.'

'What kind of car?' asked Graeme Earle.

'A Landrover, something like that.'

'A four-wheel drive?' asked Clement.

'Yes, an old, dirty one.'

'A Sahara?'

'I don't know cars. A four-wheel drive.'

'So you saw him with this woman. Did you say anything about it to him?'

She shook her head fiercely. 'I didn't want him to see me so I go.'

'You think this was why he didn't see you over the weekends? He was with this woman?'

'What do you think?' she hissed.

Clement stayed calm. 'But why after, what, six weeks did you decide to go to the beach that day?'

She was silent for a few beats then relented. 'He was acting funny those last few days, like something was up but he doesn't tell me. Like everything is good but he was trying too hard. I think he told her it was over and she doesn't like that, that's what I think. I think she gets angry and she killed him.'

Her mouth set in defiance, challenging the policemen to dispute her.

'Why didn't you tell me this earlier?'

'It's stupid. Who kills somebody because they dump them?'

Plenty of people, thought Clement, every week of the year.

Then she added, 'I was going to tell you but today, it was all ... I was in shock. And it just look worse for me.'

That it did.

Clement considered his next move. There were a number of ways he could play it from here but time was moving on. He reached into the manila folder on his desk and brought out two photos of Lauren Bagot.

'Is this the woman you saw him with?'

She spun the print towards herself, looked, then her face contorted in disgust and she spun the print back across the table.

'No.'

'Are you sure?'

'That one is small and blonde and ugly. The one I saw was taller with brown hair and ugly. Who is she?'

She jerked her chin at Lauren Bagot's photo, folded her arms and pushed back into the chair. Clement knew he had to tell her sometime.

'She is the woman Jean-Claude had been living with for over a year.'

Valentina's eyes bugged. 'No!'

'I am afraid so,' said Clement. 'She works at a mine site and is only home for the weekends.'

'That bastard.'

It wasn't exactly clear if Gomez was referring to Seydoux or Bagot but there was a veracity in the bitterness she exuded. The question was, was it the first time she'd learned of Bagot? She seemed to turn inwards, her brain processing the news, what she probably saw as treachery by her lover. Or it could have been an act.

Earle came back to the facts. 'Did you get the licence plate of the car you saw, this four-wheel drive?'

'No.'

'Colour?' asked Earle.

'Light brown.'

They showed her a photo of a Toyota Sahara.

'Could be. Like I say, cars are not my thing.'

She could give no more detailed description of the woman she had seen: twenties, brown hair, about the same length as her own but not so black, maybe a little taller.

Clement was thinking that Jacinta Richmond had only seen the woman behind the wheel of a car from a distance. She had never said she was certain it had been Gomez.

'I'll let you get some sleep,' he said.

'You think I'm going to sleep?'

Clement ignored that. 'Would you like us to drop you home?'

Her friend Wanda had offered to wait for her but Valentina had told her to go home.

'No. I'll walk,' she said decisively.

Clement got up to show her out. They had come via the rear entrance and she wouldn't know her way out if going via the front door. They passed a couple of uniforms hanging around the kitchen. As Clement was leading Valentina Gomez down the hallway near the bathroom, she suddenly stopped. Clement swivelled to find her scanning the wall, her mouth open.

'That's her!'

Clement walked back. Gomez had halted by a poster in the hallway. As he peered closer, he saw it was the drawing of the unknown woman who had been harassing mothers outside the early childhood clinic. As if Clement might be in any doubt what she was talking about Gomez said, 'That's the woman Jean-Claude was talking to.'

17

The track was narrow and would have been easy to miss if you hadn't carefully noted every physical clue the bush provided, like the tall tea-tree with the blackened trunk. She knew to cut inside after that. Mostly the bush wasn't very dense here and the gaps were wide enough to drive the Sahara through but you had to stay alert because every now and again you'd see a long limb lying where it had fallen right in your path. She didn't like that because it triggered flash images of a person with a blackened face thrashing in the dirt screaming in pain, their arm just torn from them. You had to clamp down on that, drive it out of your head. A couple of hundred metres in as you got closer to the campsite, the bush grew thicker with tall paperbarks and other small shrubs that swatted and swished against the faded duco. You had to take that real slow for a short stretch and then it opened out and there was the tent.

There was no sign of him as she came to a halt in the soft earth. She opened her door and the outside air rushed in and clawed away the veil of air-conditioning that had draped itself over her these last fifty k. She wondered why it was always her who had to go to the shops but didn't bother to raise it again. The first time she had, he'd done that sigh like the wise schoolteacher and taken her through it step by step. The less they were seen together the better, he'd said. All it is, he'd emphasised, is a few groceries, perishables like water and milk and cheese. As much as she was special, as much as he felt bound up with her heart and soul so they were one entity, the fact remained that he could complete this task alone if he had to but she might struggle to do it. And as he'd said this, he'd clasped her bony brown shoulders with his hands and stared into her eyes with those understanding eyes of his. And he was right, she knew that. Before he'd found her, she was nothing, a torn ice-cream wrapper scuttling over soulless suburban bitumen whichever way the wind blew. She'd had no ambition, no sense of purpose or identity. He had provided all that. Born into the sprawling wasteland that is south-western Sydney, raised by a single mother with a half-brother and sister, the highlight of her life had been depressing the buttons on a thousand spray-cans in rail-yards, or on sticky tar-encrusted roofs of industrial units, or in dark urine-scented tunnels. It was a wonder she hadn't killed herself with drugs. Some faint pulse of reason always restrained her from toppling into the abyss. Or maybe she just never had enough money to get the job done. At least half of those she ran with back then were now dead. Mainly from drug overdoses but one had been murdered and one had fallen through a gantry while tagging and broken her neck.

Up until she had met him, she had nothing to show for her life but her tags, and by now they would all be gone, obliterated by other taggers, or the bricks they'd been placed on smashed down so a new generation of losers could be raised on the bones of the old. From time to time, she had grabbed a job stacking shelves, collecting trolleys, tending a lunch-bar counter, although the service industry wasn't a natural vocation for her. People were stupid. They were sheep. Slowly she had progressed from being apathetic all of the time to angry most of the time. There was nothing much to do but look at your phone and read about all the ways you were being screwed. Sex was like fast food, frequent and gratifying for a very short time, with one meal much like the rest. In fact, it was at McDonald's one night that she'd got talking to Joel. Poor Joel, so earnest. He had convinced himself he was a social justice warrior but that Joel was really an avatar who the real Joel hoped might appeal to some like-minded woman enough it would lead to sex. Which in her case it had. The real Joel was never honest enough to admit to himself that's what drove his zeal. It could have easily been music or anime, he just needed a hobby he could develop that might help him find a girl. Without Joel though, she would never have started going to the rallies: anti-greyhounds, live exports, gay rights. She tagged along because by then she was his girlfriend, she liked having a target for her anger and Joel was a conduit to so many new directions for it. She and Joel lived together, alternating between a Waterloo squat and a back shed at his aunt's.

It was at a gay-rights rally that her world turned.

That's when she met him. He wasn't like Joel and the others, despite being only two years older than him. He knew things about history and books and politics and most importantly about her that she didn't even know herself. He was slim but wiry and wore a beard and those brown eyes bore right into her body and pulled out all the bullshit she'd covered herself with: the rebel, the tagger, the would-be anarchist. He told her she was playing at life, not really living it, and he dominated the landscape as surely as those big fucking steel towers where she grew up that stood astride the flat creek-land by the highway, humming twenty-four seven. She was better than what she was allowing herself to be, he'd said, and three hours later she'd had sex with him on the floor of an Ultimo squat with columns of anti-logging handouts around the perimeter, the four posts of their bed.

'Everybody says handbills are a thing of the past,' he'd told her as they lay there, her toes up against the photocopier, 'but people don't know shit. Digital is the ultimate disposable. Twitter, Instagram, Snapchat are no more than the layers of skin we shed every day without realising. They have their uses. Coordinating, yes, and simple communications, like an advertising jingle. But a pamphlet says "I am in your life and even to get rid of me you must make a conscious decision to screw me up and bin me".'

When she had told Joel it was over, he had burst into tears and pleaded with her to stay with him but that only made it worse. She knew nothing could ever be the same again. That had been three years ago.

Their camp was silent. The air crawled up her shirt like an abductor's clammy hands. She had not told him about the clinic. He had expressly forbidden her to raise a finger. There is too much at stake, he'd told her. But dammit, he didn't control her. And these stupid, sheepish women were placing their kids at the risk of autism and other shocking illnesses because they believed the giant pharmaceutical companies who only cared about profit. He agreed with her, she knew that, they had spoken about it often enough but still he'd wanted her to lay off. In the end she couldn't. She had to save those kids, or at least make some gesture, and that is exactly what she had done. It would not affect anything anyway but all the same it was better that she did not reveal her efforts. Not yet.

Likely he was meditating by the creek. She pulled out the shopping bags and trudged to the nylon tent. She bent and pushed in. Even this time of night and with the flaps up, it was stifling in here. Fortunately, he had said they would be leaving tonight. She opened the esky and whacked in the fresh ice, milk and water. Her eyes strayed to the box in the corner and she shuddered and had that image again and found herself rushing outside. Where was he?

'Thomas!' she yelled up at the blue sky, so loud she expected cockatoos to burst forth from the treetops in fright but there was nothing, not a sound.

Too late she heard the soft tread behind her. Strong hands seized her, freezing a scream in her throat. Her heart crashed wildly against her ribs like the hooves of a horse trying to escape a barn fire. She felt herself being spun. His lips found hers, the coarse hair of his beard caressed her chin and she let loose a single small sigh like a wisp of smoke.

'Any calls?' she asked.

'One. Police. I let it go to voicemail.'

A spear of fear twisted inside her. He had directed her word for word the message to leave. 'Hi, this is Kim. Grace and I are on the Gibb River Road and there's hardly any reception so leave a message and we'll get back to you when we can.'

He had been adamant that the message would ring no alarm bells.

First thing the cops would assume is that they were people who had attended his class. They'd only spoken to the Frenchman twice by phone anyway. Probably he was right. He was, mostly. But she knew sooner or later it would ring again.

18

Lauren Bagot bent at the waist and studied Lilly's drawing of the wanted woman so closely her nose almost touched it. Despite it being Sunday night she had come into the station on a moment's notice. She shook her head.

'No.'

'You're certain you don't know her?'

Clement could see her taking in every line.

'Sorry,' she said and looked up into his eyes. 'Has she got something to do with Jean-Claude?'

'We've got someone claiming they saw her a week ago at the beach carpark talking with Jean-Claude. She's wanted in connection with something else, not exactly major. We believe she is an activist: animal rights, anti-development. That kind of thing. Was Jean-Claude passionate about any particular issue?'

Bagot sighed, seemed to search through her filed personal history of her dead lover.

'He was very pro-nature but he wasn't even vegetarian let alone vegan. I guess you would say a greenie. I know he hated the tourist boats at the Barrier Reef and he said that if it got like that here he would quit his job guiding tourists.'

Not much to go on. About seventy percent of people under forty felt that way. Clement nodded to Jo di Rivi. This was a signal for her to lay an eight-by-ten photo of Valentina Gomez in front of Bagot.

Bagot had arrived at the station wearing a tank top, shorts and sandals. Winter had set in over her features, though it looked like she'd stopped crying. Clement had asked di Rivi to partner him rather than Graeme Earle. While he valued Earle's insight, he was thinking they would be doubling up on similar points of view and that especially with a female being interviewed, di Rivi might be attuned to subsonic signals that would have passed Earle and him right by. It also freed Earle to chase up who the woman in the drawing might be. Earle was excellent at procedure, tenacious and alert. He'd climb that tree and shake the branch. If there was any fruit hiding, chances were Earle would bring it to ground. But it was late at night and Clement knew his senses were blunted and likely the rest of the squad. He'd even called Josh Shepherd back in to help Manners try and track video of the Sahara.

Once more Bagot studied what had been placed in front of her.

'No.' Bagot looked up with anxious eyes. 'Is she involved with the other woman?'

'Her name is Valentina Gomez.'

He looked to di Rivi to handle it. She jumped right in.

'There is no easy way to say this, Lauren, but it appears that Jean-Claude has been in a relationship with her for around six weeks.'

Lauren Bagot's mouth opened as if to machine gun them: they had it wrong, they were stupid, didn't know what they were talking about ...

But then her mouth froze and her bottom lip trembled. Clement felt guilty that they could not spare her this embarrassment, but they had to see.

Her silence was a far better testament to her ignorance of the relationship than anything else.

Very weakly she finally managed to ask, 'Do you think ...'

But then the words ended like footprints heading into the ocean.

***

'So I won't see you for two whole weeks?' Ingrid pouted playfully. They had been playing a game of table tennis in the rec room. There had been a time in Brazil before Gabrielly when he had become quite good at it but that was only because he'd had nothing else to do with himself. Now he was below average and Ingrid was pretty terrible but that made it more fun.

'I was thinking about that.' He had not told her but he had tried to see if he could get the alternate engineer Hollis to come back early. Hollis though was hiking in Tasmania and wasn't able to oblige. If she had been a normal member of staff it would have been much easier to simply give her a furlough early, he was the HR boss after all. The trouble was her role demanded she was on the island until replaced. 'You have a week off, right?'

Her contract only gave her a week off, not the two that he got as a matter of course.

'You'd know,' she teased.

'I was thinking...' the confidence he'd had a moment ago deserted him. He looked around for it, tried to beat it out of the bushes but his tongue was tied.

'Yes?' she was on one elbow now leaning in towards him, her eyelashes batting.

Go for it, he urged himself.

'If you wanted ... only if you wanted ... you could come up to my place in Broome and spend the week with me. Then we could both come back together.' Oh shit. He began to blather. 'Of course only if you're –'

'I'd love to do that! That would be so great!' Her eyes were dazzling.

'It's not that special or anything, my place I mean, but it's near the beach. There's just one bed but there's a sofa bed too. I can sleep on that.'

'Well, I'm sure we can manage on the one if we have to,' she said with a smile.

He wondered if he was blushing. He changed the subject. 'I could pick you up if you like.'

The smaller plane that flew locally based employees would drop her at the airstrip at Onslow. He would drive from Broome to collect her.

'That's miles out of your way,' she said. 'I can find my way.'

'But it's expensive to hire a car. I keep mine at Onslow. I don't mind the drive. I might even stay around the Pilbara for a week. Couple of days, Hedland, Dampier, Onslow ...'

Paul was hoping he would find them straight up at the Dampier beach house and that everything would be settled, although his gut was already tight at the pending confrontation. Thomas was such a force, like a cyclone. But the two of them had both experienced loss and Paul hoped that he could explain to Thomas how he had come to see the world in a new light since Ingrid. If him, why not Thomas?

Ingrid was smiling. 'Well, that would be great if you could. It would be nice to drive up together but I don't expect it.'

'No, I'd like to do it, I would.'

Paul sent his Broome address to her phone so she knew exactly where they would be staying. 'I can organise you a seat on the Onslow flight,' he said. Normally, like most of the workers, she would fly direct to Perth on the bigger plane. He promised he would be there to meet her when she got off the plane at Onslow.

'You want another game?' she tilted her head towards the table-tennis table.

He was going to say 'sure', even though he had no real desire.

'Or we could go for a walk,' she said. 'And then watch a movie or something.'

'Let's do that,' he said.

He felt like he was being carried on a beautiful smooth wave but he couldn't let go yet, not completely. There was a big dark shape lurking beneath the surface. Until he sorted things out with Thomas, it would remain there.

It was close on 11.00 p.m. now and Lauren Bagot had been shuffled back to her apartment with all her humanity sucked from her, nothing but a piece of cardboard with holes punched through it. Keeble had let Graeme Earle know that there were no fingerprints of Lauren Bagot at Gomez's place or vice versa. Now she was running a quick simulation of a Toyota Sahara running over a prone Jean-Claude Seydoux.

Manners and Josh Shepherd were searching for any video of the Sahara from Thursday on, starting with the service stations. Earle had directed them to start with Willare, the closest servo to where the cycle had been found. So far nothing. Earle himself was crosschecking the identities of those who had phoned or messaged Seydoux recently, against owners of a Toyota Sahara. If the vehicle was licensed interstate, they would not get confirmation until the next day.

'We should also check driver's licence photos against the phone calls and messages, see if any match the sketch,' said Clement and went off to tell Manners and Shepherd to make that their priority at start of play tomorrow.

Di Rivi was still at her desk.

'Thought I told you to head home.'

'It's this Lizard Minerals thing. The paperwork needs to be finished.'

'I'll get Beck Lalor onto it tomorrow. You go home and get a decent sleep. You're going to need it. I want everybody in here at six thirty.'

She looked grateful despite the early start.

'And you did a good job in there with Lauren. Thanks.'

Manners and Shepherd went too. Keeble was in her office, and that left just him and Earle in the squad room. Clement welcomed the opportunity to compare notes with his trusted ally.

'She was devastated,' Clement said of Lauren Bagot. 'It was bad enough she'd lost her partner but how does she grieve now, knowing he was a cheat?'

Earle asked if he was certain now about Bagot.

Absolutely, he thought. Sitting across from her, watching her go through that, he'd been like a drum snare vibrating to a tuning orchestra. I know what you feel, he'd thought.

'I'd be flabbergasted if she had anything to do with it.'

'Gomez?'

That was trickier.

'She was angry, pissed-off with Jean-Claude. But she admitted driving him to Port Hedland right off, and she wasn't having a bar of being at the beach on Thursday. And Jacinta Richmond's statement might actually support her.'

Earle took the contrary position. 'She could have ridden out to the beach, seen Jean-Claude with our sketchpad girl and decided enough was enough. Just because Richmond didn't see her on her bicycle, doesn't mean she wasn't there.'

That of course was true. But –

'Of course,' said Earle, 'the old guy at May River said he saw a car *and* a cycle.' This was exactly the point Clement would have raised. He finished off their common logic.

'It's a lot easier to believe that car was sketchpad girl's Sahara than that Valentina planned some complicated murder that involved her borrowing a car that fits exactly the tracks at the murder scene and the May River camp.'

Keeble entered right on cue.

'About the car. A Toyota Sahara fits absolutely perfectly as the vehicle that killed Seydoux.'

***

It had been impossible to sleep. He'd lie down for a few minutes then get up and pace about the unit, round and round. He must have pissed eleven times. Ingrid and Gabrielly's faces kept morphing into one another. Eventually he had taken himself outside and stood under the stars staring. The plant was like the exoskeleton of some large, shiny cricket, the lights dewdrops.

As a child he would spend hours transfixed staring at insects in the bush. He wanted to be their protector. He was angry when other kids would kick through an ants' nest or put a praying mantis in a jar with holes punched in the lid.

He should never have become involved. Never.

Yet that was easier to see now. A few short weeks back he had no life. It was understandable. Everything had been ripped from him and what had the consequences been to the entity responsible? A swag of millions that barely affected the bottom line, some forsaken bonus options for executives already on obscenely large salaries.

He had been outraged. The company, he had come to realise, had treated them all only as parts to a machine. Fine, he was happy to embrace the mechanical him and, freed of any moral responsibility, he would act how they had in effect given him liberty to act. He had been ready, willing and, he hoped, able. And then Ingrid had happened. She was not, nor would ever be, Gabrielly. She was her own person with her own qualities that entranced him. Again, he recalled those bush walks of his youth especially after fresh rain when, strung between narrow trunks in a track, a glistening silver spider web would confront you, the spider hanging in front of your eyes like the bullseye in the centre of a target, the thread seeming to vibrate with your breath. Some kids would pick up a stick and swipe right through that. He would never do that. He would get down on his haunches and try to get under or divert around it if he could.

There was no question but that he had to put a stop to what had been set in train. He pulled out his phone and dialled. The slow empty ring reminded him of the sound of baby gulls.

Come on, answer.

The hollow electronic signal snipped through the dense night air invoking no response. They wouldn't be deliberately ignoring him, surely? No, he was the lynchpin. Without him, nothing could happen anyway. It was this vast expanse of primitive land up here with no relay, that's what it was. He would have to keep trying. And if there was still no response then he knew what he had to do.

***

It was closing in on midnight now and Earle and Clement were still weighing and sizing. Clement had finally got through to Jason, the bloke whose car Gomez had driven to Port Hedland. He confirmed Seydoux rented the car for a case of beer. The more he considered, the more Clement felt that Bagot and Gomez were innocents.

'The whole focus of our investigation has got to be identifying the girl in the sketch,' said Clement.

'That was Josh's case,' said Earle in a tone that was like a metal stamp branding the item as suspect.

'I spent a couple of hours on it.' Clement was already on his computer looking up notes. 'Those people who had Rhys – the Meadows. They knew her. At the time I remember thinking they may have been holding something back.' He was looking at the footage of the abattoir demonstration that Josh had acquired. Josh had sworn the woman wasn't on it but Clement quickly checked.

No. She wasn't visible. The Meadows' number was right in front of him. It was late but it couldn't wait. He dialled, listened to the steady burr of the phone.

'Hello?'

What was his name again ... there, Stephen.

'Mr Meadows, it's Inspector Dan Clement.'

'Oh, Inspector ...' He sounded distracted, there was a hollow sound as if his phone had moved away from his mouth. It came close up again, suddenly.

'Sorry, I couldn't find my glasses to read your name on the damn phone.'

He sounded odd, on edge.

'I hope I'm not disturbing you.'

'I'm in ICU at the moment.'

'Are you okay?'

'My wife collapsed late this afternoon on our walk. Some kind of brain haemorrhage. I'm afraid it's not looking good.'

Clement felt like his insides had been scooped out. 'I'm so sorry to hear that.' He added, 'Terribly sorry.' As if that first reaction hadn't been sufficient.

'How can I help?' asked Meadows.

As much as he desired to leave the man in peace, Clement knew he couldn't.

'I really am very sorry to call at this time. We are trying to find that young woman in the sketch we showed you. I'm afraid it's a very serious situation.' As if what's happening to you wouldn't dwarf this, thought Clement.

'Frida, yes.'

Clement's heart whammed. 'That's her name?'

'Nickname that Hazel and I gave her. After Frida Kahlo the painter who was Trotsky's mistress.'

Clement knew her. She was a favourite of Marilyn's, an eye in the forehead and Brooke Shields eyebrows. He was looking at the notes, mention of a guy with a goatee beard they had dubbed Trotsky.

'We never knew her name. Hazel is the one you'd need to speak to and I'm afraid that's not possible right now.'

There was a tremor in his voice.

'I understand, Stephen.' The man's life was on the precipice. 'I just had the feeling ... well, you might have known a bit more.'

'If we had known, we would have told you. We *suspected* that Trotsky might have had something to do with the workers' cars being set alight but honestly, it was speculation. He was a bit of a firebrand.'

'Would you know what vehicle they drove?'

A sad chuckle. 'My powers of observation are distinctly lacking. Hazel might have remembered.'

'Our thoughts and prayers are with you. Thank you, Stephen.'

'Thank you, Inspector.'

He ended the call. Clement related what had happened.

'Poor bloke,' said Earle. 'Life can be a shit. Rhys is going to be very upset. He really connected with them.'

Life certainly can be a shit. Clement was drifting home in a post-midnight fugue, a bullet in ultra slo-mo twisting through space. One second, you were 'we'. Then just 'I'. Years fuse couples. You rust into one. He thought back to the friendly little house with the Doulton teapot, the barometer, that overwhelming sense of a shared life. It was almost sacrilege to imagine Marilyn and him in the same breath. He had his albums, she had her books and clothes. Yet there had been something of that oneness hadn't there? That sense of aching loss he'd felt when she had left him, so real he could squeeze it, taste it, smell it, to this very day. Poor Stephen Meadows sitting in ICU. And what had it taken? A snap of the fingers, that's all.

You could count in hours how long it had been since Clement sat eating Hazel Meadows' slice. How kind and understanding they had been to Rhys. Now she clung to life by a thread. Time was scorching past so fast Clement could feel the heat of flames on its heels.

Rhys.

What was it? Something whispering to Clement about the case. Some fragment he had heard or seen among the thousands of tumbling pieces ...

He was almost home now. How fickle was his brain, the Meadows' plight replaced in an instant by the case.

But why? What had it been that had switched the points so that his whole body had vibrated as the express train dashed past him in the dark tunnel?

Something about Rhys.

The image he saw in his mind was that day of the protest. Rhys sitting beside him in the car, staring straight ahead, huddled as far away from him as he could get.

Hazel Meadows ...

That was it, he was pulling it in slowly now.

She had said she had seen Frida and Trotsky in town selling t-shirts. Switch: there is Rhys Earle in the car. The air-con is on. He has a jacket over a t-shirt. Switch again: the vision of the abattoir protest Clement had just watched back at the squad room. The camera panning and then momentarily lingering on Rhys Earle in a t-shirt that read *Speak For Me* with a picture of a sheep.

19

Rhys Earle sat in the lounge room in his pyjamas. Clement noted that for all the boy's recent lunge toward adulthood, the pyjamas were Star Wars. Clement vaguely remembered being caught in that awkward age between boyhood and adulthood, toy soldiers and erotic dreams. The boy's eyes were sleepy, his hair tousled but as he sipped the glass of water his father had fetched, he was like the vast inland plains coming alive after drenching rain. Earle had chosen not to wake the sleeping Barbara.

Graeme Earle said, 'Dan needs to ask you about some people who might be friends of yours.'

Too late on the scene to be 'Uncle' Dan, Clement was always referred to in the house by his first name. Rhys shot anxious glances between the two men.

'It's alright, Rhys. It's just some questions but they are important.' Clement was trying to reassure him without downplaying the gravity of the situation. 'We were following up some leads with the Meadows.'

Earle and Clement had concluded it would be better to take Dan through their questions before revealing what had happened to Hazel Meadows.

'They mentioned a young man and a woman, they nicknamed them Trotsky and Frida. They said they had a t-shirt stall.'

Rhys' eyes were darting.

Earle said, 'Dan remembered your t-shirt with the sheep. Did you buy it off them?'

Rhys hesitated.

Clement said, 'We understand you may not want to get them into trouble but the man who was murdered at Meda was seen talking with this woman.' Clement laid the drawing on the table. Rhys blinked at the drawing. He looked at his dad.

'I didn't buy the t-shirt. I didn't have enough money. They gave it to me.'

'Did you get to know them?' asked Clement.

Rhys swallowed hard. 'I met them a couple of times. First at the stall and then in the park.' There was a beat and then he added, 'And once down the beach at night.'

Earle asked his son if he knew their names.

'I only know her as Frida. His name is Thomas.'

Clement almost did a handstand.

'I don't know his second name.' Rhys looked from his father to Clement.

'They're activists. Is that right?' asked Clement.

'They care about people. And animals.' Rhys manning the barricades to defend the citadel.

'But does she advocate violence?' asked his father.

'The world is violent,' said Rhys.

Be patient, Clement told himself. 'How long did you spend with them?'

'Couple of hours, each time.'

'Were there others?' asked Clement trying to get a picture of this group.

'There were about five people there besides me.'

'Young, old? Male, female?' Clement wanted as much as Rhys could give him.

'Mainly young. There was one guy there who was older. About your age, maybe a little bit younger. Three women, three men, something like that. But not the same ones each time. Except for the old dude.'

Clement displayed a photo of Seydoux he kept on his phone.

'This guy? Was he there?'

Rhys looked closely. 'I think he might have been there the second time. It was dark. I think so, yeah.'

Graeme Earle asked if he had spoken.

'I don't remember. Thomas did pretty much all the talking.'

Clement asked Rhys to tell them everything he could remember about how he met Thomas and Frida and the two meetings he had with them.

The first time they met was about two months ago. He had been in town getting a milkshake. There was a bunch of people grouped around a little pop-up market stall, just a couple of card tables really with t-shirts. They had slogans printed like *How Would You Like Your Mother In A Burger?* And *If Animals Could Talk What Would They Say About You?*, *Coal Kills* and others that he couldn't remember right off. The little stall was doing a good trade. Rhys was admiring the t-shirts when Frida asked him what size he wanted. He explained he didn't have the thirty dollars a shirt cost, he was just looking. They got to talking then about animal rights and she called over Thomas who was really friendly. He dug in a pile of t-shirts and found one with a drawing of a sheep and the words *Speak For Me* and just gave it to him. He said they were meeting to discuss issues later up at the park and Rhys was welcome to join. With nothing to do, curious, Rhys wandered up there later and found himself part of a group of six or seven. Thomas did most of the talking. He told the little group that he had not been an activist until his mother died. Up until then he was a hedonist. He made himself blind to what was around him but then his mother got sick. She had been working in a clothing factory with a lot of harmful chemical dyes and had got cancer, as had many of the other women who worked in that factory. The authorities pooh-poohed the idea of the cancer coming from the chemicals. As they always did. But his mother died. That was the awakening he needed. Now when he looked around him with fresh eyes, he saw that large multinational companies were controlling everything important: petrol, food, medical supplies, minerals. He saw that the weak and meek always suffered, be they animal or human. He said that the ordinary people had to rise up and claim the world they wanted, that nothing came without sacrifice, that we were all going to perish unless we made a stand, that we were no different to the millions of animals made extinct each year because of fossil fuel. He said he would strike the first blow in the war soon and that it should be a rallying cry. He asked those who were interested in joining his crusade to leave some means by which they could be contacted. Rhys gave them his phone number. Not long after, he left as he had to get home, but the words made an impression upon him. Thomas had also warned them all not to go spreading this information to anybody they weren't absolutely sure about.

Clement did a quick calculation. 'This must have been just before the abattoir workers' cars were torched.'

Rhys looked uncomfortable. 'Just before. Maybe a week.'

His father seemed about to jump in but held back and said quietly, 'Did you suspect them?'

'I didn't think about it at first. Then I suppose, I did.'

Clement asked if they were living in Broome.

'I don't think so. They said something that first time that they were only in town for a day. I never saw them except selling the t-shirts.'

'Did you see their car?'

He couldn't recall seeing it. About three weeks after the first encounter, Rhys got a call from the woman saying they would be meeting at the beach

'What was the number?' Clement was ever hopeful of some slip-up.

The boy got his phone, found the number. The number was dead now. Something for Manners to chase up.

'So what happened at the beach?'

He went along. This was the time he thought the man in the photo was part of the group. It was dark, just a wood fire throwing light so it was hard to be certain. Somebody had asked if Thomas would be joining the abattoir protest. He said it had his blessing but Frida and he had something else planned and it was best they stayed out of the spotlight. Thomas' speech was much the same as the previous time. He talked again about losing his mother. He said they were all bound together by grief, with each other and the animals of the world. He said they had to stand up and strike a blow for those who were unable to, either because they were dead or because they had no voice of their own. The older man seemed to be wiping tears, said Rhys, although he couldn't be sure it wasn't just the smoke. At the end of the talk the adults all drank wine. Rhys was offered but did not partake. He glanced at his dad, who nodded approval.

Rhys, perhaps encouraged by his dad's support, then admitted that he had told Thomas he wanted to be part of the army Thomas had talked about. Thomas had said there would come that time but it was not yet. Right now, the best thing he could do was speak to his friends, awaken their consciousness. He had pamphlets he could distribute for them. And if he had any spare money, then he could donate what he could afford. Rhys had around twenty dollars so he gave it all. Thomas warned him it would not be easy. Most Australians will sell their unique heritage for thirty pieces of silver, he'd said and then handed him a shiny black lump of coal. That, said Thomas, is their thirty pieces of silver. Remember that, he said, you will need to be strong.

Rhys had tried to hand out the pamphlets at school, a few kids took them but not many. The rest, his old friends included, treated him like a freak.

'Do you have any of those pamphlets still?' asked Clement.

'In my locker at school. I didn't want Dad to find them.' His eyes slid over to his father.

'Was there any arrangement to meet again?'

'No. Thomas said, "You won't hear from us for a while but when you do, you will know." He said he would be in touch with us when the time was right.'

Clement thanked Rhys and asked him to call his dad immediately if he remembered anything more. Then Earle sent him off to bed with a hug.

But Clement's instinct told him that Thomas' efforts to withdraw from public life spoke volumes.

'They are planning something,' he said. He was at that stage in the case where sufficient facts had been collected to concoct theories. He wanted to roll them, taste them, spit out the ones that didn't fit.

'Maybe it was the clinic. They did that, right?'

'That seems pretty insignificant for all the talk,' said Clement.

'But what if it was all about money? Selling t-shirts, a GoFundMe page. All they had to do was a little something to keep the bucks rolling in.'

Clement had to concede that was possible. Earle continued as they climbed into the car.

'Perhaps there was a lot of money involved and Seydoux had a stake. Maybe he funded them and wanted his dollars back?'

Clement followed that thought. 'They pay him back but kill him and take the motorcycle planning to sell it but they panic.'

Clement fired up the car. It was possible but would you nail somebody to the road for that? Earle was already there.

'I know what you're thinking but you know what it's like with zealots. If this Thomas lost his mother, he could be a bit psycho anyway.'

The trouble was, thought Clement, we still don't have enough. It was ninety percent speculation.

'We need to speak to Lauren Bagot again and Valentina Gomez, see if Thomas is familiar. And get Rhys with Lilly, get sketches of Thomas and all the people he remembers at the gathering.'

But that would have to wait till morning, which was now only about five hours off.

Where are you, he wondered. And why would you possibly crucify Jean-Claude Seydoux?

20

He watched the illuminated blue screen pulse in the dark. It put him in mind of the translucent bell of a man-o'-war as it propelled itself beneath the water's surface. He recognised the number but chose not to answer. Paul would call again. There was no facility enabled on the phone for a message to be left. You had to be like a bushman, the fewer tracks the better. It was likely Paul just getting anxious, wanting reassurance. It was, he supposed, vaguely possible the police had somehow tracked them down and they were standing beside Paul right now. Or perhaps Paul might have recognised photos of the Sun King and then dimly tried to make sense of what had happened. He doubted it. Their paths had crossed very briefly on a dark night lit only by a low fire on a beach. The boy didn't know enough either, although he may have remembered the two of them. But he'd never seen a vehicle, never heard a surname. No. It was likely just Paul double-checking.

He looked over to where she slept in her bag on the deserted beach. They had shifted camp yesterday to be closer to their next important staging posts. So far, she had not failed him. When it had come to dealing with the Sun King, he was prepared for it, but she had not resiled from what had been needed of her. Perfidy needed punishment. That she understood. She had been insistent that they quit the May River as soon as possible. He had learned to trust her instinct. It was like she had the gift. She was the one who had whispered to him that Paul had been sent to them, he was the key. So he had proven to be.

As for any trail the police might try and pick up, he had made his list of precautions and followed them closely. First and foremost, keep the vehicle hidden at all times. He had filled jerry cans of petrol a week ago. No need to call in on servos to refill. So long as the police didn't know their names and couldn't place their vehicle, they were smoke. Nothing was perfect however. There was always a chance for an error, a piece of bad luck, or worse, a mistake by one of the others. He took a deep breath and a long moment to appreciate the natural beauty surrounding him. Eighty miles of beach they claimed.

He would like to have brought his mum out here. He didn't recall them ever being on a holiday. She was gone before they had a chance. His father was no more than the shadow cast by passing clouds. He had been nine when that man had taken himself out of their lives. Three wonderful years he and his mum had shared. Then she was gone too.

A child loses his mother at that age, it's devastating. You haven't even rebelled yet. Suddenly it is just you and objects from an outside world, cheap dressers, rusting clothes hangers. Friends are immature and inadequate, and he'd never really had friends anyway. Teachers are no more than actors on a set. Your whole life feels like a play. Each day you want the performance to end so you can go back home, but there is no home, there is no core because 'home' is where the love is. Home is the invisible but tangible emotion that exists between loved ones, that's all it is, not bricks and tiles, not a driveway with a car in it. They're no more than a sound stage.

A child needs to be able to close its eyes and still feel secure. To sense the dull rhythm of a mother's heart. That's why people put a clock in the bedding of a kitten or a puppy. Words are a very poor cousin for communication to the real thing, that bond between a parent and child, especially a mother and her child. Without that the world is sparse as an art gallery. And there is nobody to reassure you about your worth. No bosom for you to lay your head on and be gently stroked while you cry. None of that testing of boundaries either, going to the fridge one more time when you've been told to quit. Feeling yourself slowly grow into adulthood and your own entity.

His uncle, her brother, was a moron who spent most of his conscious hours in a betting shop. Aunty Jessica, Thomas was convinced, only kept her nephew around because she got some money coming her way for it. At least she fed him. She tried sometimes. But you have the overwhelming sense that you are a tolerated burden, no more. He would trawl for pleasant memories of his mother, haul them up when they bit, dissect and savour them. A time they went to the movies to see Harry Potter together. Not just locally, all the way up to the city and the cinemas in George Street. They caught a train and walked around the crowded streets before the movie, and then they ate ice-cream in the dark, his pulse racing to the action of the movie, but all the more special because she was beside him. Another time he remembered she took the morning off work to come to the classroom and see what he had been doing. Year four, around then it was. For once he had a parent who was checking out his artwork and the things the kids had built, and he felt a flutter of pride as she turned and smiled back at him in that crammed little classroom.

By seventeen, he was out of his uncle's and school but he didn't know enough to escape those dull suburbs he'd been born into where McDonald's was the Taj Mahal, and entertainment consisted of sitting on the railing by the supermarket and listening to the night-time rattle of shopping trolleys. He'd stayed with a Lebo mate whose parents let him sleep on the floor of his mate's room and use the bathroom and kitchen until he found a job. He scored one in a warehouse, where for the most part he was surrounded by more morons. He got into a share flat as soon as he could manage it but the rent left him with hardly anything to spend. Everybody he knew was dropping eccies. A few smoked weed. He started along the same hopeless path. It was an endless loop for what, two years? Working a mindless job to get enough money to make yourself mindless. Money seemed to float past him in a quick stream, never snagging. There were what passed as girlfriends. He didn't seem to have too much trouble getting sex but he had no desire for lasting relationships. Squalid was how he now thought of that phase of his life. The loss of his mother had robbed him of what should have been every child's right. He must have been twenty when he made his first important discovery.

He had spent most of his free money on pills as usual but unlike the rest of his friends had felt no desire to gobble them as quickly as possible. Then one night they were all at some rave and he found himself the only one with any pills left. His crew were so desperate they offered him twice what he'd paid. He had not a second thought about obliging. That's when he realised there was money to be made and a future to be had by judiciously buying and selling. He didn't think of himself as a dealer because he didn't even have a wholesale price going for him. It was just he had the wits to know where he could get the cheapest gear and where he could sell it for the most bucks. Like those stockmarket pricks making money out of nothing but shuffling paper. Arbitrage they called it and he adopted the term to describe what he did: arbitrage.

For a time, things went well. He kept working at the factory but the money he got from drugs was increasing. He was careful to stay out of the way of the dealers. This wasn't a career path for him, it was just something to earn more dollars, get enough to move into a flat on his own. He bought a cheap car and drove to the city where he would take in an art gallery or ramble through the Botanic Gardens. When he got bored with that he drove to national parks. He would take a quiet trail and explore, sit for hours absorbing nature around him.

Along the way he discovered that the university provided a low-risk, solid-return environment for his drug reselling, though at first he couldn't crack it with the students except at some campus raves when they were already off their faces. It dawned on him that they knew straight away he wasn't one of them. He didn't look the part, he spoke coarsely, his gaze hit women head-on instead of drifting parallel to them. He ploughed his profits into better clothes, began to dress like a student and to hang out around campus, soaking up the quality that almost all students have: entitlement. Sufficiently imbued with that, he was able to effortlessly recreate the same vibe. He was undetectable.

That was really when his life changed.

At first, he went to the rallies and talks just to fit in but then he began to listen to these student activists and what they were protesting about. It was clear most were talking out of their arse and hadn't a clue what it was like out there sleeping on the floor of your mate's bedroom or having a punch on in the deserted carpark of your local supermarket, but all the same he was impressed by their desire to change the world around them. He learned about socialism and multinational corporations, about genetically modified crops and pharmaceutical companies who basically bribed doctors to get you onto drugs you didn't need. And he thought about his mum, that stupid factory where she had worked and how she was now lost from his life. Pretty soon he decided to bypass the intermediaries – students who were spouting theories about which they had no personal experience – and to go to the library and become acquainted with the originals, old French and German dudes who'd been writing about this shit a hundred, two hundred years earlier.

At one of the campus forums one day, he found the courage to actually go to the microphone and speak. Words and ideas poured out of him and he saw he held his audience in some kind of thrall. Later, a bunch of the most committed sought him out and over bad coffee he told them his mother had contracted cancer from the chemicals at her workplace. He told them he'd been cast out on the streets. He told them that a reckoning was coming, that people didn't just stop polluting the world because it was the right thing to do, that they would only cease doing that when the pain it induced, be that physical or bottom line to their profits, was greater than the personal benefit they received.

Very quickly he became a minor celebrity. Student leaders deferred to him. Young students sought him out as a mentor. And then he learned a harsh but very important lesson that he had never forgotten. It was easy to get swept away in what might be, easy to forget what is. In this case, he neglected that a large slice of his income was from selling drugs. He hadn't covered himself with enough veils, left enough false trails, and so it wasn't difficult for the cops to track him down when they busted one of his piss-weak student clients. The dominoes fell, more clients were turned up. The cops decided he was threat enough that he should go to jail and the magistrate agreed.

He wound up getting three months. Of itself, that wasn't so terrible but now he had no job, a criminal record, and worst of all, his old hunting ground the campus was well and truly off limits. It had been quite a setback but despite that, he had gained the most valuable insight of all: what his life was to be about, how he was to make his mark in this world. He had learned too, that he held great powers of persuasion, that he could read people but that he must be ever vigilant, must eliminate errors.

The road ahead would be difficult but the destination was predetermined. And now nearly four years on from that, he was ready.

**

By the time Clement made it back to his flat, it was closing in on 2.30 a.m. When they had told Rhys about Hazel Meadows the boy had fought to stay strong but his eyes had quickly misted and a tear or three rolled, something that endeared Rhys to Clement, and made him proud. Our ability to feel, to care and to love is possibly our finest human quality, Clement told himself and yet he had so often stonewalled those impulses. For months he had fought feeling anything about Marilyn. He'd thought that had made him stronger. And then like a routed army he'd run screaming. He wished he could take back that dumb phone call. He wished their relationship had been like the Meadows'. Clement rolled into bed. He shut his eyes. He said a quick prayer for Hazel Meadows because he had told Stephen Meadows he would. He hoped it produced a better result than previous times.

Within a minute, his day ended.

21 MONDAY

It was dark when Thomas rose to the smell of ocean salt in his nostrils. For an instant he felt the deep stab of what might have been. The Frenchman had wrecked everything. Carefully laid plans, years of saving and work turned to ash. If things had gone as they were supposed to, it would have been so simple. The police would never have had any idea about them, at least not until too late. They were so far under the radar they were subterranean. For months he had kept away anything that might attract attention. But the fucking Frenchman had ruined all that.

The bastard.

Unfortunately, there were going to be consequences. As soon as they found the body, the police would have started their hunt. First step would have been identifying the dead man. That had to be delayed and that meant the motorcycle had to disappear. He had been careful from the get-go: minimal contact, keeping their identities secret, especially from the Frenchman, keeping the car out of the way and avoiding cameras, particularly servo ones. He couldn't be sure how much time he'd bought. That tattoo was going to be a signpost. But any extra minute was important. The plan had to go ahead. There could be no postponement because the longer any delay, the more chance the police might find something. Perhaps he should have been less public with that traitor. They could have dumped him in the river for crocodiles to feed on or just buried him out in the bush and likely nobody would have ever found him. But that would have been unsatisfying. Betrayal was the ultimate transgression. It mocked. It strutted. It cut the heart from the innocent. It was worse than murder because it destroyed not just the body, but our ideals, our aspirations, those fragile constituents that make us more than flesh and blood, that make us a son, a lover, a friend, that make us who we are. Despite the risk that was entailed by leaving the Frenchman there so flagrantly, it had given him a sense of completion. And if things continued as he hoped they would, it would offer a salutary lesson for any wavering followers. Still, it heightened the risk of discovery before their mission was complete, no doubt about that. The most tenuous link in their plans was the boat hire. The Frenchman had organised all of that and was going to skipper. Well, there was nothing to driving a boat, he could handle that himself, but the Frenchman knew the waters, the reefs, the tides. Nonetheless, he was confident he could handle all those so long as he got the boat. But would there be any snags with the boating people? They knew Seydoux, they trusted him with their boat. Would they insist on somebody else taking his place?

His heart had been in his mouth when he had called yesterday and made out like he had no idea what had happened to the Frenchman. Hello, my name is Thomas, I organised a boat with Jean-Claude. He mentioned he was hiring from you but I've been unable to …

'Oh no,' he had gasped, 'that's terrible!' when told that the Frenchman had been killed. 'That's awful.' And then after the appropriate shock and expressions of regret he had made like he was clawing his way through fog. Is it possible we could hire the boat still? We have travelled all the way from Perth. We've been planning this trip of a lifetime for years. It had been easy to fudge how Jean-Claude was an acquaintance of a mutual friend who had met the Frenchman while diving in Perth, and how he had recommended they get in touch with Jean-Claude about diving the islands off the north-west coast. That way he didn't need to act too distraught, or have the hire people tell him to see the police.

Yes, he had lied, my partner and I are both experienced divers. The problem, had explained the man at the boating place, was that this was peak tourist season and that he didn't have anybody spare to act as a guide.

This was perfect. It made things simpler.

We don't need anyone, he'd said. All we need is a boat and a trailer because Jean-Claude had said diving and fishing would be better a bit further south and it would be better to drive.

The man at the boat place had agreed with that.

'We could leave a deposit, a bond?'

The man had asked what they had agreed to pay Jean-Claude. Clearly, he expected Seydoux would be adding a mark-up for himself on top of whatever Seydoux was paying for the boat.

'Two thousand eight-hundred for everything, trailer included, for three days.'

The man had thought about that and said they could leave it at that then. They could direct-deposit the money or use credit card. He would need a passport or driver's licence and that was about it. The boat would be fitted with all safety gear.

'When would you want to get it?' he had asked.

'Say seven tomorrow morning, if that's alright? We'll be driving up from Hedland. We left Geraldton two days ago and dived at Ningaloo.' He'd thrown that in just in case the police asked about the boat hire. It would make it seem they hadn't been anywhere near the Kimberley. Then he sputtered some more nonsense about how he couldn't believe Seydoux had been killed.

'Not that I knew him personally, but it must be a shock.'

Yes, it was a shock the man agreed. It sounded from what he could tell, he said, that somebody might have killed Jean-Claude and stolen his bike.

'That's just awful,' Thomas had said. 'I'll let my friend in Perth know. He'll be upset I am sure. So, seven?'

The man had given them directions to the marina. The tide would be a bit low but it would be sufficient.

After that call he had breathed much easier. He was sure the police weren't onto them. The guy would have been more agitated and would have asked for names and all sorts of things. It was possible, he thought, that they might still get away with it. Initially that had been his intention. This would be just the start of a series of events where he would strike out at those multinationals who controlled energy, food, medicine – all our essentials. He had, however, always been prepared that there could be consequences to himself: incarceration, injury, death. That was the price you had to be prepared to pay to create lasting change. And it would come with a bonus: global recognition.

Oh, how the world had kowtowed to Greta, that snub-nose little Swedish twerp. How did she deserve it? What had she given up? What had she lost? How many nights had she slept on the streets, scavenged dustbins? Had she lost her mother? Her home? No, her mother was a fucking opera singer, her father some musician. They'd spent their lives sucking off the teat of cultural institutions, travelling around famous European cities, whereas his opera house was a McDonald's carpark. He'd arbitraged his way up the ladder with drug-commerce. Well, what he had planned would put little Greta well and truly back in the Swedish shade where she belonged. He was sick and tired of these arseholes who jumped on the bandwagon: gay marriage, Black Lives Matter, you name it. Not the ones, anonymous like him, who'd been in the vanguard and taken the hits, and stood on cold corners with chilled fingers shovelling out flyers, but those that thought they could get a piece of righteousness by sticking a stupid logo on their Twitter or Facebook, or by joining a rally march because all their cool friends were doing it. And no institutions did he loathe more than Facebook and Twitter and Instagram and Snapchat with their jeans and t-shirt moguls congratulating themselves on their 'disruptive' philosophies. Not that he would tell them that, ever. For they were the ones who would spread his notoriety. They ultimately were his conduit to power.

When he had planned to remove the Frenchman his first concern had been, could the offensive part of the plan remain intact? His answer to that was, yes, with a few potentially minor alterations. The bike had to be removed, they would need to cover off the couple of calls they had made to him on his phone for when the police checked, but that was about it. So, the action could still go ahead. Initially his answer to the second question – Could they still escape after the action? – had been, probably not. But when he teased it out, he had become more optimistic. If all went to plan, they would be well clear before the actual detonation. With the Frenchman gone, that left Paul as the biggest single pointer to their involvement. But Paul would not be there at the time. Eventually he would be questioned and he might well fold. By that time, they would be in another state or even another country. And if things got really hot, there were contacts he'd made over time, people who could hide them, get them out of the country. Look at Baader-Meinhof, the Red Army Faction. They had been headline winners in the 70s, not just in their German homeland but all over the world. Or the Weathermen from the US. They had survived for years, and they had been the real deal. They were what this apathetic, over-stuffed world needed to regain its dignity. But they were all long gone and there was a void to be filled. He was the one to fill that void. And it was time now to embark upon the last leg of the journey. He shook her awake.

'It's time.'

***

Earle was a dab hand with the frypan. The pancakes were first rate.

'You've been keeping this talent from us,' said Clement squeezing fresh lemon over the neatly circular piping-hot pancake, then sprinkling a smidge of sugar.

'Years of camping and fishing. The skillet is your most useful tool.'

It was 6.30 a.m. and Clement's whole team was assembled in the station kitchen. Earle had rocked up with the pancake mix, lemons and maple syrup, for which Clement was very grateful. For one, he was hungry; secondly, he knew they all had another huge day in front of them and this was a good way to bond and get them enthused. Keeble had already delivered bad news on any chance of fingerprints from the pamphlets. If there were prints other than Rhys Earle's they must have been on the pamphlets he'd already given out. There was only one set on the sheets she'd scooped up an hour ago. They would be Rhys'. Manners was pessimistic on getting anything from the phone number that had called Rhys.

'We need to find this couple,' said Clement aware that he was stating the bloody obvious since he had already briefed them all on what they had discovered the previous night.

'While we cannot rule out Bagot or Gomez, I can't justify further investigation of them at this time. The uniforms will follow up the beach carpark, see if Gomez might have been there Thursday but so far their alibis, while not proven, are most certainly intact. So, it's Thomas and Frida, front and centre.'

Clement had left a message for Lilly asking her to get to the Earle household as early as she could this morning so Rhys could help her sketch a likeness of those he'd met. 'Hopefully we'll have a sketch of Thomas and possible others soon.'

'I've already got the girl's poster to every police station in the Kimberley and Pilbara,' said Mal Gross. 'When I get the others, they'll go straight off.'

Clement said, 'I want uniforms covering the town from top to bottom with the sketches. I want them asking pubs, roadhouses, cafés everywhere. Jo, I'd like you to hit the real-estate agencies, you never know, maybe they are staying local or did at some point in the past. Josh, matching the vehicle to CCTV. And just a heads-up everybody, I might have to call Perth in.'

There was a sense of disappointment.

'We've done well but these guys could be in Perth or interstate by now.'

Clement reached down and picked up the t-shirt the couple had given Rhys Earle.

'No point trying for prints, this shirt has been worn and washed. If you see anybody wearing a t-shirt like this with activist slogans, ask them when and where they got it.'

Earle, only sitting down now, being the cook and the last to eat, said, 'I'm going to try the shops in town to see if they bought any t-shirts or took some on consignment. I'll also chase up who distributes this brand. It seems to be called Golden and is manufactured in Vietnam.'

'Let's go, people,' said Clement and they scattered.

***

She felt like she needed to pee again. Nerves. She still hadn't told him about the early childhood clinic. Nobody there had known her name and she hadn't seen any cameras but it was possible she'd missed one. She was more certain about fingerprints. She'd been careful, hadn't left any. Anyway, so what if somebody had told the police about her? She'd been nowhere near the car. Without her name she was a phantom.

These reassurances didn't quite work. There was a shade of doubt that crept back like a plucky cat after you'd shooed it away. What if somebody *had* seen her getting into the car? Then the police might somehow track back from the car licence and identify Thomas' car with the mystery woman. Last night he had been in a good, positive mood and she had very nearly told him. Something though had stopped her. She knew he would vent. He'd never been violent towards her but he'd had no trouble planning how to kill Seydoux. She'd agreed with him about that. The bastard had double-crossed them and jeopardised everything they had planned. She felt no sympathy towards him. Long ago, she and Thomas had talked about the sacrifices they might have to make to spread their cause. She was ready for death if it came. Not that she desired it. If she could she would avoid it but if there were no way out, she was prepared. Life without Thomas would be meaningless anyway and she knew he was ready to die.

Even so, her muscles felt bunched as they drove through dark just starting to fracture with the sun's slow rise. He was anxious, she could tell, because they were heading back to Broome and even though the marina was on the southern outskirts, if the police had made any links, they must be looking for them. Had he known about the clinic, he would be much more anxious. Yes, it was as well she'd said nothing. Thomas was always going on about betrayal and though she did not think what she had done was in any sense a betrayal, maybe he would see it differently. As if reading her mind, he turned to her.

'Don't worry. I don't think they would have linked us yet, and when we leave here, we'll be towing a boat on a trailer. They won't look twice.'

He can't be that confident, she thought, or he wouldn't have insisted they both cut their hair and change into neat, suburban arsehole clothes. He was wearing a polo shirt. He never wore those. This one had a rugby look to it, horizontal fat stripes followed by thin stripes. He'd let her be except for snipping her hair and having her change into a sunhat and a pair of clean jeans. She would keep quiet about the clinic. This time tomorrow it would all be over, so why create a potential drama now?

***

As soon as Risely had entered, Clement had gone to his office and briefed him.

'Should we go to the press?' asked Risely.

'You're asking me?'

'Yes. What do you reckon?'

Of course, he had been thinking about what was the quickest and best way to find Thomas and Frida. The phone call to Rhys proved a dead end. The phone had been reported stolen from a youth hostel and the service terminated later that day by the owner.

'It could help. But it also might tie us up with a lot of false reports. Manners and Shepherd are crosschecking calls and messages to Seydoux. They'll try and match the callers' details to driver's licences and vehicle licences. Maybe they'll get a driver's licence photo match to the Frida sketch. And they'll also check to see if any of the callers might own a Sahara. Either way we could get their real names. Hopefully they'll get something very soon. They're also checking CCTV. We can backtrack from the car regos. If Thomas and Frida know we're onto them they might ditch the car.'

'Let's give it till lunch,' said Risely.

Clement found Beck Lalor waiting for him outside his office. He had forgotten he'd messaged her.

'What did you want, sir?'

'Di Rivi is flat out on the Meda case and she has some unfinished stuff on the Lizard Minerals case in Halls Creek. I was hoping you might help out?'

She beamed. 'Love to.'

He told her to sort it out with di Rivi and not to hesitate to ask him if she needed help. Then he turned and saw Mal Gross escorting Rhys Earle into the room.

'How did it go with Lilly?'

'Yeah good, I think. I did my best,' said the boy shyly.

'Thanks for that.'

Mal Gross said, 'I've got them and they're going out any minute. Here are your copies.'

He handed photocopies to Clement who only now noticed the boy was carrying a Tupperware lunch box.

'Dad forget his lunch?' he asked.

The boy bit his lip. 'If Thomas has a criminal record, his fingerprints would help, wouldn't they?'

'They certainly would. But we won't get any off the t-shirt.'

'I was thinking you might get some off this, but.' Rhys peeled off the top of the lunch box.

Clement found himself staring down at a shiny black rock the size of a clenched fist.

'It's the lump of coal Thomas gave me. I haven't touched it since the day he gave it to me.'

22

They were sitting having coffee in the canteen when the hum of the approaching plane reached them. The main flight direct to Perth had already left. Most of the workers took that. A few of them though lived in the Pilbara or Broome and they travelled on the small plane the short trip across the ocean to the mainland. It was a fairly quick turnaround for the flight back and even though it was only a few hundred metres to where it would land, Paul knew he should get moving. He reached for his bag.

'I had better head out,' he said.

'I'll miss you,' she said.

He was too embarrassed to say he would miss her too. He reached down and picked up his backpack and was about to head out.

'Hey, no goodbye kiss?'

Before he knew what was happening Ingrid had leaned over and kissed him on the lips. 'Plenty more where that came from,' she said and smiled.

'Thank you,' he said, feeling that was inadequate.

'You're welcome.' Her smile showed dimples, made him feel good.

He walked across the linoleum floor to the door and turned for one last wave but she had already headed off to her work and was almost out of the canteen. He stepped out from the air-conditioning into the heat and watched as the plane landed. Walking was effortless. But as he reached the plane his gut tightened. He was not looking forward to what lay ahead.

***

'Real nice set of prints,' said Lisa Keeble. 'Well, two sets of prints, one being Rhys', but the other set is now in the system.'

Clement knew she would let him know as soon as there was any hit. Rhys had headed off to school. His father was still in town trying to get a lead on the t-shirts.

'I've got her!' Josh Shepherd was across the room proudly bouncing on his toes like Steve Smith at the batting crease. Then he tempered that. 'At least we're ninety-nine percent –'

'Tell me,' said Clement. Ninety-nine percent he would take in a heartbeat.

'Annika Styles.'

Shepherd placed a New South Wales driver's licence printout on Clement's desk, the sketch Lilly had done beside it. 'No criminal record.'

Clement had no doubt it was the same woman as in the sketch. Shepherd continued.

'There were two calls between her and Seydoux, one on the day before he died.'

'How come we didn't find her before? I asked Manners to call everybody who had contacted Seydoux's phone number.'

'She was the one who left a message saying she and her girlfriend were driving on the Gibb River Road.'

Clement remembered now.

Shepherd continued. 'She used a fake name. The phone company details said the phone was owned by Annika Styles. No one of that name with a driver's licence in WA but her name popped up in New South Wales and her licence photo matched the sketch.'

Styles and Thomas had bought themselves time. They could be in Melbourne by now.

'What about a vehicle?'

'She is not registered as the owner of any vehicle anywhere in Australia,' said Shepherd.

So, the car likely belonged to Thomas.

***

Paul looked down through the windows of the small plane at the ocean below. There are plane rides, or more generally journeys in your life that impress themselves on you like a hot iron on soft skin, he thought. You know at the time these are moments you will either want to never forget or never remember. His first arrival into Brazil had nothing about it that announced it would be a defining moment. He was excited, yes, a new culture and all that, but he had not yet met Gabrielly, was not even aware of her existence. On the other hand, on the flight back to Australia he felt that all his insides had been hollowed out and bales of straw stuffed in their place. With each passing second, he was rocketing away from the only place in his whole adult life where he had felt joy. It was the end, a finality that could not be massaged, nor argued with. The only impetus for leaving was that to stay would have been worse. It was a time in life where the practicalities offered an excuse you could gratefully accept.

Apart from today's, all the other flights to and from the island since he'd started had been as inconsequential as a drive into the office. They had nothing to say about who he was.

Today was different.

This moment, suspended in the air between departure and arrival, was a metaphor for where he found himself in life, between past and future, despair and hope. He had read with amazement about how great men had experienced in their lives some epiphany where all the pieces of their previous life coalesced, where the flashing neon sign said *dig here*, where their lives made sense, their purpose suddenly made clear. Yes, he thought he too had been gifted that – the books he'd found, Thomas, the ideas and experiences they had exchanged, flowing out of them like lava. But up here, looking down like an osprey, he had his own epiphany – that you never quite knew where you were in the chain links of your own story. He could never be happier than he had been with Gabrielly, and he had thought, erroneously, that meant he could also never be happy again, but that doesn't have to be true. And the evidence was right there in front of your face every day, even in signs as simple as an old person shuffling off to buy some meagre essentials for life. Their youth has gone. It will never be recaptured. Their loved ones are likely gone too. And yet they can find some pleasure, even if it's only feeding a pigeon.

What lay ahead of him would not be easy. Thomas would resist, he was sure, at first. But perhaps he could explain it to him just as he himself was thinking this through right now: that we don't know for certain that some path has been predestined for us. Yes, based on past experiences, we might convince ourselves with absolute certainty this is why we are put on this earth, but we are looking at it from the limited perspective of men. From up here, like an osprey, we see that when you are standing on the ground things can block your vision. There is no way you can know what may be around the corner, possibly even ... hope.

***

Rhys' lump of coal had come up trumps. They had a match. Clement sat there absorbing the news, relief infusing his body. Earle's quest for answers on the t-shirts had proven fruitless but the hot chips he had brought back suddenly tasted like the best he'd ever had.

'Thomas ...'

'Berryman,' said Keeble and spelled it for Clement so he could write it on scrap paper in front of him. 'Born fourteenth of June nineteen ninety-three, Liverpool, New South Wales. Drug-dealing bust nine years back. Looks low-grade. I'm copying you the file now.'

She stared down at her phone and pressed. Beat the old fax machine.

He called Manners immediately with the good news.

'Need you to do the electronic legwork: car registrations, credit cards, phone records, money, everything. And call Perth and get them involved with all this. Banks, social media, you know the drill.'

Graeme Earle was gobbling chips and grinning.

'Told you it would work out.'

They were flying now: two names, Thomas Berryman and Annika Styles. He reined himself in. Okay, these two had lied or at least been deceptive but that didn't mean they killed Seydoux. They could be freaking out about the clinic and nothing more than that. But it was progress, and if Keeble could get her hands on Berryman's vehicle, it might be game over.

Berryman's criminal file gave as next of kin a Jennifer Davidson of Fairfield, New South Wales. The phone number was a landline that rang dead.

'Shepherd,' he yelled and Josh appeared in the doorway.

'I want you to track down Jennifer Davidson. She was in Fairfield, New South Wales nine years ago.'

Shepherd took the note Clement had handed him and dashed over to his computer. By the time he reached it, Manners was standing in front of Clement, flushed with excitement.

'Berryman is the registered owner of a tan two thousand and four Toyota Sahara. Perth licence plates. I've copied Mal Gross and Risely. No hit on any credit card.'

'Keep looking for anything and everything.'

Earle said, 'Why don't I give Jo a hand. Check caravan parks, real-estate agents, motels, Kimberley and Pilbara.'

'Good idea.' The car registration would make things so much easier. 'And could you check with Mal, make sure he's across the rego and every eye we have is looking?'

Earle left for the front area that was the domain of Mal Gross.

Clement was so pumped he nearly smacked a fist into his palm. It was all coming together. He looked out to see Beck Lalor hovering by Graeme Earle's desk, obviously looking for him.

'He's with Mal. Can I help?'

Lalor flushed. 'It's about the Lizard Minerals case. I noticed something I thought might be … it's probably nothing.'

Five minutes earlier he would have told her he was too busy but now he was feeling like a surfer on a good wave.

'What is it?'

She came towards him holding a sheet of A4.

'Lizard Minerals supplied a list of all past and present employees and there's a name here that you'll know.'

She pointed and passed over the paper.

The name stuck out like a seagull in a murder of crows.

Lauren Bagot.

She had been an employee at Lizard Minerals from last November to early February. Clement cast his mind back to the interview with her. What had she said? She and Seydoux met a little over a year ago in Hedland then came up here where she did some temp jobs before getting her new job.

'Well done, this could be important. Just keep going with the rest of the paperwork.'

'Sure thing.'

Clement got up and found Earle heading back with a phone to his ear.

'I've started on the caravan parks.'

Clement told him about what Lalor had discovered. Earle's brain made the connection quickly: Lizard Minerals, explosives theft, Seydoux a commando.

'Shit,' he said.

23

She felt more relaxed now as they headed south, Eighty Mile Beach somewhere beyond the scrub to their right. It wasn't like she had no anxiety, there was still a heap lying under the mat like dirt. But Thomas was right, towing a boat made them invisible. Even if the cops were looking for them, the boat was perfect camouflage. The guy had been at the marina waiting and was satisfied with the direct deposit screenshot on her phone. They had made out like the Frenchman's death had been a total surprise, promised to return the boat on time and driven off with a fully fuelled and equipped boat. They'd had to fudge about where they intended diving and the guy had been overly helpful with his suggestions so she was getting toey about ever getting away but eventually they were done and now here they were barrelling down the highway.

'This might be our last free day in a long time,' she said, wondering if he'd been thinking the same thing.

'Freedom is only an illusion they allow us to have to further the growth of their capitalist philosophies.'

'Maybe that's true but right now I feel free.'

He nodded thoughtfully. 'You're right that there are degrees of freedom, or more accurately non-freedom.'

'You think we can get away?' She knew he didn't like talking about that but she pushed. It was too late to pull out of their enterprise now anyway. She expected him to avoid answering.

'You know I don't like to talk about it because it might jinx it but the only way they get to us now is through Paul. They will find two phone calls between you and Jean-Claude. You will say that he came

205

to our beach meetings a couple of times, that's it. They will look into Paul. They will find a couple of calls between him and me. Again, the same explanation.'

'But if they connect us, and they will, then it all depends on what Paul says.'

'Paul won't talk,' Thomas said with finality.

'You can't be sure.'

'He won't. I know people.'

Except you don't know me, she thought. Then she turned her gaze back to the endless road. It was pointless worrying, she decided. What will be, will be.

***

Lauren Bagot had come to the station as quickly as she could. When Clement had called it sounded like he'd woken her. Understandable; Clement would want to sleep forever too, anything but face reality. All up it was a shade under twenty minutes. Yes, he could have just asked her his questions over the phone but he wanted to check her reactions in the flesh. Graeme Earle sat beside him in the interview room. He had asked Bagot if she wanted a coffee or tea but she had declined. He had provided water and she sipped it now.

'You've been in touch with Jean-Claude's parents?' he asked. Though itching to move on, he did not want her to be defensive.

'Yes, thank you.' Her eyes were as dull and flat as her answer. He wondered if she had told them about Valentina Gomez.

'You mentioned to us before that when you first came to Broome you worked a couple of temporary jobs.'

'That's right.'

'Where were they?'

She looked like she was confused as to where this was headed but she played ball.

'For about a month I got a job at the Mimosa doing basic kitchen duties. The pay wasn't anything like I was used to with Rio so I looked for a mining job and got one at Halls Creek for about three months.'

'Lizard Minerals?'

'That's right.' He could see she was anxious to know why he was asking this.

'What were you doing there? Cooking?'

'Cooking and cleaning.'

'Jean-Claude didn't work there?'

'No.'

'Did he visit you there?'

'Yes, a couple of times. I was working fourteen days on and a week off. It was a pretty small operation. We got permission for him to stay overnight.'

Clement said, 'Was there blasting going on in the time you worked there?'

'Yes. What has this got to do with Jean-Claude's death?' She appeared to be genuinely lost, and Clement was relieved to see that.

Graeme Earle said, 'Somebody broke into the magazines and stole boosters. They also broke into the bulk storage shed and grabbed a bag of explosive mix. We think it might have been Jean-Claude.'

Her mouth moved in preparation for words but none were forthcoming.

'We're thinking that might be where he got his cash,' explained Clement. 'Selling those explosives.'

'To who?' she asked in a daze.

***

The trip south had proven uneventful but long, the 850 kilometres like convalescence, with strength being drawn from what lay ahead. Annika had fallen asleep after a couple of hours, which was sensible because the coming night would be taxing. Careful to attract no undue attention with his driving, the trip that he would normally make in around nine hours had wound up nearer ten. It was close now. For so long he had wanted to slay a dragon so large that it would inspire others to follow and – yes – carve his own name in stone. This is what Bin Laden had achieved with the twin towers and while that was well out of his league, and he did not share the man's ideology, the point remained that if you showed people a dragon could be slayed, it gave confidence to others that they could do the same, make their own mark. He did not wish to cause anybody's death. Hopefully that could be avoided but there was no guarantee, and as he had explained to the others, if you choose to suck on the teat of big industry, you can't complain when you wind up sick. Paul understood. He grasped that while he had not actively caused what had occurred in Brazil leading to the loss of his partner and unborn child, his very employment was a collusion with the powers of evil, and a tacit endorsement of their inhuman actions. Just like those fucking fly-in fly-outs on the mines. All they cared about was making a buck. They didn't give a stuff about anybody but themselves. The Frenchman's death did not worry Thomas in the slightest. He'd made noises about being green but there was no commitment. And in the end, he had revealed the fault in his weak personality. Unable to take the final step. And worse, trying to hold Thomas to ransom. There was no greater sin than disloyalty.

But now there was a link through him to them. It could have been so easy. They would have simply driven to the marina, joined the Frenchman on the boat and begun the long trip south to the target. And when it was over and the police were still trying to figure out what had happened, they would be long gone, back to the marina and vanished for the next strike. That target he'd already picked, the Queensland coal mine.

But Seydoux was a snake.

He had taken their money, bought himself a new motorcycle and then turned around and said 'no'. Thinking he could do that, change his mind midstream. 'I'm not going to do it. People could be killed.' Of course, people could be killed. Initially he had fudged that with the Frenchman because he needed him, but finally the rogue – for that's what he was, a rogue; wasn't that a French word? – had figured it out. Actually, he likely suspected all along and just wanted the money. Perhaps he had put blinkers on, allowed himself to believe what he wanted to believe. But then to turn around and order Thomas to 'pull the operation', to blow up something else instead, something harmless like the abattoir ... even now his blood boiled as he recalled that. Just who the fuck did the Frenchman think he was?

He had stayed calm, told the Frenchman that wasn't going to happen, that everything had been planned and was in readiness. If the Frenchman wanted to pull out, fine, just give him back the money. The Frenchman had refused. He could do that. He still had the bomb that he had built and the spare booster.

'What are you going to do? Go to the police?'

Cocky, the big tough commando, calling the shots. It wasn't that hard to lure him out to Meda, not with the arrogance of the man. He just had to pretend that he was cowed by the commando, that he was craven and had seen the error of his ways. Yes, he'd told the Frenchman, he'd thought it over, Jean-Claude was right, but he had another idea that would involve only the loss of some cattle at the worst. But he must bring the bombs, they had to have mutual trust. He knew the Frenchman would go for it. After all, he had been quite prepared to blow up the abattoir.

'What is it you are planning?' the stupid Frog had asked.

'It's easier to show you when we're there,' he had said.

And the fool had driven out there and shown them how the bomb worked with a simple timer, and how you could detonate the booster too with as little as a rock or hammer. The booster was a TNT charge and would be perfect for a localised smaller explosion like a car, say. He sat drinking wine with them. Wine laced with sedatives.

'I don't know if you need these,' he'd said, showing a small box of long spikes. 'They were in among the explosives. I didn't realise.'

An idea was already forming in Thomas' brain about those spikes and how to make use of them on the so-called Sun King. Once the arrogant fool had passed out, he went to work giving the traitor what he deserved.

But attaining justice for himself had created problems. Like having to avoid cameras. Without the Frenchman, there would have been no trail; with him, there was. Despite carrying jerry cans of petrol, they would have run out of petrol before Dampier had they not stopped at Sandfire for a refuel. He had paid cash. Left his sunglasses on, pulled down a worn xxxx cap, done his shirt up over a bunch of those little plastic inflated bags they used now for fragile parcels. Made himself look like a fat redneck. It passed without incident as he was pretty sure it would. The problem that bastard Seydoux created was not so much what was going to happen before they struck, as what would happen afterwards. The police would trawl through videos and they would find the Sahara trailing a boat, and look him up and maybe even connect him to Seydoux. They would have to be pretty thick not to put the pieces together. However, that would take time and time was this friend.

Thomas felt his excitement growing as Dampier drew closer. A few years back when the big energy companies had still been able to silence scientists and green politicians on the growing threat of global warming, Dampier had been booming. There were tankers coming to fill giant gas tanks, there were tugs and oil rigs and all the other ships and maritime business you needed to go with that kind of industry. The dockyard was glowing nine hours a day with rooster tails of welding sparks, there was banging and clanging and the whirr of forklifts. The world's stove was burning twenty-four seven and those big basins of gas out there under the ocean just off the coast were being sucked and funnelled and bottled to keep the flame going. But finally, there were enough floods and landslides and droughts and weather turning upside down that the arm-wrestle for public opinion started to go the other way. More greenies got elected, hippy tech-billionaires got a sizeable bite of the media, and they started running the old jokers out of town, the suits with head offices in Houston and Dubai, pert blondes with low-cut dresses who fronted nightly news with every story but melting icebergs and dwindling species, got bumped aside and in their place came dull experts with no dress sense but a heap of facts and figures. You had Al Gore making it sexy for Establishment people to have a moral conscience about the environment. The Woodstock generation convinced themselves they were young again and seized the chance to absolve themselves of a half-century of profligacy. Some even gave up flying. Carbon footprint became a word as real as Subway. And voila, next thing you know the prices at the petrol bowser have shrunk like a cheap t-shirt and the ships don't need to come here anywhere near so much because the Houston and Dubai people suddenly want less oil and gas out there, not more. Dampier goes back to being a little coastal town. The parasite FIFOs were now all back in their hometowns eating fat food and guzzling beer while savings from their overblown pay-packets lasted. Yes, it still has big industry all around it. They're still pumping gas that they already know about but it takes a lot less people to watch a pot on a stove than to find the ingredients for the meal. Dampier wasn't bust but it was no longer booming, thought Thomas as he cruised through.

It was just after five when he swung into the little yacht and boat club. Being a Monday was a good thing. Nobody firing up a barbecue or kayaking with kids.

'First thing we do,' he said to Annika who had been sitting up beside him the last hour listening to podcasts or something, 'is get the boat in. Then we get the car out of sight as quick as possible.'

24

Scott Risely was reeling like a batsman who had ducked a fraction late.

'A bomb?'

'Or bombs plural, that's what we think.' Earle had joined Clement in their boss' office. Clement continued. 'As a matter of course, we need to consider the abattoir but this could be bigger.'

'Like what?'

'They've got grievances against everything. Mining ... tourism.'

'Shit.' Risely's thoughts were transparent: people being blown apart at the Mimosa.

Risely said, 'Run me through it. How you think we got here, what's next.'

Though he was still forming the whole pattern in his own brain, Clement did his best.

'Seydoux was a French commando. He could handle and rig explosives. He comes into the orbit of Berryman and Styles. Maybe he's an activist or maybe he's just in it for the money but they pay him to make them some bombs.'

Earle took it up. 'Di Rivi and I were looking into theft of explosives at Lizard Minerals up in Halls Creek about four weeks ago.'

Clement said, 'Lauren Bagot had a job there early this year for a few months. Seydoux visited. He was familiar with the place.'

Risely shifted in his seat. 'You think she's involved?'

Clement said, 'We don't think so. Seydoux compartmentalised his life and kept this from her. I think she wants to help, find out who killed him.'

Risely flicked a finger. 'Go on.'

'Seydoux and the others have a falling out over something. Maybe money, maybe he got cold feet. They kill him and take the bombs.'

Risely stuck his elbow on his desk and massaged his forehead. He grasped the situation. 'They're in the wind and they're primed. We know if they have any other weapons?'

'Not that we know of. We have to assume they do.'

Risely concurred. 'If they killed Seydoux, they're serious.'

Clement said, 'They could rig the car full of explosives and drive it into their target. This station even.'

The terrifying abyss that had opened beneath Risely was growing wider by the second. The target or targets could be anywhere.

'We need to get eyes on all the main roads looking for them,' he said. 'I'm going to issue a media alert.'

Clement expected as much. It was too late now for the laying of careful traps. Prevention had to be the uppermost consideration.

Earle said, 'Mal Gross has contacted all agencies with a description and the rego. So far not a peep.'

'They could have ditched that vehicle by now,' said Risely. 'BHP, Rio. We need to let the miners know.'

Clement said, 'Mal contacted Pilbara directly and they are alerting all the mine sites. I've got di Rivi and Shepherd trying to find the couple's family and friends. Maybe they let something slip.' But Clement's hopes were flimsy.

Risely said he would alert the Federal Police. 'Maybe they have turned up on their radar. They have to know anyway. Shit, we better make sure the airport is locked away.'

Clement and Earle took their leave and found Shepherd waiting.

'I located Jennifer Davidson in New South Wales. You want me to call her?'

'Thanks but I'll handle that.'

Shepherd passed across a number to Clement.

'Tracked her through her driver's licence,' said Shepherd, who obviously wanted a pat.

'Good work,' said Clement, already dialling. Things were moving fast. Too fast. Berryman and Styles had a good lead on them. The call was answered.

'Jenny speaking.'

'Jennifer Davidson?'

'Yes,' came the voice, suspicious.

Clement introduced himself. 'I need to speak to you about Thomas Berryman.'

'Is he alright?'

'We urgently need to speak to him in relation to some very serious matters. May I ask your relation to him?'

'I'm his aunt. I'm married to his mum's brother. What's going on?'

Clement wished he had a full and complete answer to that.

***

Paul had resisted the impulse to call Ingrid. For now, it was better that she was an island on an island, cut off from this. He had retrieved his car from the carpark where he had left it and was relieved it had started straight off. Some of the other workers disconnected the battery and he supposed he should probably do that too but then the last year or so he'd really not had much energy for anything. The trip north to Dampier had passed like a day when you were sick in bed as a child. Life seemed to be happening outside but you were in your own cocoon. All you noticed was sunny rays turning to lengthening shadows. He'd never been that much into music. He'd always just gone to see whatever bands his friends wanted and bought the same CDs as them to fit in: Foo Fighters, Kings of Leon. Gabrielly had loved Madonna. She liked Katy Perry too, Lady Gaga, a few others, but for some reason it was Madonna that she loved to sing along with and dance to, swaying her hips suggestively at him, hands in the air as if they held castanets. In his unit on the island, he didn't bother with CDs. Like everybody else, if he wanted music, he just streamed it or listened to the radio, although in truth he'd gone back to a life without music. The flood had leached all the joy from his life. It had only been the last few days he'd found familiar melodies swimming through his head once more. Ingrid, he supposed. In his car, an old Corolla he'd bought cheap in Onslow, he still had a stash of worn CDs that he had brought back to Australia from Brazil. Driving towards Dampier, he had listened to Madonna and imagined Gabrielly beside him laughing and singing, and in the back a small child, a girl, with black thick hair like her mother, smiling as Gabrielly sang 'Papa Don't Preach', playfully poking him in his shoulder with her finger. He had a pang of deep sadness bordering on panic, as it occurred to him these fancies might vanish as any relationship with Ingrid flourished. He didn't want to lose them. Guilt swam through his veins. 'You don't get nothing unless you give up something,' Gabrielly used to always say.

Yes. But I don't want to give up you.

When he pulled up outside the house, evening had arrived soothing as the tone of a French horn. He removed his sunglasses, the glare reduced now to a single biscuit left on a tray out of politeness. Even though he had been the one to rent it, he'd only been to the house once before, but he remembered its plainness, the salmon brick, the smell of near ocean. He would like to have been here a couple of generations earlier when he imagined there might have been just a few beach shacks, red earth and the green-blue water. There was no vehicle at the house. He hoped they might have been delayed, that he could say he assumed that they had got cold feet, come to their senses, that he had waited and then, realising it was hopeless anyway, had left. He got out and stretched his legs. There was nobody visible on the short street although he fancied that he heard children's voices floating out from a backyard somewhere.

It was what, three months back, that Thomas had told him that he must give them some proof of his commitment by renting the house.

'You won't live in it. You will come only by invitation. Understood?'

He had said he understood and then dutifully found the place online. His story made sense. He was FIFO on the island. He paid a month in advance. He had handed them the keys in Broome. Three months. An eternity and an eyeblink.

When he saw the car swing into the carport his heart sank.

Thomas and Annika climbed out. Thomas offering a short wave, Annika going straight to the house and opening it up, Thomas grabbing a plastic car cover from the garage.

'Give us a hand,' he said. Paul dutifully went over and helped pull the cover over the car.

'Won't you need it?' Paul asked.

'We'll walk back to the sailing club. The boat's waiting.'

Thomas said it with the sort of quiet discretion that people remove fishbones from their mouth.

'Inside,' directed Thomas and Paul led the way. Paul was disappointed that Thomas shut the door after them.

The house was stifling, and had that smell houses get when the pipes have not been running and the windows shut, a hint of stagnant water. Annika was sliding windows open. Eventually the breeze would make a difference but not yet. Thomas switched on an ancient air-conditioner and plugged in the fridge.

'We'll wait a couple of hours before setting out,' said Thomas and pulled up a chair at the kitchen table.

Paul followed suit.

'You have the passes?' Thomas asked him.

Thomas had told him to get three identity passes and had supplied photos. It was probably unnecessary, really. The chances of a security person actually seeing them and stopping them was low. The more important part of the pass was the barcode that needed to be scanned to open the gates that gave access to the heart of the train. Although now he had no intention of handing them over, whatever Thomas said. He had only brought the passes with him because he wanted them to know he had been genuine.

'Where's the other guy?' he asked. He noticed a look between Annika and Thomas and wondered what that meant.

'He stayed with the boat,' said Thomas, not looking him in the eye.

Paul did not know the other man's name. He had made up aliases to go with the photos and then once the passes had been printed, he had deleted all records. Back a couple of weeks ago, he'd had no intention of trying to get away with anything. This was going to be his chance to go public and speak about why this had happened, the callous indifference of big companies. It had never unduly worried him before that the company against whom the attack was to be carried out was not the same company whose greed had killed Gabrielly. Now, however, it did. He wriggled uncomfortably and wished there was something cold to drink. As if reading his mind, Annika placed a plastic shopping bag on the table and pulled out three cold cans of lemonade.

'So hot in here,' she said placing one of the cans in front of Paul.

'Got them from the machine at the sailing club,' said Thomas popping his can. Paul saw there were half a dozen chocolate bars in the bag.

'Something for our trip,' laughed Thomas and held up his can for a toast.

Paul half-heartedly responded. He had to tell him. He'd just get a little lemonade into himself first.

***

'They have to be somewhere,' said Earle. Their optimism had been slowly evaporating.

Mal Gross said, 'We've got eyes on every major road but they could be off the beaten track.'

Clement, Earle and Gross had joined Risely in his office. Despite the air-conditioning, Clement could smell sweat.

'That's probably a good thing if they are hiding out,' said Risely, nervously shredding tiny pieces of paper with his fingers. 'The longer they take, the more chance we'll nail them before this goes south.'

Risely had ordered light planes and helicopters into the air but all they had come up with was a couple of false leads. And now it was dark and there would be no more air surveillance till dawn.

'If they left right after they ditched the motorcycle, they could be in Darwin or Adelaide or beyond,' said Clement. 'On the other hand, if they want to inflict damage locally, it makes sense they'd wait until dark.'

'Thanks for that cheery thought,' said Risely. 'The Federal Police are scrambling. Apparently these guys were not even a blip on ASIO's radar.'

'The aunt couldn't help?' Mal Gross had not been present when Clement had briefed Risely about his conversation with Jennifer Davidson.

'Not as to their current whereabouts. She last spoke to Thomas more than a year ago. She hasn't seen him for four years by her reckoning.'

Clement gave a shorthand description of the conversation he'd had with the aunt. It had been revelatory but not encouraging. 'She said he had been angry more than half his life.'

'Now he's found something to target his anger on,' said Risely.

But what exactly? wondered Clement. He couldn't help feeling that he was missing something.

Earle said, 'We got even less from Annika Styles' mother: "Don't know, don't care." Styles left home seven years ago and has pretty much never been in touch. No dear grandmother, no best friend.'

'They probably exist,' added Clement, 'but by the time we turn them up it might not matter.'

'Facebook? Photos? Phone?' Mal Gross knew they would have canvassed all these but asked anyway.

Clement told him what they had gleaned: nothing.

'They've been planning this for a long time. Perth is chasing up every phone number. They'll let us know if they hit paydirt. Manners is trawling their social media. Berryman doesn't have a bank account at all that we can find. Styles' account has been dormant for three months. They're either living on cash or they have some account under a false name, or both.'

There was a rapid and loud knock on the door. Gross who was standing closest caught the nod from Risely and pulled it open to reveal Jo di Rivi. She seemed bursting to tell them something. Please don't let it be a bomb, prayed Clement.

'Just had a call from the Mimosa security head. A man and woman in their twenties in the carpark acting suspiciously. They haven't approached them yet.'

'Go,' ordered Risely.

**

Paul rolled the light aluminium on his fingertips. No more stalling.

'We can't do it,' he said.

Thomas had his head back and mouth open relishing the last drops of the sweet soda. Now it swung towards him like a gun turret. For a moment the only sound was the mechanical grunting of the barely functioning air-conditioner. Static crackled, the sound of the can being crushed in Thomas' hand.

'What?'

Paul felt himself swallow. 'We can't go through with it. It's a mistake.'

Frida, he was sure that wasn't her real name but it was what he knew her as, had been out of Paul's vision but now she appeared and moved to stand behind Thomas' shoulder.

'You can't back out,' she said. 'Not now.'

Paul took a deep breath. He knew it would be hard for them. He understood.

'We can't be sure nobody will be hurt.'

'We always knew that,' said Thomas slowly, probing with his gaze.

Paul could feel anxiety rising like a tide. 'We don't know what the explosions might do. They might set off other explosions. Gas, fuel.'

'So? Firefighters and security are like soldiers. They get paid because there is a risk.'

'Look,' said Paul. 'Nobody understands more than me, what you have lost. But you have each other. You can still protest. Still fight against the greed of the multinationals. But this isn't even the company that cost me Gabrielly.'

'They are all cousins with the same pedigree,' said Thomas.

'But they are not. These people are innocent.'

'Where is this coming from?' asked Thomas, still poking like a cold surgical instrument.

Paul ignored him. The three security passes he had printed were hanging on lanyards around his neck. He pulled them out from his shirt and brandished them.

'Look. I did like we discussed. I got the passes. I was ready. But I met someone. At work. And I realised that what we are doing is wrong.'

'You "met someone".' Thomas smashed a sneer as if it were avocado. Paul felt colour rising. Be calm, Paul told himself as Thomas turned to the girl and repeated, 'He met someone.' Throwing his hands up in a theatrical gesture.

'Yes,' said Paul, resolute. 'It showed me. There is hope.'

'And she's on the island?'

'Yes.'

'Why not just send her off?'

'It's not that –' no, he didn't want to become mired in what was irrelevant. 'We shouldn't do it. We won't do it. It was wrong from the beginning but I didn't see that. Gabrielly wouldn't want me to do this. And I know you lost your mother but I'm sure she wouldn't –'

Thomas stood from his chair with a frightening suddenness. 'Don't you tell me what she would or wouldn't want. We agreed on a course of action. You gave your commitment.'

'Yes, but I was wrong. We're allowing our personal grief to create more grief. I don't want that on my conscience. You don't want that on yours.'

Paul swung towards the girl looking for her support but she was like a new sheet of A4.

Thomas moved around towards Paul. Paul was forced to stand in order to not have Thomas looming over him.

'So, you have reconsidered for all of us?'

'It's the right thing.'

'Perhaps,' said Thomas reaching over and fingering the lanyards, 'it is. Perhaps it was inevitable.'

Relief flickered over Paul like a welcome breeze. Or maybe it was the air-conditioning finally kicking in.

'We can still protest. We can still expose hypocrisy.' He wanted to reassure Thomas that what they had shared had not been false, nor in vain.

Thomas put his hand on his shoulder. 'We can. Maybe not you, but we can.'

It felt like a punch to his side near his ribs. He was so stunned he did not move though he knew as he looked down and saw the knife in Thomas' hand that he had been stabbed.

'No!' he tried to shout and felt another punch near his kidney.

Blood was leaking out of him. Whether it was the shock or actual blood loss, he didn't know, but he felt strength going from his legs and he gripped the chair for support.

'You don't decide for me,' Thomas hissed at him and he felt the lanyards being lifted over his head.

He clutched the back of the chair with increasing desperation. It was as if the hands of devils were pulling him down. Thomas leaned down towards him.

'Gabrielly would be ashamed of you,' he said.

Something hard slammed into Paul's head. The resistance went out of him. He felt himself crumple onto the lino, a limp piece of lettuce fallen from a plate. It was growing quickly darker around him.

'It's not true,' he tried to say but wasn't sure if he actually spoke. Gabrielly was not ashamed of him. She wasn't …

25

A young man and woman siphoning petrol, that's what the Mimosa alert turned out to be, a complete waste of time. Shepherd, Earle and Clement had tooled up with firearms and vests. The assault team had been readied. The two miscreants weren't much more than kids, frightened as bunnies when the lights hit them. Clement and the others had made it back to the station for the loss of ninety precious minutes. Although, thought Clement, whether they were precious was moot, for in the last two-and-a-bit hours they'd uncovered nothing new.

It was going on for 10.00 p.m., close to sixteen hours since Earle's pancakes. They'd discovered much yet accomplished nothing. He'd already sent the others home. Risely had gone an hour back with an order that Clement should follow suit and get some sleep. Everything was really out of their hands. Other people were watching computers and social media and phones and highways and byways. Clement's phone would ring as soon as something was turned up and only then would he be needed. And quite possibly not even then.

'Perhaps we should call it a night,' suggested Earle.

'You're right,' he said.

His legs were stiff. He looked at the whiteboard in the big room and saw all their wild theories written up there. Not even erased yet because there had been no time. All those hours pushing ideas through tired, dark brains trying to feel the slightest tickle of a clue: the two women in it together, wildlife smuggling, Seydoux diving for drugs.

Clement checked he had his phone and wallet. He'd not spoken to Phoebe for days. He needed to give Bill Seratono a call, gently prod him about a boat. He was at the threshold to the back corridor that led to the carpark, Earle politely waiting for him, when he felt that sharp prick you can get when you're groping around and almost accidentally stab yourself with an idea you knew was out there somewhere.

'What?' said Earle recognising in his partner a change.

'It might be nothing.'

Clement found himself drawn back towards the whiteboard. Somebody, Jo di Rivi probably, somebody with neat small writing had listed dot points under the heading Sun King Phone. Clement pointed at the almost invisible, until now forgotten entry.

It read *boat hire*.

'Seydoux was in touch with ...' he looked for the name on the other part of the board, found it, '... Coleman from Deep Adventures about hiring a boat for him to take some divers out.'

'You called him, didn't you?' said Earle, curiosity pulling him closer too.

'Yes. He said Seydoux occasionally made some money with a hire but I didn't ask him about this one.'

'You're thinking Berryman and Styles might have organised a boat?'

Clement was already dialling Coleman's number. 'It's smart. They can disappear anywhere up here ...' Clement's finger traced over the huge expanse of coastline, oceans and tiny islands, '... and all the time we're out blocking roads and looking for them on land.' That was the thing about the Kimberley, thought Clement. Only a few roads for thousands of k's, easy to be hemmed in, but on the water, the escape routes were endless.

Coleman's phone rang and then almost immediately a message kicked in. '*Hi, I'm out on a charter right now and might be out of range but you can try our office ...*' he ran through the number too fast, as people familiar with their own number are wont to do. '*Leave a message and I'll be in touch as soon as I can.*'

***

Ingrid was holding his hand and pulling him towards the water, urging him but he just wanted to lie there on the sand. He didn't want to move. The water would be cold. He was already cold but she was laughing and urging him.

'Paul, come on. Paul, please. For me.'

It was as he went to lift himself from the beach and suddenly found he had no strength, and that his muscles had melted into the surrounding sand, that he woke.

It was dark and he was very, very thirsty. His first thought was that he was on a floor surrounded by spilled Coca Cola. That's when he remembered. Surprisingly knowing it was his blood didn't reduce him to a million pieces. Instead, reason kicked in. He wasn't dead yet. He had to stop them. Ingrid was in terrible danger. He felt for his phone but it was gone. They must have taken it.

He'd been lying over his left arm and it had very little feeling. He tried to haul himself using the kitchen chair but he hadn't the strength. He oriented himself, discerned the outline of the front door. He part crawled, part slithered towards it. After each couple of advances he was forced to stop to regain his breath. He was so thirsty. Now he was at the foot of the door. He reached up and turned the doorknob. Locked.

He wanted to shut his eyes and sleep. Pain shunted through his body like carnival bumper-cars. The back door, would it be locked? Probably. But he remembered something from his conversation with the realtor when he hired the place. She'd said, 'You might want to get a new clip on the bedroom window. It doesn't really work.'

He'd forgotten all about that until now. He hadn't remembered to tell Thomas. He began to haul himself towards the bedroom.

'I must have leaked a lot of blood,' he thought. He supposed that the exertion would make it spill faster, tearing open any clotting. It had to be done. His left arm was still useless so he would stretch out his right arm and then pull while pushing with his feet. An image came to him of one of the statues in Gabrielly's mother's house, Jesus with his palms pointing out and blood flowing from them. He did not think of himself as Jesus but he did whisper to Gabrielly: 'Help me.'

And somehow, he made it to the foot of the worn bed with the sagging mattress in the stale-air room. He was feeling light-headed but he dared not stop. He seized the bedpost closest to the wall and hauled himself up. The curtain was rough and stiff and smelled like it had been stored in an attic. He stuck his head under and reached for the clasp on the sliding aluminium window. Broken it might be but it still had some grip. He squeezed and it gave. He slid open the window and felt moving air. Flywire. Damn. He didn't have the energy to return for a knife. He pushed his head into the flywire but he was too weak to break it. He hauled his whole body onto the bed and pushed. This time his weight was enough.

It wrapped around his face like a veil and he pitched forward, out of the open window, his stomach across the sill, his knees and legs still on the bed inside. He put his hands down and his fingers touched the gravel side of the house. He thrust forward and felt himself tumbling.

The slight breeze with an ocean tang revived him momentarily and he made a few metres crawling quite quickly to the front of the house but then the effort told and he felt faint and dizzy, only worse than before. He took a long moment to get his breath and pushed again. Then again.

He could barely lift his head now and there was a dull humming in his ears. He thought he heard Gabrielly's voice above the hum and he rolled on his back and looked up and she was looking down on him, the light in her eyes a zillion stars. Sometimes he and Gabrielly would sit out in front of her little house and look up at these same stars. How many million people had they seen die in their lifetime he wondered? He had been a lucky man to have found Gabrielly and Ingrid. But Ingrid was in danger. Because of him. He rolled back onto his stomach and dragged himself forward. The humming was really loud now and everything was even blacker. He tried with all his might to go forward but he was immobile. He did not think there was enough liquid in his body to cry but he did. He thought he lifted his chin but he couldn't be sure. Dark swirled, the buzz in his ears grew louder and a last jolt of panic shot through him.

He was about to die. His last conscious thought was that this was his last conscious thought.

26

The hire boat could do eighty k per hour but there was no need to open it up and attract undue attention. Thomas pointed it generally west, angling to the south towards the island. The night was a low fever but as the boat surged through the dark it produced a palliative breeze. Paul had assured him that at night they would be able to bring the boat in close to shore without being challenged. If they were challenged, they would have to anchor further out and swim in. His biggest worry was the explosives getting wet but Seydoux had assured him the bomb was waterproofed, the explosive in plastic rammed into a PVC tube, closed at both ends apart from the line to the booster. There were places you could take the boat right up onto the beach but it being night and Thomas never having been here before, he would play safe, get within fifty metres of the shore, and swim the rest of the way.

It had not been his original choice to despatch Paul but he had to admit that it actually worked out well for them. Paul was the weak link, and while he had believed Paul was to be trusted and would never have given them up, it had turned out quite clearly that he had been wrong. Still, Paul had suffered and, unlike Seydoux, was more cowardly than treacherous. Even had there been time, Thomas would not have crucified him. His pulse was gone when they cleared out. By the time the police eventually linked them, they would be well out of the area.

It had been foolish of Paul to lose his burning demand for retribution because he had met some woman. Most women will betray you. He stared through the plexiglass at Annika sitting cross-legged on the foredeck. She was different, one in a million.

An image of his mother began to pry open a box of memories. He tried to push her out but she defiantly kept her toe in there. He shook his head to clear her. It wasn't long now and he'd be able to burn the hurtful memories on a giant pyre. The lights of the island showed as small white globs on the horizon.

Soon.

***

Of all the dumb things I've done, thought Clement, this is possibly the dumbest. Aloft in this dark sky, a metallic reverberation travelling up his backside and through his body the only thing to connect him to the real world, while his thoughts galloped unfettered. They had travelled over a vast continent of memories and emotions, from Phoebe and fatherhood to his unfortunate experimentation with being a sex-machine. They had trawled through the ashes of the case, the false leads, his own shortcomings. The whole two-and-a-half hours he'd been in the air, they were being funnelled to the same end point: Was this a wild-goose chase? Would Risely crucify him if it turned out to be so, and probably more likely, would somebody crucify Risely if he didn't?

The word 'crucify' pinched him.

That was where this case had started after all. He couldn't see Earle in the seat behind without twisting and he wondered if he might be similarly troubled on Clement's behalf. Clement being the senior man had taken the seat next to Cindy, their pilot, and, being the senior man, he would also be the one where the buck stopped. Yes, he could have called Risely, woken him and laid his cards on the table.

'Listen, I have this hunch about what Berryman and Styles might be up to.'

The trouble was his cards were all twos and threes. Risely would have said, 'Well what do you have exactly?'

And he would have tried to talk up his case. Somebody had booked a private boat-hire with Seydoux. This, through his own fault, had until this evening been overlooked. It seemed inconsequential. Until you started to ask yourself, well who did book that boat? And why would they have gone through with it?

At which point Risely would, quite correctly, have asked what he'd been able to find out from the people who hired the boat. This is where it got sticky. Mark Coleman was currently incommunicado somewhere at sea. There was no reception on his phone at the moment and until he radioed in no means of immediately contacting him. And time might be of the essence.

Clement would explain how he had tried the Deep Adventures after-hours number and got the office manager, Safavi, who knew hardly anything about the hire because it wasn't an official hire. But she did know that the hire had gone ahead. Coleman had headed into the marina early this morning with twin outboards and a trailer for Seydoux's client. But that was all she knew, no names, no numbers and no gender. The client's driver's licence and a copy of the deposit would likely be with Coleman on his phone. He would have snapped those but had probably not yet had time to upload because he went almost straight out on the charter. The contract might be somewhere at work but it could take time to dig up. Time Clement felt they might not have. He had asked Safavi to please get into work and try to find that contract and send an electronic copy to him as soon as possible.

Nothing yet. And he knew what Risely would say, would be obliged to point out, that it may simply be a normal hire.

Of course, it might not be Berryman and Styles. But to ignore that possibility was to Clement negligent, for the boat might be less about escape and more about completing a plan of action. He would have said to Risely exactly what he'd said to himself.

'Think about it. Maybe the target isn't on land. Maybe that's why Seydoux was so appealing, because what they wanted to blow up had to be approached by sea. What if they wanted to make an almighty political statement? What target would serve that purpose best?'

And there he had come up with one obvious answer: a gas train. If that was the target, you would strike at night and from the water. He felt a tap on his arm and saw Cindy pointing to a yellow-white halo in the darkness below. The island.

***

He motored in slowly now as quietly as possible. They had approached from the opposite end of the island to the long jetty where ships berthed and filled up with their LNG cargo. Paul had told them there were no tankers scheduled for this evening and that would mean less activity in general. It was also only a thin moon so they were close to invisible as the bright mushrooms of light where the main plant was located did not reach this far. It was a little after midnight now and close to high tide. While it meant they had to swim a short distance to shore, it was preferable to arriving at low tide when they would be stranded further away. The slow bass chug of machinery reached out from the island and brushed his ears but he heard no voices or rushing vehicles. They would be able to walk unhindered towards the plant's outer fence, cut through that and advance to the gates of the inner fence for which, thanks to Paul, they had passes that would enable them to stroll in through the gate. Then it was a matter of planting the bomb, setting the timer and retracing their steps. If all went smoothly, he would also set the booster to detonate but if there were any problems, he would keep that in reserve. He cut the engine and dropped a light anchor. Then he fetched the small plastic raft from the cabin where it was already inflated. His eyes met Annika's and he was taken by surprise when she swept into his chest and raised her mouth for a kiss. He detested such dramatic gestures but he went along with it.

The shore was no more than about thirty metres from them and though extremely venomous jellyfish could be found in these waters from November on, he considered the risk low given the short time they would be in the water. Even had the water not been so warm as it was, he would have avoided using a wetsuit because the sooner they were in land gear, the better. He had debated whether to leave Annika with the boat, the original plan, with Seydoux and him going ashore. In the end he thought it was better that she joined him. They stripped down to their bather bottoms, both of them electing to go bare-chested. After carefully loading the backpacks containing the explosives into the raft, they added plastic bags with 'work' clothes, boots, tools and torches. Then they slipped on fins. He sat on the edge of the boat and dropped in first, like a teabag in the tepid water, he thought to himself. She carefully handed down the little raft with the backpacks, the bombs inside. The water was calm with very little movement. She followed his lead and they began quickly kicking towards the rocky shore. They were there in no time. He felt his fins dragging over rocks and went horizontal, pushing the raft ahead. Using the fins as protection he clambered the last couple of rocky metres to land. Annika followed. They slipped off their fins and opened the plastic bags, dried themselves with a small towel then pulled on dark blue drill pants and orange safety jackets with silver flashing. After putting on socks and boots, they clipped their passes to their hips. He made a neat pile of the fins and bags and slipped on the first backpack. It wasn't heavy at all. He helped Annika with hers.

'Like going for a hike,' she whispered and it was the first either of them had spoken for minutes. From the plastic bag he retrieved wire-cutters, a torch and a lethal-looking knife which he slipped into a scabbard on his belt, hidden by the large jacket. Seydoux had warned him against trying to acquire guns.

'If we need guns, we haven't done it right,' he said. 'And the police are always onto that sort of thing. Where are you going to get a secret gun from? Bikies? You can't trust them. And the police could be monitoring them. All you need is a diver's knife, just in case something unexpected crops up.'

They made ground easily, heading two o'clock in direction. It was about one hundred metres of low rock, tufty scrub and sand before the outer fence. The only cover came from a few giant termite mounds. Thanks to the narrow moon they were in darkness for more than half of this journey, however as they drew closer to the perimeter fence, talons of strong artificial light stretched towards them. According to Paul, this outside fence was not alarmed or electrified although there were intermittent cameras, not in this little quadrant though. As he reached for his wire-cutters, he remembered what the Frenchman had said.

'Get the best make you can. It's a lot harder to cut through wire than you think, especially if it is fairly new. This stuff you see on TV where they snip away like with paper is bullshit. Make sure you practise.'

And he had taken the Frenchman at his word and practised regularly, strengthening the muscles in his hand. Of course, they could have taken the risk and gone in through the gate using their passes but if anybody saw them, two workers coming in from outside the perimeter fence might arouse unwanted curiosity.

'What's up?' 'Is there a problem?' He could imagine the conversations and then he would need convincing answers.

No, this was better. As he started cutting the first strands of thick wire, he heard a droning hum above the bedrock noise of the plant. It took him a moment to place it but then he realised what it was, the engines of a light plane. From the sound of it, it was drawing closer.

***

Because they had left with such haste, there had not been time to forewarn the island of their take-off, and they had been well into their flight before pilot Cindy had been able to raise the island's command centre to prepare them for the landing. She assured Clement and Earle she could manage regardless.

'There is so much light from the plant I might as well be flying into Perth,' she laughed. 'But best to make sure there's no grader sitting on the strip when we land.'

Clement had her alert the island command centre that two detectives were on their way in and Clement identified himself and explained that while they should not be alarmed, the security staff should be well and truly on the alert if they weren't already. It was just as well that Clement did this, for the notification they should have received already had fallen between the cracks. Perhaps whoever had been told to alert mining companies about the bomb threats had taken that literally and neglected other resource companies.

Regardless, it was the first they'd heard of it.

The small plane dove through the black curtain towards the artificial light, descending into the giant metal maw: all around them were ladders, tubes, pipes, cylinders, fences, platforms. They touched down on the strip, bounced for a few hops and then coasted to a halt.

***

The strip between the fences was around seventy metres wide, mainly low scrub with a rim of gravel bordering the outer fence through which they had just crossed. They were in full light now and heading like they belonged towards the gate that Paul had assured them would take them to the inner sanctum. Thomas was feeling confident. Surely had the security people suspected anything they would have been patrolling the waters. But when he was only about twenty metres from the gate, he heard shouting. On the plant side of the fence, men sprinted from a donga and headed to a brace of four-wheel drives parked out front. As they powered up, a golf cart containing two men came speeding along on the strip between the two fences where Thomas and Annika were currently trapped. It was about thirty metres back, gaining quickly. These men did not wear the bright jackets that matched their own and those on a few other workers in the inner area that Thomas could see. Those in the cart and the ones who had sprinted from the donga wore navy-blue overalls: security. Annika swung towards him, her eyes wide with panic. His own heart was thumping. He swung the backpack off his shoulder and slid open the zip. His fingers could flick the detonator timer on from there. The golf cart was hugging the narrow gravel strip near the outer fence, the passenger shining a torch at the wire. It had already passed the point where he and Annika had entered. From the looks of it, it might not have spied the damage. He didn't think they'd been seen yet. His brain was spinning. Stand? Run? Detonate? The light plane – had that brought news? Had Paul been found? They stood stock-still as the cart passed them. Then it swung around and came back towards them. He debated, the knife or the bomb? There were two of them, they would overpower him if it was just the knife. The fingers of his right hand were inside the bag now, touching the timer.

The cart's lights hit them in the face. They had come so close. Defeat tasted bitter at the back of his throat.

'We've got a report of a potential security threat,' said the broad Australian voice from behind the light. 'You haven't seen anything?'

He was shaking his head before he'd thought about it. 'Nah. What sort of threat?'

He saw the man's eyes flick over their security passes, satisfied.

'Not sure. Disgruntled greenies, I think. Keep a lookout.'

Then the cart looped back and continued in the direction it had been heading. But now he could see the four-wheel drive was leaving the inner compound via a boom gate.

So, somehow or other they had discovered something was up.

It had to be Paul. Somebody must have found his body in the house.

'What do we do?' Annika pressed into him.

He didn't answer. It was obvious what they had to do: set the bombs and get the fuck out of there. The guts of the whole plant were just the other side of the fence, ten metres in. Once they slid into the metal maze, they would look like any maintenance worker. Thirty more metres in and a bit to the right was where Paul had said the explosion would do the most damage. He jogged to the gate and scanned his pass. There was no click. He pushed hard against the gate but it did not shift.

'Fuck!'

The buzz of the plant machinery was like a pump to his bloodstream. He could see more blue security uniforms about two hundred metres inside. He tried the pass again. The gate remained steadfast.

'Try yours,' he almost yelled it, conscious now how exposed they were.

Annika scanned but got the same result.

'We need to go.' She was fretting.

Maybe they had changed the security code already? Or more likely, he thought, his anger rising, that fucktard Paul had not given them a working pass in the first place. Protecting his fucking fucktard girlfriend.

Fuck.

He reached back into the backpack. The pipe bomb and its booster filled it completely. The timer could be set to a maximum of forty minutes. But that was too long. They'd find it before then. The Frenchman had said the bomb would be very powerful. Thomas set the bomb to ten minutes, stepped back and, seizing the backpack by its strap, hurled it up and over the ten-foot fence. Even though he'd been told it would explode only via the timer, he flinched as it landed with a soft thud on the other side among the outermost pipes and machinery.

'Come on,' he shouted and began running back to where their entry point had been.

He could hear the noise of a larger vehicle, probably a four-wheel drive coming from the opposite direction to which the cart had travelled. Welcoming shadows that marked the external fence were drawing closer with every stride but so was the vehicle.

Darkness. Annika just behind him. His boots pounded through the rocky scrub. He wasn't sure he would find their exit point.

'There!' Annika pointed and ran and tumbled over. He reached the fence as she righted herself and held up the wire.

'Quick!'

Annika slid through on her elbows, her backpack with the booster bomb intact snaring the wire.

'Here.'

He yanked the pack off and she scrambled through. He pushed the backpack through ahead of himself. On the outer side now he got to his feet and charged into black, stripping off the jacket as he ran. He heard the sound of the vehicle slowing, sensed a strong light. He grabbed Annika and pulled her to the ground behind a termite mound. There was the sound of a car door opening and a radio, but the security people were staying at the fence, which likely meant they hadn't seen them yet. He put his finger to his lips, stripped Annika's jacket from her, slung the backpack over his own shoulders and started in a hunched run in the direction of the boat.

***

It should have surprised Clement but it hadn't that there were only ten security staff on the island. Six of those had been sleeping when Clement had first made contact from the plane. Australians had a notorious 'She'll be right' attitude to life. Largely inured from war and famine, the nation had referred to itself as The Lucky Country with good reason. Though the world had long been global, the Australian psyche was still back in the days of biplanes.

'There's really only nine of us who actually patrol or supervise,' explained Gus Nordling, the head security officer. If size was a hallmark for security excellence, then Nordling had it in spades. Broader than a North Queensland accent, he stood at least 195 centimetres. Nordling had revealed he was ex-army.

'We have a two-man patrol nightly. They use a cart, get out, walk around. Another two personnel are on call in the security station. We're a mix of ex-coppers and service.'

They were in a cart heading onto the long pier where the ships docked to have giant tanks pumped full of LNG. Clement had taken advantage of guaranteed phone reception to wake Risely and explain the situation. On the whole, his boss had taken it well.

'You knew if you called me before, I would be in an awkward position and might tell you not to go till we had more to work on,' he'd said. Before Clement could spin any bullshit, Risely had said, 'Don't bother answering. I trust your judgement and there's no police presence on the island any more so it's a smart move. I'll get onto Dampier in the morning and get a couple of bodies over there. Wake me again if you need.'

Nordling's big body bounced as the cart hit ruts.

'We've got two boats we use for patrol. One of my people has gone ahead to ready them. If we had a ship in, we'd have a couple of people down at the dock.'

He swung off to where two motorboats, each with twin outboards, were moored at a lower pontoon.

Clement and Earle were just heaving themselves off the cart when an enormous bang punched through the air. Clement spun to see a huge bell of dust rolling upwards through the artificial lights back at the plant.

27

After an instant of shock, Nordling was on his radio. Clement and Earle stood watching the dust drift. Despite the harsh metallic bark from the radio, they could make out the response from whoever Nordling was in communication with.

'This is Delta. Large explosion.' Delta then shouted across to somebody else unseen, 'Is there fire?' Then back to Nordling. 'Doesn't seem to be fire yet but I can see stuff-all. It's thick with dust. Casualties unknown.'

'On my way,' snapped Nordling. Earle and Clement were about to climb back into the cart when they heard the unmistakable hum of powering outboards off the coast. They couldn't see the boat in the dark but they could hear it until an alarm cut through, drowning everything else. As Nordling jumped behind the wheel of the cart Clement made a snap decision. He pointed out to sea.

'We'll go after that.'

Nordling nodded. 'Edwards will take you.'

Edwards turned out to be a woman about forty, her blonde hair tucked under her cap. She was standing on the pontoon, the powerboat, about thirty-feet long Clement guessed, at her back.

'Fire her up,' Earle bellowed to Edwards. 'I got this.' He raced for the mooring ropes, slipped them off their bollards and tossed them into the boat.

'We need to catch that boat.' Clement charged across the small gangway behind Edwards, fumbling for his phone. The big engines roared to life, the vibration driving up through the soles of his feet. He sensed Earle arriving in a blur, then dragging the gangway on board.

'Clear,' yelled Earle and then the boat was moving fast through the black.

As the island receded and with it the alarm, Clement got through to Risely who answered immediately.

'There's been an explosion on the island. We don't know the extent but it was a helluva bang. We're on the water in a boat. Hopefully on their tail.'

Risely snapped a good luck and rang off, further talk superfluous.

The noise of their own engines was so loud it masked any from the other boat. Edwards snapped on a searchlight that illuminated more than fifty metres ahead. Earle swung it in an arc but there was no sign of their quarry.

'How are we going to find them?' Clement asked. Earle gestured to Edwards who was steady at the wheel.

'We're catching a bit of wake. She knows what she's doing.'

Showing no indication that she had heard, Edwards continued to make adjustments to her course.

Clement was growing alarmed. They appeared to him to be heading further and further away from the island and in the opposite direction to the coast. He said as much to Earle. Unfortunately, there was no chance to whisper. Edwards turned and without expression said, 'Given this course, I'm pretty sure they're heading to the Montebello Islands.'

All Clement knew about these islands was that the British had tested nuclear bombs there and a bunch of Australian servicemen reckoned they had got cancer from it and were still waiting sixty years on for some recognition.

'How far away?' he asked.

Earle, who Clement guessed had probably fished here more than a few times, said, 'At this rate, about another half an hour. But there are lots of coves, right?'

Edwards nodded. 'There are quite a few little islands and plenty of spots in there.'

'How many islands?'

'Try fifty if you count the tiny ones. More than a dozen you'd call small,' said Edwards. 'Two major ones. But mostly it's as bald as a billiard ball on them. There's nowhere to hide long-term.'

Edwards' radio crackled and she answered quickly. Clement tried to catch what was being said at the other end but it was too hard. Edwards listened without interrupting. The boat thumped over the swell. Eventually he heard her say, 'Yes, I will pass it on.'

She ended the exchange and yelled over to Clement, 'No known casualties to this stage and no fire. The bomb detonated just inside the inner perimeter. The boss says it has caused a fair bit of damage and there's a crater but it hasn't ruptured any feeder pipes so the fries are onto it. No suspects apprehended but they found the outside fence cut and work clothes for two people down at the shore. He also said that for now we're on our own. He has nobody he can spare.' She shouted to Earle, 'We might be better to douse the light. Use these instead.'

She was holding what Clement recognised was a night vision monocular. She bypassed Clement and handed it to Earle, who killed the searchlight.

'Go for'ard. The windscreen isn't as clear,' said Edwards.

Earle took himself towards the bow and squatted down. He put the instrument to his eye. Time passed. Clement found it hard to judge on the water. He was hoping like hell nobody had been badly hurt in the blast. It seemed a big one.

'Got them.' Earle used his left hand to indicate the direction they needed to pursue.

***

'I think they're still back there.' Annika was gesturing wildly behind them.

Thomas tried to turn to see for himself but it was too hard to steer at the same time so he bored on. At least when their pursuers shone the big light you knew where they were. He was still churning inside. When he heard the explosion just as they had begun to leave the island behind, he had felt elated. But that emotion was quickly swamped by bitterness at what might have been. Damn Paul. Had he given them the correct pass it would have been so much better. The fucking bomb worked! The Frenchman had known his stuff. There had been virtually no defence on the island. Putting it together in his head as he was dashing for freedom was hard, snatches of reason, ideas tumbling like boulders but he couldn't stop himself trying. It must have been Paul or Seydoux. Maybe Seydoux left a trail. Everything his end was watertight. Well, they still had one booster and if they wound up cornered, he could use that. He would be a hero when word got out. Shit. They had been so close. There hadn't been any patrol craft to stop them so his best guess was that whoever was on the plane came with information. The explosion was terrifyingly loud. Surely it did some major damage. If it had created some conflagration would that be visible from here? Probably not.

Another island loomed ahead. He could make out the outline. He did not know the waters, that had been the Frenchman's job.

Again, he cursed him. He would have put a nail through the Frog's skull this minute if he could. He headed right, keeping the approaching landmass on his port side, not getting too close because of potential reefs, although there was a depth sounder onboard, he had now discovered. Other islands began to appear. He decided to follow the largest island's coastline. He kept the island to port, correcting so he was heading due north. It wasn't long before he found himself at the end of the island's eastern flank that ended in a bony extended finger. Rounding the tip, he plunged back south on the other side of the peninsula. So now they were heading up the left flank of an n-shaped bay. Directly ahead and to starboard the ground swept up into low hills. He looked keenly for a cove. He would need to get closer to shore and trace the n but not at this speed. It was dark and the coastline looked rocky. But if he could find a cove, it would be difficult for any posse to find them on this night almost devoid of moonlight. He cut the engines.

***

Earle had lost sight of them once they rounded the peninsula. Edwards brought the boat around but the sea was empty.

'Nothing,' said Earle scanning all around.

'I don't think they could have made those yet.' Edwards pointed at the closest small islands.

'You think they're here?' Clement was checking out the bay of the larger island.

Edwards nodded and cut the engines. Clement strained, hoping to hear the noise of an engine but only the throaty sputter of their own was audible.

'If I were them, I'd make for one of the coves. There's quite a few. And the reefs aren't too large,' said Edwards as she steered the boat on low revs down into the n-shaped gap of what Clement supposed resembled the inner space of an upside-down fishhook. To their port side now was the short, or hook side, dead ahead the belly, and then the longer side was to starboard with maybe four hundred metres of water between the two sides. They stuck close to the port flank of the island. It was low and flat at the tip of the peninsula, nothing but scrub and rocks, but then the ground started to rise to form a rocky cliff that extended for most of the island, though here and there this disappeared into nothing but tufty hill. Now they were close enough to use the boat's spotlight to illuminate the shore. While Clement trained that, Earle checked out the higher ground to the right with the night vision monocular. They saw nothing. They continued along the bottom or belly section where there was an inviting small and narrow beach but it was quite open. A cliff rose above the beach and beyond that appeared to be the highest point of the island, a hill higher than Clement would have expected out here in the middle of the ocean. They continued to cruise, turning north so the longer flank was now on their port side. There were several coves and Clement raked the light over them as the boat ticked slowly by, but saw no sign of life. The radio buzzed. It was Nordling. He reported that the previous assessment was confirmed, no casualties and miraculously no fire at the plant but there had been extensive damage, fortunately not to any of the gas pipelines themselves. Clement told him the current situation.

'I'll send the second boat over there,' said Nordling. Clement informed him he had no phone reception and asked if he could call Risely and give him a progress report. Nordling assured him he would do that.

When they reached the top of the long side of the island, Edwards asked what Clement wanted to do now.

'You don't think they could have got over there?' Clement indicated the nearest islands.

'I don't.'

'Let's check again down these coves. If they are there they're not going anywhere.'

They started back in the opposite direction this time, so the long flank and its coves as they headed south were to starboard. Those near the northern end were protected by small reefs and these prevented them getting a good look inside the coves but Earle said he didn't think the other boat would be able to get in there without a lot of luck. When they were almost back to the bottom of the fishhook where the belly started, Clement's light hit a crevice in the rocky cliff that had not been visible when coming from the other direction.

'What about there?' he pointed.

Edwards asked him to shine the light near the narrow entrance to the cove, and seeing there was no sign of a reef, progressed very slowly through the gap. Clement and Earle drew their Glocks as a precaution. The bow nudged through the gap into a small cove shaped like a character's thought bubble in a comic. A boat, around thirty feet in length, lay anchored on the right-hand extremity. Clement shone the spotlight over the boat. It was deserted. In this cove, the cliff behind them through which they had entered gave way to a barren rocky hillside and the spotlight was able to sweep some distance up this but it illuminated no movement, human or animal.

'It's over, Berryman,' yelled Clement above the sound of the outboards. 'Give it up.'

They were met by silence.

Edwards brought her boat alongside the other, and now close up they could see it was deserted. The boat was anchored about ten metres from the shore and the approach to land was all low rock.

'It looks like it's around two point three metres deep right here,' said Edwards checking instruments. 'But in about ten metres you'll be able to stand.'

'Are there sharks around?' asked Clement, dubious about going in.

'You bet. And deadly jellyfish,' said Edwards. 'Fortunately I've got this.'

She pulled a small inflatable raft out from under the seating.

We must look like Laurel and Hardy, thought Clement as he and Earle paddled the short distance across to the rocky shoreline. He was in front, nominally Laurel, while Earle sat behind. They had removed their shoes and rolled up their trouser legs for disembarkation. Regrettably they had not worn boots, not expecting to find themselves in this situation. The water was warm and the rocks large and not sharp, so it was easy to disembark and find their way to land. They pulled the raft up and dried their feet as best they could. Then they put on their shoes. Earle had brought the monocular, Clement a flare gun with two flares. They had left Edwards on the radio informing the other boat, which had just left the island, of their location.

Clement and Earle began to climb using small torches to guide their way. The cliff face quickly gave way to a hill covered in low scrub. There was a bit of wind but the night was still pleasantly warm. They walked in three-to-four-minute bursts then stopped and listened.

'We should kill these,' said Clement, indicating the torches, and Earle immediately switched his off. They had no idea where their quarry might head. With scant moonlight, bare as the terrain was, it was no certainty to find them. Each time they stopped to listen, Earle pulled out the monocular and scanned. It was on the fourth of their stops, a little more than halfway up the hill, that Earle spotted something to their left about two hundred metres away, slightly above them.

'I saw something,' he whispered. 'Could be an animal, could be them.'

Clement nodded and they continued, moving swiftly up gradually rising ground towards the position where Earle had sighted movement. Every now and again there would be a fold in the hill. If their quarry was down in one of those, it would be easy to miss them. Now Clement could clearly make out some old ruins on the hill's crest. He guessed they must have been some army quarters from the atom bomb testing seventy years back. It was eerie to think all that time had passed while these man-made buildings slowly rotted. Clement stopped their advance and indicated Earle should check the landscape ahead. He put the monocular to his eye, scanned, then shrugged. There were three possibilities. Berryman and Styles and whoever might be with them had managed to crest the hill already; they had doubled back down one of the little hollows; or they had realised they were being pursued and were hiding, either amidst the few boulders or up in the ruins. Clement doubted they had crested the hill yet. But they could be lying in wait, and armed. It was also possible they would split up, and that would present major problems. He loaded the non-distress white flare cartridge, pointed the gun to the sky, aimed over the area they ought to be, and fired. The projectile shot up through the sky. There was a crack and then the earth lit up stark and white. Earle and Clement might not have spied them had they remained motionless, prone behind a few scattered low boulders. But they must have panicked as, before the light had been sucked back into the night's belly, two figures sprang from the ground and ran towards the ruins. Earle set off at the same time as Clement. Despite his size, he was only a fraction slower.

It was possible that the fugitives would head for the ruins only to use them as cover in order to slip away and make for some other part of the island. But unless they had another boat stashed, there was no escape. It was more likely that if they were armed either with guns or explosives, this might be where they attempted to eliminate their pursuers. And there could be others waiting to ambush them. But Clement had no choice. Those he was pursuing had no way of knowing how many they were either. They were all truly groping in the dark. Still Clement was absolutely certain of this – Berryman was prepared to kill. Clement and Earle advanced rapidly to within a hundred metres of the ruins that seemed to be remnants of one hut-like structure; no roof or windows, gaps in the walls, and a few scattered pieces of heavy iron lumps that may once have been additional parts of the building or ancillary machinery.

Clement signalled they stop. They squatted low while Earle used the monocular and Clement loaded the flare gun with the remaining cartridge. This was red for distress.

'Can't see them,' he said.

'You guard the front here,' whispered Clement. 'I'll circle around the back. Keep an eye out in case there are more than those two coming up behind. Sorry, I better have that.' Clement took the monocular and both men drew their pistols. Crouching low, Clement moved to his right, feeling his muscles tense. There was no cover and if whoever was up there had night-vision goggles, he'd be a sitting duck. As his angle took him to the back of the little structure, he brought out the monocular and swept the back side of the hill but could see nothing. Now he turned it up on the ruins. He was no more than eighty metres from them but still below the crest of the hill, and the insides of the ruins were obscured. Mostly he could see just the tall, mainly intact side wall. He needed to improve his angle, so he crawled on his belly further round and closer still. Around fifty metres from the ruins, he could look up to where the back wall had disappeared, leaving just some wooden beams and then inner partitions. He put the monocular to his eye, and by one of the remaining inner partitions could see somebody's back leg and foot. They were still facing the front. To his right and ten metres up was a mound of some old rubbish that offered slight cover. He got to his haunches and, gun ready, dashed to it. Immediately there was noise within the ruins. They'd heard him.

'Thomas, Annika,' he called. 'I am Detective Clement, Major Crime, Broome. There is no way off this island for you. If you have any weapons put them down and come out with your hands open and above your head.'

There was no response. Clement couldn't be certain it was them and not some associates but he tried again.

'Thomas, please –'

'We're not surrendering, ever.'

It was a man's voice, Clement assumed Thomas. And now there was movement and he could see the outline of two bodies in the gloom of the ruins.

'Does Annika feel the same way as you?'

'Yes,' came the response from a female.

Okay, Thomas and Annika. Hopefully nobody else.

'We are not going to subject ourselves to minions of the multi-nationals!' the man he assumed was Thomas bellowed.

They advanced further out towards the back of the ruin facing him, and now Clement could clearly see the two of them standing there.

Clement called up, 'We're employed by the people of Western Australia, not multinationals.'

'You're their lapdogs, though!' It was Styles this time.

Clement said, 'Are they your own words, Annika, or his? Because Thomas, you and I know this whole thing isn't thanks to something those big companies have done. Not really. It's more to do with your mum, isn't it?' In the dark, from the distance, Clement couldn't see facial features to judge how effective his torpedo had been but he counted Berryman's silence as a hit. Again, it was Styles who led the counterattack.

'They killed his mother. As good as murdered her.'

So she didn't know.

Clement said, 'I don't think Thomas has told you the whole truth, Annika. I spoke to his aunt yesterday.'

'Shut up!' snapped Thomas.

'His mother is still well and truly alive and living in Queensland, Annika.' The girl swung towards her partner. Clement had the blade in the crack. He kept working on widening it. 'Thomas, I understand. It's a traumatic event. You're ten years old and your mum runs off with a bloke and dumps you with your aunt and uncle because her boyfriend won't have her kid around. I get you're angry. You have every right to be. But you need to be honest with Annika, let her know you're doing this because you're a damaged soul. The bloke who took your mum away was a FIFO miner. That's your real gripe, isn't it?'

'Thomas?'

Clement just made out the word from Styles. He could imagine the confusion swimming in her head. Good.

'Shut up, you lying pig.' Clement could see he was holding a backpack. Did he have a weapon in there? Clement's gun hand was steady but his heart pounding.

'We both know I'm not lying. Your aunt gave me your mother's phone number. Put your hands up and walk out and we can call her.'

Clement thought he could see Thomas' body trembling and took a few steps closer. They were maybe thirty metres apart now.

'Is that why you killed Seydoux?' Clement was pushing. 'Did he find out it was all a lie? Or was it because he was only after the money?'

'I don't know what you're talking about,' muttered Thomas.

'Come on, mate. Nobody has been hurt in the explosion at the plant. And Seydoux, well, you can tell us your side of the story. I mean I guess you weren't planning to kill him, or Annika wouldn't have smashed up the childhood clinic.'

'What?' The word exploded from Berryman.

She stammered, 'I wanted to tell –'

'You stupid bitch!'

Before Clement could react, Berryman had seized her and even in this low light Clement could tell he had a knife or something like it at her throat. Styles half gasped, half screamed.

Clement shouted, 'No, Thomas. Don't destroy what you've achieved. Right now, you get to tell your side of the story. People will give you a fair hearing. But you hurt her ...'

It was like speaking to stone.

'You stupid, dumb bitch! That's how they knew!'

Clement hoped Earle had followed the exchange and was moving up from behind. There was no way Clement could take a shot. Annika was wailing.

'I'm sorry. I didn't know it would matter.'

Keeping the Glock trained on Thomas with his right hand, with his left Clement felt for the flare gun. Berryman and Styles went at it.

'Didn't know it would matter!' Berryman mocked.

'I didn't know you would kill him!'

'*We* killed him. Us. Together.'

Clement fired the flare. The whoosh swung Berryman's head. Styles took her chance, shoved him and threw herself forward. As the flare burst overhead, Berryman roared and lunged at Styles with the knife. Clement fired the Glock. There was a thud and Thomas Berryman went down. Moving too fast for her feet to balance, Styles sprawled forward and tumbled down the hill towards Clement who caught her, then threw himself over her to shield her from Berryman.

Clement pulled up the Glock and aimed with the flare's last gasp. Berryman was gone.

'Thomas?' cried Clement out in the new dark but the only answer was the clatter of shoes on stones heading down the hill to his left.

***

Emotion and reason rushed through Thomas, intertwined like dirt and rain in a flood down a gully. For as long as he could remember, this had been his life, cold and alone. So what if his mother's desertion had burned like acid? That didn't invalidate everything he'd worked for. These corporations were vile ogres and those in their service were complicit zombies. He'd sold drugs to their children at university. He'd stood outside the red velvet rope at their private functions. But even though they had kept him in the shadows, even though he was as smart as any of them, they had ensured he remained dispossessed. And the new generation with their beards and groovy tattoos were worse, manipulating his life with their Facebook and Instagram as surely as if they had been KGB. Everybody had betrayed him. His mother, Seydoux, and now Annika. That was his own fault. Hadn't she abandoned her old boyfriend to be with him? He should have known, should have smelled her weakness.

All of a sudden he felt light-headed, the strength rushed out of him, his legs went.

'Thomas!'

Berryman heard the cop yell his name. He was cold now, his legs growing numb. The gunshot wound must have been worse than he realised, his adrenaline getting him this far. Maybe if he surrendered he could survive. But what was the point? A trophy for those bastards. No way. And even Annika had ultimately let him down. He reached inside the bag and slid out the booster. Seydoux had attached a cap that could be detonated by a hard blow. His hand crawled across the earth and wrapped itself over a rock.

'Thomas!' yelled Clement and started after Berryman.

'He's got a bomb.' Styles' voice sounded so thin it might have been stretched across the Grand Canyon.

Clement hesitated. An image of Phoebe flashed through his brain. He couldn't lose her. Then before he was aware that he had even made a decision, he was charging. 'Thomas! This is pointless.'

There was one of those dips in the ground ahead. Clement bolted down and was on his third stride up the other side of the gully when the earth exploded.

28

After the red flare burst, Graeme Earle had decided to leave his position. He had closed the distance to the ruins by half when there was an almighty bang from somewhere to his right. The shockwave rippled his clothes. Despite ringing ears he could hear high-pitched screaming. His thoughts dived headlong towards Dan. He dashed to the old ruin through clouds of dirt. Out the other side he saw Annika Styles standing there, face in her hands.

'Where's Clement?'

She pointed over to her left. Earle ran that way, yelling for Dan. As the dust cleared, he saw a large crater and something mangled. Earle started running towards the crater. There was a fold in the hill just in front of it. As he was about to start down, he saw Clement. Lying on the bottom, spreadeagled on his back, his shirt torn from his body and most of his pants ripped away.

***

Clement was dead. He must be. He was in a soundless, dark space. A light was hovering. When you die you must move towards the light, he remembered his religious aunty telling his mother. The light is your guide. He tried to reach for the light but the spirit world was different to a human life on earth and you had no limbs. You must have to think your way there. He tried to transport himself to the light by thinking it. It was working! The light was coming closer and closer. And then God's face loomed above him and smiled. God, it seemed, was the spitting image of Graeme Earle.

29

Clement sat up in his hospital bed. It was now fourteen hours since he'd been airlifted from the island by helicopter but the first seven of those had passed him in a blur: sleep, headaches, pain, scans, some delirious snatches of slumber, more pain, a lessening of his deafness. The only sense of his that seemed unaffected was smell. That was working fine and told him he was hungry. He'd just eaten some egg sandwiches. The painkillers must have been working for he was not experiencing pain except when he'd turned to his left side. The poor doctor had been forced to brief him twice because the first time he'd not retained a thing. Being ninety percent deaf didn't help of course. A broken rib and hopefully only temporary deafness, the doctor had declared. Apparently, he'd been lucky he'd been below Berryman by a metre or more when the booster detonated. The angle of the blast had meant the lower part of his body was mostly unscathed. His chest and head had borne the brunt of the blast and resulted in a bad concussion but his neck and spine and skull appeared to have no fractures though a small rock had done its darnedest and he had a very large bump on his head.

Berryman had been a different story.

He was no more than a lump of seared flesh.

Scott Risely had flown down to Karratha Hospital and was sitting with him now. Graeme Earle had been there the whole time until a couple of hours ago but had been allowed to head to the motel to get some sleep.

'The Dampier police took Annika Styles back by boat. Graeme stayed with you.'

Clement knew Risely was shouting although it sounded like a whisper.

'How come Dampier cops were in the chopper?'

Risely had a soft satchel across his lap. He reached in and extracted a photo and passed it across to Clement. It showed a middle-aged man Clement did not recognise. He looked dead.

'His name is Paul Isegar. He worked in HR at the plant and we guess he must have been the inside man. He was found stabbed, barely alive on the road in Dampier. Looks like he crawled out of a house there. He was wearing a pass with Jean-Claude Seydoux's photo on it. One of the responding cops was sharp, recognised the face and called me. I told them to grab a helicopter or plane and get to the plant as quick as they could to support you. They were almost there when Nordling told them to go to the Montebello Islands. They saw the flare ...'

'Is he dead?' Clement handed back the photo.

'Touch and go but they're pretty sure he will pull through now. When you're feeling up to it, Internal will interview you. Styles says she has no idea if Berryman lunged at her with the knife like you said, but confirms he had one and was on edge. I'm sure you'll be fine.'

Clement was sceptical. Somebody on social media would decide he was a trigger-happy cop but right now he couldn't give a toss. Despite it all, he couldn't help feeling for Berryman. 'When can I get back to Broome?'

'Three days observation at the very least here. My orders. The concussion was severe and they need to monitor your hearing.'

Clement had seen a Fellini film on SBS once. That's how the night passed. Fragments. Terrors, pain, equanimity, Phoebe age six in a tutu, Berryman screaming, bursting flares lighting up his parents sitting in fold-out chairs in the old caravan park they owned. Doubt. Lucinda. Marilyn.

Darkness.

Graeme Earle dropped by the next day and was pleased to see his mate conscious and relatively unscathed.

'I brought two,' said Earle pulling two beer cans from a paper bag.

They sat quietly drinking. Clement had no idea what the time was except that it was some time after breakfast.

'I got Keeble to check Seydoux's space at Deep Adventures that they let him use. They found another four grand cash stuffed in a duffle bag and traces of ammonium nitrate and various wires and shit.'

No doubt that was where he had been disappearing to, building the bomb for those hours.

'I should have seen it,' said Clement bitterly.

'Come on. Nobody else saw shit. If it wasn't for us, they'd have more than a dozen dead at the gas train. At least. The whole island could still be on fire.'

'I see you're writing yourself into the script.'

'Fucking oath.' Earle took a pull on his beer. 'I thought three grand was a bit light for breaking into Lizard, stealing the shit and building bombs.'

'How is Rhys taking it?'

'Pretty good but shaken up. He liked those guys. But I told him, good people do bad things.'

'He saved lives.'

'I told him that too. He can't get his head around it. Hard enough for me.'

Ain't that the truth, thought Clement.

Earle said, 'I know Styles can't confirm Berryman was lunging at her when you shot him. But I can. I was standing on the hill looking through the ruins.'

Clement put down his can. 'No you weren't. And they'll prove it. Don't worry. I'll be right.'

Three days later, Clement was looking forward to the drive back to Broome. He'd been so exhausted from the injuries and the investigation that he enjoyed having the second day in bed. But by the third day he was ready to move on. His hearing in his right ear was fine. His left ear still had some problems, and every now and again his cracked rib sent a jolt of pain through his body. He spent long zoom chats with Phoebe reassuring her he was fine. She offered to ditch the band tour to the US but he told her not to be silly, he would be okay and they could still do stuff in January. He then put a call through to Deep Adventures and spoke to Mark Coleman, wondering if there might be any places in January on a diving safari. Coleman said he would ensure those places and offered a two-for-one deal. Clement accepted. Bill Seratono had called, so Clement rang, assured him he was okay and informed his friend he was no longer in need of a boat. They arranged to meet at the Anglers Club as soon as Clement was back in Broome. There were numerous well-wisher calls from all the bods at the station. Keeble said she had been praying for him because he still owed her two bottles of Kahlua. Clement rang Lauren Bagot. She was back at work and sounded miserable but thanked him for his efforts.

He felt he was a fraud, a thief posing as a security guard. Valentina Gomez had not answered. He had left a message but she had not responded. Why would she? He had spoken to his elderly parents as soon as he could. They would be worrying. His sister had called to wish him well. So had Marilyn. Earle had informed her that her ex had been blown up but not so badly you'd notice much difference. She had finally called Clement and the conversation had lingered and set off far more pain than the broken rib. Had there been a frisson or was it his concussion talking? It was safer if he ascribed it to the latter. He had even found two voicemail messages in his phone from Lucinda, the brief fling that had ended in tears. He couldn't guess whether she was going to wish the blast had killed him or was offering sympathy. He decided not to find out.

By day four, dressed and packed, Clement was itching to go, although the air-conditioning was something he could get used to. He inquired from the staff about where Paul Isegar might be found and was directed just one ward away. Apparently Isegar was not considered a flight risk. There was no policeman guarding the door and he was not cuffed to his bed. The plastic tubing pumping various fluid into his body and the leads for constant monitoring were anchor enough it seemed. Isegar still looked weak, not as white as he had in the photo but in far worse shape than Clement had been. He was, however, quite conscious.

Clement introduced himself. Isegar looked anxious.

'It's okay. I'm not trying to trap you. I've been in the next ward. Berryman blew himself up and nearly took me with him.'

Still Isegar seemed wary.

Clement said, 'Truly, I wanted to thank you because I think you saved my life.' Clement told him what had happened. 'I don't know if you only dragged yourself out of that house to save yourself. I don't care. If you hadn't, I don't know how I'd have done. Maybe I would have been okay. But it saved hours.'

Isegar spoke, though he seemed understandably constricted, the words taking an effort

'I lost my partner in Brazil. And our baby. The tailings-dam burst.'

Clement had not forgotten the news reports.

'I died that day. My whole life. And I was angry and I wanted to punish people who I thought were responsible. Probably still do. But not that way. I wanted to help Thomas. Then I realised ... Gabrielly ... she wouldn't want that. She would have said no ideology is worth hurting innocent people. I met someone, a lovely woman at the plant. I didn't want anything to happen to her. I tried to stop them. I thought I could talk them around. But just in case, I never encoded the passes. They couldn't get into the main compound. I'm not trying to excuse myself. I just wanted to save Ingrid. That's why I crawled out onto the road. I wasn't being a hero. I just didn't want her to get hurt.'

Not for the first time, Clement felt that there was no fairness in the world. But at whose feet do you lay the blame? Berryman, whose mother ran out on him when he was ten? The resource companies, who existed because they produced what we demanded?

'Has she been in to see you?' asked Clement. 'Ingrid?'

Isegar shook his head. 'I called her. The police had been in touch about me. She said she wants nothing to do with me. I can't blame her.'

Clement reached across and took his hand. There were tears in Paul Isegar's eyes, and Clement thought there might have been tears in his own.

EPILOGUE

Clement rang the doorbell and waited. Beyond the flywire door were shadows of the entrance way, the front door propped back. He heard steps coming towards him. The smell of hibiscus hung over the newborn year.

'Oh, hello, Inspector.'

Stephen Meadows swung the door open.

'Hi there, Mr Meadows. I felt terrible I didn't get back to you.'

'Stephen, please. Totally understandable. Would you care for tea?'

'Please.'

Clement followed him into the room he remembered so clearly. The barometer was exactly where it had been, the Doulton teapot looked the same.

Meadows fussed with the tea. 'Young Rhys told me you had been injured, and then I read the reports.' He swivelled and checked him over. 'I was worried you might have lost an arm or fingers.'

'I was lucky.'

'No slice this time, I'm afraid,' said Meadows. 'But I do have some very nice shortbread biscuits I got for Christmas.'

They sat in the comfortable chairs under the cooling breeze of the fan.

'She never regained consciousness,' Meadows said, nibbling a biscuit, legs crossed, his eyes on the watercolours his wife had painted. 'We got your card. Thank you very much. It was so kind of you to think of us.'

Clement wasn't sure if Meadows was using the royal 'we' or more likely, he thought, including his wife as a living presence. Though Clement had sent a sympathy card, and despite his natural inhibition, he had felt impelled to visit personally.

'I couldn't get this place out of my head,' he said as he sipped tea. 'Or, more precisely I guess, I couldn't get the two of you out of my head. You seemed, not so much a couple but one person. You don't even really know me so I apologise if I'm ...' Clement had led himself into a dead end, '... and I envied you that. My own marriage didn't work out.'

Stephen Meadows looked at him intently, without judgement, patient.

'We met so briefly but Hazel made such an impression. You both did.'

'That's very kind of you. Yes, Hazel was hard to forget. Swept me off my feet when I was twenty-two. She was a fabulous dancer.'

Clement said he could believe that. He wanted to say he was worried for Meadows, worried he would be bereft at the loss of his soul mate.

'It must be very hard,' was what he finally said, and bit the biscuit.

'Sometimes, yes. But you know, I think about it, how fortunate we were. We did everything but die together.'

'Do you have children?'

'A son and daughter. Daughter lives in England married, two grandchildren. She came out for the funeral. So did our son. He's in Boston. My daughter prodded me about going to live with them but you know, this is home.' He looked around, breathed in the air. 'I still feel her here. And I love the climate. I don't think I could handle those cold English winters any more. Or summers for that matter. And you? Children?'

'Yes, my daughter, Phoebe. She's around Rhys' age. She's coming up here to spend her holidays with me. We're doing a diving safari and Graeme Earle has a couple of days where I can borrow his boat.'

A thought jumped into his head and Clement, so rarely impulsive, said, 'Would you like to come out with us for a day? With Rhys.'

Meadows' eyes sparkled and he uncrossed his legs, put down his cup and leant forward as if sharing the most amazing piece of gossip.

'I would love that. I really would.'

'Good.'

There was something about this place that relaxed Clement and made him able to drop his natural defensiveness.

'What was your secret, do you think? You and Hazel?'

Meadows sat back, recrossed his legs and tented his fingers beneath his nose. Apart from professorial robes, he looked just like how Clement imagined an English academic. Meadows took his fingers away, sat up and said, 'You know, I think we just got lucky. I hear people say all the time you have to work at a relationship but I don't think that's true. If you have to work at it, then perhaps there's a fault in it. I'm not saying we didn't quibble, or have the odd row over nothing but almost every day of our lives, we enjoyed being with one another.'

That's how it had been with Marilyn at the start, thought Clement. Actually, for quite a long time. He wondered where he had gone so badly wrong. He had almost finished his tea but felt no inclination to leave this space.

'Another?' asked Meadows reaching for his cup.

He was on leave, Phoebe was still two days away. 'Please,' said Clement.

When Clement finally emerged and walked to his car, evening was falling slowly like a hood. Thunder was close. He thought of the contentment of Stephen Meadows and how it contrasted with the despair of Paul Isegar. Both men had found their soul mates and yet fate had treated them completely differently. Isegar's life had been buried in mud. Then when he had finally found another person to love he had lost them too.

Our past is always dogging our heels, affecting our judgement. Isegar had become a pariah in the eyes of the woman he loved, even though he had nearly died trying to rectify his error. Had he not done what he had, maybe Clement wouldn't be standing here now sniffing encroaching rain, savouring the advent of Phoebe's return. He thought of Lauren Bagot and Valentina Gomez and wondered if their lives had been scarred forever. He hoped not.

He looked at his phone. There were still those two Lucinda voicemails demanding attention. He'd never played them. He dropped the phone in his pocket. Then he pulled it out again. You couldn't live your life like that, running away. He hit the dial button and put the phone to his ear.

ACKNOWLEDGEMENTS

I am very grateful for the assistance of a number of people. Pat Fairchild and especially Daniel Prowse, thank you so much for your help in regards to the availability, storage and protocol for explosives in Australia's north-west. Neil Fergus, I greatly appreciate you directing me on the kind of security operations that might be in place in the locations called for by my story, and for a little mining anecdote or two as well. Bullbar, thanks for your assistance as always, and Steve Mitchell and Pumper, your assistance in describing your experiences in mining and energy work, explosives, security, and the marine geography of the north-west of Australia was invaluable.

Jed Elderkin, your knowledge on powerboats was gratefully received and if I sell a couple of hundred thousand copies of this book I'll buy a boat from you.

To my editor, Georgia Richter, thank you again for guidance and intelligence, you make each novel so much better with your input.

My wife Nicole, thanks so much for believing in me from the first till the present.

ABOUT THE AUTHOR

Dave Warner is an author, musician and screenwriter. *After the Flood* is his eleventh adult novel, with previous novels winning the Western Australian Premier's Book Award for Fiction, and the Ned Kelly Award for best Australian crime fiction. *After the Flood* is the third in the Dan Clement series (*Before It Breaks*, *Clear to the Horizon*) set in Broome and Australia's North-West. Dave first came to national prominence in 1978 with his gold album *Mug's Game* and his band Dave Warner's from the Suburbs. In 2017 he released his tenth album, *When*. He has been named a Western Australian State Living Treasure and has been inducted into the WAMi Rock'n'Roll of Renown.

ALSO BY DAVE WARNER

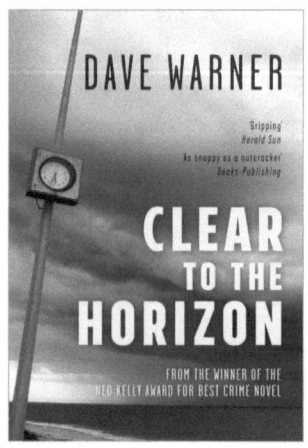

FROM FREMANTLEPRESS.COM.AU
AND ALL GOOD BOOKSTORES